I0680688

This Starry Deep

Adam P. Knave

This Starry Deep
Adam P. Knave

ISBN: 978-1926946-030

Trade edition.
This book is also available in ebook formats.
©2016 Adam P. Knave, all rights reserved.

Published in Canada by Creative Guy Publishing
Victoria, BC, Canada

Cover art ©2016 Dylan Todd

THIS STARRY DEEP

ADAM P. KNAVE

Thanks to:

Lauren for her always deft editing,

Ariana for helping me realize the story I needed to tell, and for all the naming assistance,

and of course N&N, A&A, and J&A for all that they are, together.

Chapter 1 – Jonah

THE MIDDLE THIRD of the tree exploded into burning splinters. The shrapnel flew with certainty and speed, but the needles embedding in my face didn't even register at first. I focused on dodging the upper third of the tree, suddenly airborne and quickly remembering gravity.

"What do these guys have against trees?" I said as I landed, figuring I wouldn't be heard over the echoing crash of the tree trunk. The impact shook the ground just enough to upset my footing as I sprang back to my feet.

"Stop changing the subject," Shae said. She glared at me, pushing herself off the ground. Her face bled, but she paid her wounds as much attention as I did my own. No time to be precious and feel pain.

I checked the charge on my Acadian blaster and grinned. "I'm not changing the subject. Just trying to not get killed, either. Look, fine, let's focus. What are they firing?"

"Tankos high-yield slugs. The ones you said I shouldn't bother buying last resupply. You thought they were wonky."

"I thought they were useless. Slug throwers. How often are we on planets?"

"We're on one now, if you hadn't noticed."

Orsid. We were on Orsid. Not my favorite planet, but far from the worst I've had to set foot on. Though the ground felt too springy for me. Just moist, really. "I noticed. All right, sit rep. Both our

GravPacks are damaged and the emergency jump ship won't get here in time. We still have to blow the silo."

"And then find a way off this rock," Shae said. "This really moist, humid rock. If we can find a small jump ship, anything that can clear atmo, I can get it started." She fired two shots from her sidearm, energy blasting off into the forest in the rough direction of where the last shot had come from. "So that's settled. Now. Jonah, can we talk about this?"

"I don't see your problem, is all."

"We can't raise a child living like we do."

"I don't see the problem." I tapped my ear twice, and switched to coms. That way we could still whisper while we snuck forward. Not the best protocol, but this wasn't the first time. I liked talking to Shae. Hell, I liked talking to Shae enough I'd married her.

"We can't bring a child into combat, for a start." Two more high-yield shots came in and missed us, exploding and sending the ground up into the air where it blinded us. The good news - they still weren't sure where we were. Or they were terrible shots. Either way, it helped.

"So we leave the kid with whatever base we depart from on a mission. I think we'd be good parents, Shae."

"Damn it, Jonah, of course we would be. But not if we abandon the kid at every turn."

I used my blaster to cut a tree down, not that I had anything against them, and shoved it in a direction we weren't. Both of us sprinted as it fell, making sure we found cover quick. Chances were they'd investigate that.

"All right, so we leave the kid with your father."

Shae's hand sliced through the air, two fingers extended. I nodded and crept in the direction she pointed. Dead on, there were the Orsidsians, trying to figure out why a tree had just fallen out of nowhere.

"The one who doesn't talk to either of us?"

I elbowed the first idiot in the back of his neck and smiled at the other as he turned, startled, at me.

"I bet he would if he was a grandfather," I said as the second, still confused, idiot, reached for his communication device. Before he could get to it, Shae's foot cracked against his skull and he sank down into the forest, unconscious. No need to kill them, no point. Wouldn't unless they forced the issue.

"I wouldn't want to leave my child with him any more than I'd want to live with him now myself."

"Base care is good, Shae."

Her initial reply was drowned out by the sound of blaster fire from above. Great, those two called the cavalry before they investigated. Stupid efficient guards.

We huddled near a decomposing mass of leaves and detritus. Its heat would help hide us. "What was that?" I asked while we waited for the air support to get tired of blind fire.

"I said, next thing you'll suggest we just take a child with us on missions."

My blaster could do damage to their ship but I'd need to be closer. No way, yet. We crouched, thinking over options. "Well, a blast-proof armored papoose, maybe a small gravity shield, why not?" I smiled at the thought. Gave me an idea. My GravPack was busted, Shae's too, but if I could get a field working at all, it might buy us the time we would need for a better plan. All too often, my life was just a way to stretch two minutes to five, and then using those extra three to stretch circumstances into survival.

I unslung my pack and started cracking open the casing. Shae nodded and did the same. We'd had to do this once before, back on King Seven. Between us we'd have the parts to make this work. I hoped. "Now you're just messing with me," she said.

I stopped working and looked her in the eye. "We'd be great parents, baby."

"I know we would, Soldier. I just don't know if this is the right time." A small shrug as she handed me components. I slotted them in place and jammed the housing closed. This wouldn't be pretty, assuming the pack didn't just explode in my face.

"We'll use that as an excuse forever. Don't you want a kid?"

Before she could answer I pulled up a selection screen, aiming the GravPack in the general direction of the ships above. Still firing. They didn't give up. Then again, neither did we.

I hit the makeshift switch and tried to force myself to not flinch as I did. A wave pulse rippled the air, almost too fast to see. Trees wobbled. My inner ear spun. Both ships got tossed like they were at the end of a whip and hit each other.

"I'd love a child. You know that," Shae said as we watched the ships try to stay airborne. They managed it, but one of them sparked badly from the gun mount.

Fine, we'd reduced the rate of fire from the sky by half. I'd take it. "Then we'll find a way," I said, giving Shae the signal to start running. We needed them to follow us now, to see us and try to fire. If they didn't know their gun was out, things could get ugly for them quick. Sure enough, the ship throwing sparks started to belch smoke as well and we heard the low, rumbling cough of an interior explosion.

"Fine, we'll find a way. Now can we blow these idiots up and go home?" The smoking ship hung in the air, and I could see, mentally, the crew trying to put out fires and get things working. They hadn't dropped out of the air yet, so they were doing something right. Good on them, I suppose. Damn it.

"Got the grenades?" I asked. We ran from strafing fire. I'd lost patience.

"I'm insulted you'd ask," she said, patting a few pockets.

"Then let's blow them up, already. We take one ship semi-functional and we have line of sight to target and then we're off-world. From there, home." I turned and fired back, knowing my blaster wouldn't take them out. Still, might make them flinch. And did. I stood there, waiting. Either Shae's grenades would hit the ship right or I'd be a pair of flaming boots in about a minute. I didn't even consider it an option. I trusted her. We worked.

"Deal," she said, and let three fly in graceful arcs across the sky.

Damn, all told that had been a good day. A good day a lifetime ago. I smiled and pushed up against gravity harder.

Sweat rolled off my forehead and slid down my temples. I closed my eyes. My arms resisted, but I forced them to lift the weights again. My left shoulder shook, the muscle straining hard, but my arms straightened anyway. I held myself there, arms extended upward, flat on my back, and took two deep, slow breaths. I exhaled through my mouth and lowered my arms.

Eyes still closed, I lifted again. This time I held the weight for a ten count. I focused on everything but the urgent burning in my shoulder: the sweat-slick feel of the leather padding under my back, the soft breeze that played over my body, cooling my chest and legs, the new beads of sweat that formed before they slid off, following gravity down.

I lowered the weight and held it against my chest. I opened my eyes. Above me a few clouds drifted, but most of my field of vision was taken up by a dazzling blue sky. I smiled up to greet it and hefted the bar again; it felt somehow lighter this time.

I always exercised outside if possible. The sky, that clear land above my head, had captured my imagination as a child, and I still loved it dearly. I loved it almost as much as I loved the blackness that perched above it, the parent to all of the skies in the universe.

The potential up there - the freedom and, damn, the joy I felt when I went to greet it each time - those things still got a rise out of me. I studied the sky, watching the higher winds etch patterns in clouds, and lifted that weight again and again. I felt my shoulder reach the point of no return, so I set the long metal bar in its cradle above me and just laid there a while.

My left shoulder hurt like a bitch, a knife's hurt. I lay prone under the sun and let my heart rate ease off, stretching my arms. They ached, not as much as my shoulder, but it was a healthy ache. The shoulder, that wasn't healthy: that was damage born of countless abusive moments.

I treated my body like a temple, but it was a temple that I raided for goods as often as prayed at. I got what I got, and considered every inch of it worthwhile. Still, it hurt. It would always hurt, unless I let them replace the thing with an alloy-and-synthetic model.

I lifted my legs and glanced down at my right knee. Same story as my shoulder. Neither joint was quite right anymore, and both "should have been" replaced. That is, in the opinion of doctors who didn't understand me. I wasn't against replacements, in general. But at my age, I didn't see the point in deep-tissue surgery followed by months and months of rehab all for new joints that would possibly need further replacement a few years down the road.

Not when I was pushing 60, at least. I felt past the point of needing bits and pieces swapped out: I'd grown used to the problems and worked with them as much as possible. More than that, I let go.

I stood and rubbed at the sweat coating my body with the towel I'd brought out. I padded inside, rubbing the towel along my head, feeling my grey hair bristle against the fabric.

Shae sat in a long recliner, reading. She looked up as I entered and closed the book slowly on her thumb, marking her place. Her black hair stuck up along her head, much like mine did, except hers

7

would probably come down to her ears if she let it hang naturally. She looked around at me, her eyes a rich hazel in the day's light, and I felt myself smile in reaction to the smile that crept across her face.

"Hey, Soldier," she said, resting the book on her lap, thumb still in place.

"Hey, baby," I said. I hung the towel around my neck and glanced off toward the bathroom. "Just gonna grab a quick shower, and then lunch?"

"Sounds good," she said. "How's the shoulder?"

"For shit," I admitted.

"So the usual, then?" she asked.

I nodded and shrugged. Cooling off inside the climate-controlled house was starting to produce a chill. "I should get a haircut," I told her, stopping to run a hand through my hair again. It felt long, or at least longer.

"Yeah, it might get long enough to lay down," she teased.

"Because you keep yours so long," I said, smirking.

"Well who wants long hair—"

"In a combat helmet," I finished for her. We both laughed, an easy laugh born of an old joke. Neither of us had seen the inside of a helmet, combat or otherwise, in years. We didn't plan on it anytime soon, either. Maybe, if we got really bored, we would take a cruise up and out, but not this season. It had been a bunch of seasons since we had.

Cruise ships don't like it when you go armed, and neither of us felt comfortable going bare hipped. Old habits die hard, and ours were born of more incidents than we could count.

"Didn't we both retire?" she asked me, picking her book back up.

"We're just old creatures of bad habits, baby," I told her, the old, familiar reply. "I'm gonna go grab that shower, then we'll have lunch."

"Already planned," she muttered, lost again in her reading.

I turned the shower up as close to scalding as it would go and stepped into the fray. Jets shot water from all sides and I turned, letting the heat and pressure massage my hard-worked muscles. Every time the water hit scar tissue the sensation of the hot, stinging spray dimmed slightly.

The sensation dimmed a lot. My shoulder and knee, of course, were knots of scar tissue and damage. Ugly as sin to look at but still functional. Scars crisscrossed my back and sides as well. A few dotted my chest, including one thumb-sized welt of a scar on my left side where I had taken a slug back when I was still a kid. That was the shot that should have killed me, but I was too young to die, then.

I rubbed at it, lost in memory for a minute, and stared along the thin line of wax-like flesh that ran up from my right wrist all the way to my elbow. Laser fire isn't pretty to take, and it makes sure you remember it. My legs were just as bad as my torso, and sometimes I admit to wondering if the ratio of good skin to scar tissue had crossed the fifty-percent mark yet.

I turned off the shower and grabbed a clean towel, rubbing myself dry in the steamy, ceramic-coated room. The air was thick and hot and I took long, slow breaths to fill my lungs. I started to stretch, extending every muscle while they were still warm, and then opened the door. Cool air slapped at me and I walked quickly to the closet, grabbing thin white slacks and a matching shirt.

I wandered into the kitchen, the stone floor piercingly cold against my bare feet. Working quickly and without much conscious thought, I tossed together two salads and set them on a black stone serving tray. I added a pitcher of iced tea and glasses and headed back out to join Shae.

The tray went on a table between us, and I eased myself into the chair across from hers. She took her salad and made a soft noise of pleasure at me, like a hungry cat. I nodded and poked at my own salad, the two of us eating in companionable silence.

"Heard from Mud recently?" she asked after a few minutes.

"Newt is fine," I told her after swallowing.

"So that's a no?"

"That's a no. He's a grown man, Shae. He'd call if he was in trouble."

"Sometimes it'd be nice if he called when he wasn't in trouble," she said. She poured both of us some tea and gestured with her fork. "And you should start calling him by his name."

"He claims I never say it right, anyway."

"So learn," she insisted.

"Newt is fine," I told her with a grin. "Besides, what does it matter what I call him if he doesn't get in touch?"

"Don't start," she said, shaking her head.

I poured myself a second glass of tea. Shae and I had met when we were both just kids. We would've each hit you rather than let ourselves be called kids, but the older I get, the more I realize how much of my life I spent being just a kid. "Just." Ha.

Still, I knew the moment I saw her that I was in love. And what held true almost forty years ago is still true for me. I love her. Better yet, she loves me. We had spent innumerable days just like that, sitting and enjoying each other's company. We both find it easy to enjoy the quiet times, considering that as much as the quiet days couldn't be counted correctly as they blurred into one another, the noisy ones always outnumbered them.

We had saved each others' lives, often. When I first met her, Shae was a slip of a girl. She lived with her father, Doctor Williams, at the time. I knew the Doctor through his work perfecting the adjustable gravity engine, the thing he'll go down in history for. It was during a visit to test his engine that I met Shae, who brought us each a drink shyly before she slid back out of the room on whispers and silent glances. She wasn't silent anymore, thankfully; I couldn't have counted her as the most amazing woman I knew (though I admit to bias) if she were always quiet.

But regardless, we courted, she got kidnapped and I saved her, and we started seeing each other when I was on-planet. The Doctor found our romance agreeable, giving us his blessing easily. We grew old together, weathered adopting Newt and the passing of the Doctor as well as countless other things: wars, spies, abductions, supposed death, and long trips to the short end of the universe.

Which is why, even though I did it on a regular basis, I still smiled as I got lost in her eyes. I was sitting there, sipping my iced tea and doing just that, when the chirp of the house phone broke the moment. The glass clinked against the table as I put it down. I shifted out of my chair and took three quick steps to the nearest phone, grabbing the earpiece and pushing it around my ear.

"This is Jonah," I said curtly.

"Captain Madison, this is Lieutenant Mills calling for General Hodges, sir," replied a young voice. I knew his type instantly. A personal assistant, good at his job and efficient, but lacking the ability to go off-script.

"Just call me Jonah, son, I'm retired."

"Captain Madison—"

"Jonah," I repeated.

"Captain Madison," he insisted, "I am calling to inform you that your commission is being reinstated."

"Bull. I'm retired," I turned to Shae and shook my head, the frustration in my eyes easy to read. "You can't call me back up. What the hell is going on?"

"Sir, I am not at liberty to discuss that at length on an unsecured channel."

"Then call me back on a secured line. My unit can handle it. I'll wait."

"Very well, sir," he said, and he hung up.

I turned to Shae, throwing my hands up in anger. "They want to call me back up!"

"Easy, Soldier," she said, rising to cross to my side. She rested a hand on my shoulder as the phone rang again.

I hit the side of the earpiece to activate the call and braced myself for the static tweet of a secure line. It came and I winced in spite of myself. Those things were loud.

"Captain Madison," Mills started, without waiting for me to greet him this time, "the situation is grave."

"It always is. Son, just tell me straight what's going on and why Hodges didn't call me himself."

"General Hodges," he said, stressing the man's rank, "is busy, Captain."

"Fine. What's going on that you think it's a good idea to bother an old man during lunch?"

"Captain Madison, sir, our entire system is about to be wiped out by an invading force."

"Well now, that we probably should discuss," I told him, raising an eyebrow at Shae.

Chapter 2 – Shae

JONAH KEPT HIS EYES on me while he started to pat down the desk near the phone. He grabbed the second earpiece and tossed it at me underhand–I snatched it out of the air, fitting it in place quickly. I flipped it to monitor-only so the mic would pick up no noise and stood, watching Jonah.

"Captain Madison," I heard a young voice say, "we have credible reason to believe that a full-scale invasion force is moving in from out-system."

"Define 'credible,'" Jonah said. I could hear the sigh in his voice and reached out to touch his arm. The kid on the other end was obviously nervous. Besides having to deal with a Big Event, he'd gotten suckered into calling on the reluctant cavalry. Not a great place to be in that early in his career. Still, if it didn't drum him out, it would help forge him into someone worthwhile.

"We've lost contact with King Seven, sir, all contact. As well as Bulk, Athena Fourteen, and Mast's Prayer. All within the last three months," the kid said. He was holding it together pretty well.

"They're all far spun from things. That far out, can you discount natural occurrences?" Jonah looked to me and I shrugged. Both were possible. Planets that far from the center of things had gone dark before. Natural occurrences of all types can arrange for that, it didn't have to be anything sinister.

"We think so, sir. We've had reports of brightly colored ships across a growing number of planets,

14

and not long after each reported incursion there have been multiple missing-persons reports."

"And they line up?"

"Excuse me, sir?" the kid asked with a growing agitation.

"The missing people line up exactly with these incursions?" Jonah asked.

"We think so," I could almost feel his nod.

I wandered away from Jonah and grabbed up the remains of lunch. No matter which way this fell out, I knew from experience that lunch was over. We were either about to go back to war or we would solve it from here, but either way we wouldn't be sitting down to relax again for a few hours, minimum. I kept the earpiece in to hear exactly how things fell out.

"You *think* so?" Jonah asked. I put the pitcher of tea away and glanced out to where Jonah stood, looking at the sky as he talked. He liked to stare toward whoever he was talking to.

"Captain Madison, sir, the data are listed as credible," the voice on the other end repeated.

"In other words, you aren't allowed to see the actual hard data." I laughed at that. I remembered when we were younger and Jonah had been issued top-secret documents that I wasn't cleared to see. Treason, they threatened, if it was known I stole a look at them. Except we were married and working on the case together. Sometimes they trip over their own feet making up rules.

"No, sir, I'm not cleared for that." Exactly.

"Great," Jonah groused. "And the ships?"

"We have not yet captured one, Captain. It's only a matter of time, of course, but from their design, they are unknown to any records we have."

"So let's see," Jonah said, "you have some planets out on the fringes who have stopped talking to you, and some new ships flying around on rare occasion. When those ships show up, you have an increase in missing-persons reports from the planets those ships scout near, and from all of that you draw *credible reason* for a full-scale system invasion?"

"Ye-yes sir," the kid's voice broke, but I knew something he didn't. Jonah couldn't resist a good invasion, theoretical or not. There were enough blocks in this one that stood up at a decent angle to make me interested. If I was interested, then I knew Jonah would be as well. I headed back to the bedroom and started to access the lock-closet that led to the weapons and supply stores. Time to start taking a current count of what we had on hand and what we would need to requisition. I knew, at the least, I would need new grenades. The ones downstairs were underpowered by today's standards.

"Not interested," Jonah said harshly in my ear, and I dropped my hand to my side, starting to turn back toward the outside of the house.

"Excuse me, Captain Madison?" the kid asked. Good question, kid: what the hell what Jonah playing at? I didn't know, but I intended to.

"You heard me. This is thin. I'm retired. I don't do *thin*."

"But, sir—"

I stood in the doorway and glared at the back of Jonah's head until he felt it and turned to face me.

He shook his head at me once, curtly. It just made me angrier.

"No. Have Hodges call me back himself if it's so blasted important. But this is flimsy and far from anything you need me for. I'm sorry to send you back empty-handed, son."

"Captain Madison—"

"Don't argue with me, son," Jonah said, staring at me. That man did not know what he was playing with. Correction, he knew full well what he was playing with, which made it all the stranger.

"But sir, it wasn't a request. I have orders from the General here and—"

"And he can come serve them himself," Jonah cut him off, "with *all* of the data in hand, or he can damn well leave me alone. This call is terminated."

He took the earpiece out and set it down. I grabbed my own and yanked it out, throwing it onto the table. We stood there and stared at each other for a moment, as if daring the other to make a move.

Jonah and I didn't fight *that* much; we worked together better than anything. But still, in life, there are times when eyes don't meet, and sometimes when that happens you need to hit at them until the swelling helps them line up again.

The thing was, under my anger was concern. This wasn't like Jonah, not at all. I tried to think of another time he'd refused a commission. It had happened, sure, but over much bigger stuff than this seemed to be.

We were both retired. We had done far more than our share of time, and it was over. But that wasn't exactly a new situation. Six or so years ago we got called back in. Goodness, was that really six years ago? It felt a lot more recent until I gave it some turning over.

Even so, I didn't like this. We stared at each other and his cold blue eyes tightened as he considered what to do next. He ran a hand through his hair, stopping to rub his scalp for a second, thinking. I crossed my arms and just stood there, staring.

"Shae," he said after a while, "I don't know why you're so upset."

"Yes you do, Jonah. Yes, you really do."

"Look, you heard Mills, too. They think they might have a problem." He shrugged, as if that explained everything.

"Oh so now he's 'Mills' and not just 'son'?" I asked, giving him a light laugh.

"What's that supposed to mean?" Jonah scowled down at me. His six-foot-four frame towered over my own five-foot-ten, but I could match him in attitude any day of the week.

"When he's an annoyance to you he's just 'son,' but when you need to suddenly puff him up a little bit, make him someone to listen to, he gains his name back. Jonah, it's an old habit, and it doesn't work with me."

"I'm not playing any sort of game here, Shae," he insisted.

"Whatever. Look, there's no reason we can't go check it out, anyway."

I started to turn away, my arms still crossed, but he caught me by the shoulder and held me there. I didn't resist, letting him turn me back to face him. His face grew solemn and he glanced up before looking back down at me.

"Yeah, there is. If we let them call us back at every dropped hat they find in the road, we might as well not have retired in the first place," he said. I caught a note of sadness in his voice, but dismissed it in annoyance.

"And maybe we shouldn't have!" I yelled at him. I was just a girl when we first left planet, together, and never looked back to wonder if it'd been the right move. Now suddenly he was looking back and sounding like he saw nothing but dust back there.

"We're old, Shae! Look around you!" he yelled back. Then he took a deep breath and calmed down. "Damn, I'm not as fast as I was and I have to work twice as hard to keep in shape. It's time to let them grow up and take care of themselves. We can't have the entire military as our children."

I heard the words, I realized the truth in them, but I didn't like it. Not at all. Besides, my own anger wasn't quite spent yet and he was pissing me off. "Not that we treated our actual child like one, either," I shot back.

"You raised him, too, baby," he said, as a slow grin spread across his face.

"Maybe we both did a shit job at it."

"Maybe!" he said loudly, as the grin fell away fast. "Except you know damn well we did a great job, and Newt's a great kid."

"He really is, huh?" I shook my head. Mud was terrific and he might not have been ours by birth, but he was ours. And Jonah was right, the old soldier. Our little newt had grown into a strong man.

"Yeah, he is. And we're old. And maybe we should act it for a change, not run off guns blazing for once, and let the people who do our jobs now do them. For a change. Just to see what happens."

"I don't like this, Soldier."

"I know, baby. I know. No one wants feel old."

"I didn't until now."

"I have for years."

"Then why let it stop you now?" I asked. My anger was gone and that note of sadness in his voice was back. But the question was an honest one.

"I...because it's time, Shae, all right?" he answered.

"All right," I answered.

Except it wasn't all right, it wasn't even half right. He refused to go, felt old and unneeded. I knew better, and I wasn't going to let him wallow in his own self-imposed uselessness, wasting away. It wasn't right, not for either of us.

I patted his hand and left him outside to stare at the sky and think a while. I knew he would stay there, giving me space as much as needing it himself. I kicked off my gray slippers and padded around barefoot on the cool stone floor.

The thing of it was, I couldn't just force him to go. Not directly. But if I left without him, well, that would get him going. I would need some time; pulling together an excursion package without being noticed by your own husband is a bit of work. But not the roughest work ever, it'd just slow me down.

That kid, Mills, would report back to his boss and it would take a few days before they thought to call again. And I knew Hodges would call again, this time in person, to try and talk Jonah into the trip. I also knew Jonah would say no, again. So I had to be ready.

20

When Hodges called, I would be ready to run a trace on the signal. That was crucial. If I offered to go myself, without Jonah, they would say no. It was an oversight, and a stupid one, but I held no rank. They couldn't really call me in solo. With Jonah I was a freelancer, part of his team and accepted. But solo? Solo I hadn't bothered accepting a rank. I hadn't felt the need.

Now I did, but I couldn't fix that right away. I'd get around to it. Probably once I was up on Hodges' ship. Given the nature of his offer, I figured his command-class ship was nearby. No further out than Mars. I could rent a skimmer to get that far without worry. But the command ship would be cloaked, on principle, and guarded.

One did not simply walk in the front door of a command ship. Not without explosives and a secure force of at least ten people who knew what they were doing. The explosives I could drum up; the people would be a different problem. But, I reminded myself with a laugh, I wasn't invading them, I was going up to offer my own help. Which meant I could go up to the front door and ring the bell. If I could get myself that far. But no.

Getting in the front door without asking always proves a point about your usefulness. They couldn't say no once I did that. We'd both worked that game before. It was almost expected, I assumed. And I didn't want to disappoint.

So that was it, that was the plan. Wait about a week and then sneak off, heavily armed and prepared, break into a hidden command-class cruiser and offer my services. Once I was signed up, Jonah would follow. And he'd see it had been the right move all along. Sometimes I had to drag him in into realizing his own needs. It worked out.

I grabbed a bag and dropped a few hand blasters into it. Little things, not much battery or punch to them, but they were worth lugging. I would have to find those new grenades and sneak them home, somehow.

I stood there, staring at a mirror and grinning at my own reflection, and started to plan in earnest.

Chapter 3 – Mud

THE SONIC BLAST SHIMMERED the air near my head. It missed me, but the problem with sonic weapons boils down to the wave spread. They didn't have to hit you directly. The left side of my head felt squishy as I fell against a nearby wall. Sonics wreck your sense of balance, they feel like someone scraped your skin with a palm full of tiny needles, and they have a tendency, for me at least, to leave you feeling ... soft.

Luckily, none of the effects last long without a direct hit. Unluckily, even a short duration was longer than I had to recover. All four of the Reclaimers moved toward me at once, fencing me in, my back quite literally to the wall.

"Guys," I said, my voice deep and lumpy, "can't we discuss this? I know a good bar a few levels down."

Their leader shook his wide, flat head and croaked a laugh. "Exile-traitor, there is nothing to discuss."

I wondered if he practiced that kind of line in the mirror at night when his men weren't looking. Probably. Hurkz who worked for their Off-world Reclamation Project tended to be deficient in humor and oration skill. They lacked wit, but made up for it in perseverance.

This group, or ones like it, had been after me for a while now. Ever since I hit the Hurkz age of adulthood. Twenty-seven Earth years, roughly, but Hurkz had its own rotational speed and solar orbits to worry about. Me, I counted Earth years. I was raised there, mostly. And that was the crux of the issue.

I stopped thinking of the past and considered how I could end up with a future instead. I leapt, arms outstretched, and grabbed the sonic shooter's shoulders. We went down together, but I made sure he was on the bottom, taking all the force we managed to sum up between us on the way down. I rolled, catching a glimpse of the other three, and took the shooter with me as I did. He made good cover - they didn't want to harm their own man, after all.

I tucked up, my feet planting solidly against the shooter's chest, and shoved. He described a pretty arc as he flew right into one of his teammates. I took the second or two worth of confusion to get my own feet under me and run.

I had to get off the station, that much I knew. As long as I remained aboard I was too easy a target. One place - even a large one, if contained - is too easy to deal with. Open space – that's another matter.

I ran down a hallway, knowing it led ... somewhere. Well, somewhere I wasn't, and certainly somewhere my pursuers weren't, so that made it a better bet than anything else I had.

The corridor was well lit and brightly marked; the station's designers didn't want anyone getting lost. That was fantastic unless you were trying to get lost. I kept running, keeping an eye out for any decent-sized pool of shadow. Nothing caught my eye. I kept moving, my legs pistoning.

The hallway cut a sharp right turn. I took it, of course, and noticed the glowing sign cut into the wall as I moved past it. I was six levels up from the space dock, and on the wrong spiral arm of the station for my own ship to boot. Right then, running the whole way and avoiding the Hurkz stopped being viable.

I dropped and rolled to a halt, shedding momentum and changing direction as I did. Popping up, I slapped at a door panel, trying for access. The door opened and I slipped inside, knowing that the Hurkz team would be close enough to hear the door seal shut after me.

The room stood dark. I adjusted my goggles, resettling them over my large eyes, and took the few seconds I had to think. What I needed was a plan of some sort. Something beyond getting to my ship and getting off the station. If they caught me, it would be a long, painful trip to Hurkz followed by a short, painful execution.

Hurkz can camo themselves, to a degree. Their - well, our - skin may be a solid, unreflective midnight black, but there are markings along our skin that secrete light-activated chemicals. Those markings stand out in neon colors, but they're also what gives us the ability to camouflage ourselves. Each family has their own set of markings, given to them by evolution to help avoid predators in the distant past.

They run along our chests, backs, limbs, and faces. They stand out and declare to all other Hurkz who we are, what family, tribe, and country we come from. Unless, like me, you had been stolen as a child, slaved, and ended up with the markings tattooed over in the same black as your skin.

Then all you ended up with was a series of incredibly painful memories, bad ink, and the subtle glow of what you had lost. That tattooing ruined the glands, ruined the ability to hide. Which is why it was done in the first place. Which is part of why I needed to be put down, according to Hurkz law. I was tribeless. I was nothing.

And sure, a case could be made for that. I was a cripple. I couldn't camouflage myself, I couldn't belong to any family on Hurkz, I couldn't be a part of what I came from anymore, and that embarrassed them. It scared them.

Of course, I thought with a grim smile creasing my wide face, what nature gives technology can replicate. I hit the wrist controls on my thinsuit. The suit was as black as my skin, and specially coated. Where my markings were ruined, the suit would serve. The shadows in the room were dark, but not black enough to hide me. The suit helped. It quickly changed to match the bulkhead behind me as best it could. It only took a few needles to do. I felt them prick my skin and snarled briefly. The jolts of pain remind me of tattoo needles, every time.

I pressed back against the wall and stayed as still as possible. The suit was one of a kind, and it worked by taking the minimal secretions of my marking glands (what was left of them), enhancing the effects, and acting much like my skin would have.

The bulkhead door was cracked open, leaving where I was obvious to anyone who'd seen me running down the hall. I stood there, as hidden as

26

possible, and waited. I saw their shadows before I saw them, and I tried to press myself closer to the wall. My back itched. I fought down the urge to rub it against the molding.

One of them entered the room and glanced around quickly. He didn't see me. My luck was holding. He waved the others in and they started to search the room, closer. Much closer and I would be spotted. Instead of waiting around, I ducked back out the door and started to run, turning off the suit's camo effect. Drained the batteries, anyway.

I padded down the corridor, trying to be as quiet as possible. I hit the emergency ladder hatch and yanked it open, but the damn panel stuck, and it clanged as it tore free. I shoved myself into the ladder area and started down, knowing the chase was back on.

This was getting me nowhere. I exited two levels down and started to move off along a corridor, but knew I was wasting time. Look, if I ran and kept running maybe I could reach my ship first. But the space dock I'd parked in was probably the same one they had used, so that wouldn't buy me much time. No matter how much more trapped I felt in a station, I wouldn't really be freer in my ship.

No, running only prolonged dealing, as my father liked to remind me. Not that he knew about this - Mom either. I didn't want to bother them with it, and I didn't want them to step in and deal with it for me. I was an adult. So the running had to stop.

I stood near the ladder and waited. Sure enough, they were coming down after me. I grabbed the ankles of the Hurkz Reclaimer furthest down and dragged him out of the ladder well. His face hit the floor, my boot hit his head. When he didn't raise it I kicked him aside, hoping the other three would be just as easy.

Nope. The next guy had thought to look down before he came into grabbing range. Must've looked down before that, even, smart one. He dropped, free-falling, into sight and grabbed at the ladder to stop himself, already firing. Sonics flashed out into the hall. I dove for some sort of cover, finding the unconscious Hurkz on the floor adequate. His body quivered as the sonics hit. I grabbed his blaster and fired back.

Somehow, possibly since I hadn't done anything but run until this point, they weren't expecting that. He went down hard, catching the waveform full in the chest. Too bad he hadn't gotten out of the ladder well first. I heard him bump into things on his way down. It was only another four or so levels until the bottom. I'm sure he landed fine.

I fired again, this time into the metal tube that held the ladder. I wasn't trying to hit anyone, I just thought it might rattle them. Sadly, station rules worked against me. They could carry limited weapons as agents of their government. I was a no one and so I was unarmed, also held to station standards. Hardly fair.

I thought it through. Right about now, Dad would be going in after them, bringing the fight right to their faces. Mom would sneak around them and blow them back to where they came from. Neither option suited me.

The only way to truly stop them was to kill them. I didn't want to kill them, truth be told. Killing them would only make it harder to get off the station, and would also manage to ensure that the next Reclaimer team sent after me would have more guys with bigger guns. It seemed that running might be my only good call in this. After I disabled them, of course.

I fired into the ladder tube again, springing into the opening after my shot. The two Reclaimers were holding onto the ladder tightly, weathering the blasts and preparing some sort of answering shot.

They *really* didn't expect me to come in after them. I fired twice, straight up, and wrapped my arms around the ladder tightly as the sonics reverberated back down the tube at me. Damn, I hate sonics.

I think, right then, they hated the sonics more than I did. At least that's what the looks on their faces told me as they started to fall past me. I knew that the drop wouldn't actually kill them. A leg broken, maybe. A concussion, bruising, and a general feeling of "that wasn't pleasant" could all result, but death? Doubtful.

I jumped back out of the ladder well and took off again, toward the hanger area. I passed all sorts of people, being in a much more populated area of the station. They looked at me. Part of those looks was just annoyance at someone running past them, shoving them when needed. It wasn't polite, and I resisted the urge to apologize as I went, saving my breath for the running.

The other looks, though, those I had gotten used to. Correction: I had tried to get used to them. The looks that spoke of an alien in their midst. The mistrust, the distaste, those looks of mild horror.

We all hit space at some point, but we don't get past a base us-versus-them mentality all too often.

I took the turns and level changes of the station as quickly as I could until, slapping the access plate hard, I entered the hanger area that held my ship. My ship hung there, held in place by a good-sized clamp, waiting. I saw the Hurkz Reclaimer transport a few docks down. Smart guys, they parked close to me. As I approached my ship, feeling home free, I sighed. Above my ship, the dock light flashed red. Which meant that my ship was in lockdown.

Stupid, stupid, stupid. Of course they had contacted the station authorities and had my ship held. Why wouldn't they? Pure amateur move on my part, but it wasn't the first today. I was sloppy and I knew it. No time for berating myself, though. There would be time later, once I got my ship free.

Dock locking didn't prevent me from entering the ship and I hurried aboard, scrambling down the thin hallway that made up the center of the ship, until I got to the cockpit. I turned the atmo cleaners up high and leaned back as the air grew warm and thick with humidity. My goggles came off, letting my eyes relax in the wet air. I sighed deeply and considered my options. Grinning, I thumbed the communications array.

"This is Reclaimer Squad Seventeen," I said in my best Hurkz. I didn't know too much of the language, but Mom insisted I learn it when I was kid. Wanted me to know where I came from and all that.

"Repeat, please," came the Station's reply.

Bingo. They didn't speak Hurkz. Why would they, it was rare that a Hurkz ship would stop here and rarer still that they wouldn't speak a more common tongue.

"Repeat, please," they said again.

"Reclaimer Squad Seventeen, requesting dock freedom," I said in Hurkz.

"Docked ship T194-MURT, please reply in a common field language."

I laughed under my breath and let out a loud rumble. Directly into the mic. I followed it quickly, though. "Reclaimer Squad Seventeen, request this ship release, for compound," I said in thick, halting English.

"T194-MURT, this is Dock Captain Byrne, your ship is being held by..."

"Know why! We are ones who did," I shouted. "And now need ship. Let free. Authority Hurkz government."

"Dock release in seventy seconds, sir," they replied. This was perfect. They were just dumb enough to think we all sounded the same, and my scenario seemed reasonable enough that they could be lazy. These guys sat in a room all day just telling people how to back up; they aimed at lazy whenever they could reasonably get away with it. They didn't even think to ask for a pass code.

The clamp holding my ship released and I eased out of the dock, slowly. No sudden moves and no one will notice what you're doing. I backed the ship out and turned it, also slowly.

Once I was clear of the dock, I shifted my ship over to the side and aligned it with the Hurkz ship, tail to tail. I backed it up nice and close, looking exactly like what I said I was, before I fired the main thrusters and took off. The wash from my engine melted, bent and otherwise screwed up their propulsion system but good. The Dock Command would see it as some sort of stupid flight accident.

At least at first. By the time they knew better, I would be off and slipping through space. I accelerated hard and thought about how I intended to clean this mess up without letting Mom and Dad know about it.

Chapter 4 – Meanwhile

THE SCOUT SHIPS SAT docked comfortably in place. The pilots sat around and bragged, telling tales about how they had grabbed up each specimen right from under the noses of the locals. They told stories, to each other and anyone else who would stop, heightening their skill and determination to phenomenal levels.

They cheered and drank and drank and cheered. They celebrated and knew that they had earned the right. Thanks to them, the fleet could go on and their race could survive.

Meanwhile, in other parts of the fleet, scientists carefully analyzed the data brought back. They dissected new specimens and ran tests. Though they didn't boast, working long hours, each one of them planned their nights out for later dates when they could sit and quietly tell stories of their work. They, too, wanted to strut and impress. But first, like the pilots had, they needed to prove themselves, yet again.

Another world, another set of data to pore over. They worked as quickly as the pilots. Efficiency could not be overrated. Time was against them, as ever. Still, they did their work and passed it on, with only one word stamped on the cover of their reports: Acceptable.

The reports landed on the desks of generals and field leaders. They took the baton of information and ran with it. They were well trained, each one hiding their impatience at useless delays.

The fleet moved on with purpose.

The planet Tenzil sat fat, blue and green in space. It rotated on its own axis, as well as rotating around its primary star. Tenzil whipped through space, just like millions of other planets did.

On its surface, life varied. Different landmasses held different cultures, each a strain of the other, and all looking quite similar to someone from the outside who simply didn't know better.

Without understanding the nuances of Tenzil's life forms, one could easily mistake it for a planet conquered by one life form at the expense of all others. Taking it further, from space, the cultures - each of which considered itself unique - looked so close to each other that the differences became local color.

Wars hadn't broken out on Tenzil in centuries, though each faction still held itself up as the true and right one. They worked together under a green sky, pregnant with ghostlike algae that floated through the upper winds, giving the planet a hot, humid atmosphere.

When the scout ships first came down onto Tenzil, the locals dismissed them. While familiar with space travel and life on other systems, the entire existence of aliens still seemed, to most, like the concern (or ramblings) of a select few. A few factions even resorted to blaming neighboring factions for making the whole thing up in an effort to destabilize global politics.

Into that mindset the fleet descended. Tenzil, to its credit, caught on quickly but still scoffed a bit. How do you, they said, thinking themselves smart, invade an entire planet? It was a question posed by the fleet itself once. But then they remembered that they weren't invading: they were harvesting, and that was a different game altogether.

The attack ships screamed down into the planet's atmosphere, sending whorls and eddies of algae spiraling out of control. They rushed down - no warning or preamble given. Then they opened fire.

The ships could outfly anything on Tenzil, and they knew it. They targeted defense positions across multiple land masses for simultaneous destruction. Before Tenzil knew what hit it, the fleet had laid waste to their defenses. It didn't take long after that.

Mountains were leveled, simply to see how fast they would crumble. Natives were gathered up and dissenters shot. Cities were razed to the ground as quickly as fields were set on fire. No one bothered to contact any of the governments on Tenzil, no one offered surrender as an option or even announced an intent. They effortlessly came down from the blackness of space and opened fire on anything that seemed worth firing on.

Some of the attack was distraction. Some designed to negate any force Tenzil could muster. The pilots grinned in their ships, opening throttles wide as their engines bit air, and let themselves enjoy their work. They knew, though, that their destruction wasn't the point of the exercise. The harvesting was.

Two out of every three people on Tenzil found themselves being loaded aboard large transport ships and flown back to the body of the fleet. That third person in each statistical group only found themselves shot, crushed, burned or otherwise killed. If they had known what awaited the others, they might have even considered themselves the lucky ones.

The ones who ended up on the transport ships were packed in like so much waste, crammed and shoved hard. They broke limbs and lost meager lunches when the acceleration hit, the transport ships lifting off toward the main fleet. At the other end they were dumped out onto wide floors, cold to the touch. Then they were herded and pushed, into processing plants. The sound of gears, the feel of searing heat, and the vibration of heavy machinery were the last things they remembered.

Tenzil went dark within three days. The fleet stayed another two, cleaning up and ensuring they had gotten every life form worth getting into their processing plants. Satisfied, the fleet gave everyone two days off, knowing from their advance scouts that they could afford it.

The fleet leaders also knew that such luxury would not always be the case. The deeper into the systems they went, the less time they would have. Word would spread, and they couldn't stop it. They also couldn't stop their trek or alter their path. They knew it as certainly as they knew that Tenzil's unwilling sacrifice had ensured that the fleet would last a while longer.

Before they left for good, they paused to give thanks to Tenzil for providing life for them.

Solemnly, all forms of celebration ceased on order, and the entire fleet stopped to give thanks for their boon. Not one of them took it lightly.

Hours after the thanks were given and the fleet had restarted, the advance scouts went off again, even as the longer-range scouts returned. The short-range scouts sought the next system, not even stopping to welcome the long-range scouts home. They launched and continued their trek across the galaxy. Soon enough, they reasoned, the time for celebration would come again.

Chapter 5 – Jonah

MY HAND RESTED lightly against the rough bark of a tree. I trailed fingers along the surface, letting the rough ridges implant their sense memory in my mind. I told myself I stopped here to feel that tree, to remember it. Not because I couldn't run anymore.

My right knee bitched at me, throbbing blindly. I had run a sprint into the woods, a few miles from the house, as part of my workout. Working off lunch, I told myself. Working off anger was the truth. I resented the hell out of being called. In the past I would've vented it, fought and railed against it. These days, I moved off into the woods and got my aggression out.

Sometimes, though, my aggression got me instead. The sprint started fine, and I reveled in the force of my legs pumping under me. Then, as it did when pushed too hard, my knee buckled. I didn't fall. I didn't go down on one knee. I just limped, at speed, to a nearby tree.

Which is where I stood. I wasn't even winded. I drew a deep breath anyway, tasting the clean air, and then exhaled. I forced my lungs to deflate as much as possible, good spacer technique, and held myself there. No air, nothing for the body to work with. I held it, and then I held it some more. My chest started to burn, but my will was stronger than my flesh. I waited until I felt lightheaded, just the start of it, and then allowed myself to inhale again. Not deeply: normally.

I had been out about three hours. Before I left, Shae and I talked for a while, quietly. We agreed that we would call Mills back and maybe work out some sort of advisory plan. We could suggest some people to replace us.

My fingers worried at the bark unconsciously as I listed names in my head: Hendricks, Shaffer, Turk, Grayson, Tucker, Dansk, Glurt, Dugan, Po'Leen. All dead. All under my command at one time or another. Together we'd made the best insertion team anyone had seen.

Each of them, after a time, got unlucky. Over the years they'd joined up, each one replacing another irreplaceable officer. Over the years, each had met the same fate. Fighting for something bigger than themselves, they'd fallen while under my command. Shae and I were the only ones left.

It made me wary, some nights. I didn't drag myself over coals for them - no nightmares of lost comrades for me - but I still felt their losses one by one. I counted them, on the bad nights, the way some men count sheep. Who was left, damn it all, to do this job? New kids, people I hadn't met yet. It was that simple, and I forced smooth the rough edges of the truth that threatened to rankle.

I reached down, instead, and felt my knee. Bits of bark flaked onto my leg and I puzzled for a second before stopping to glance at the tree. Gaping rents in the bark showed me exactly how much those deaths did bother me. I brushed my hand off, wiping it across my chest, and reached for my knee again.

Swollen, but serviceable. I decided to risk another sprint. I got maybe fifty feet before the knee gave out again. My wordless rage scared a nearby bird or two. Retirement I could deal with. It was, I realized, safe. Safe was acceptable. I had done enough and more than earned my rest. The betrayal of my body, however - that burned and ate at me like a fire.

I started to walk back home. There was nothing else to do. It was getting dark, anyway. Soon working off lunch would become missing dinner, and Shae was going to grill some steaks.

I walked, keeping a normal pace. About an hour out, the sky flashed white for a second. Several sonic booms sounded off at once and I stopped to listen and watch. I couldn't make out the ships in question - they rose too fast. Their engines didn't sound familiar, either.

That kind of flash was a scatter tactic, a way to keep people from pinpointing you on their systems or with their eyes. There was no reason for it unless you were going out of your way to be untraceable. Generally it only worked with a cluster of ships, to confuse the enemy as to which ship went where. Good for double-blinds and switching out payload vehicles. Useless for what looked like two ships.

I couldn't tell where they launched from, exactly, but it had to be within fifty miles of the house. Shae would have picked them up and scanned them. I figured she'd let me know what they were when I got in.

They might've been coming from the house itself, and maybe Shae was in trouble, but we'd each had a sub-dermal panic tracker installed years ago. It hadn't gone off, so I didn't worry. She could, I knew

40

all too well, take care of herself. And the house, with any sort of warning, was a small fortress when need be.

I kept walking, picking up my pace anyway. My knee complained, but I was careful to move only as fast as I could without crossing over the line to disabling myself. She was fine. I knew it. I didn't slow down, regardless.

The house looked fine from the outside. It's when things are quiet, when the picture you see is exactly what you expect, that everything is likely to be wrong. I picked up my pace and, knee be damned, sprinted the last bit to the front door. I rested, leaning against the outside wall of the house, my hand cool against the siding. I allowed myself three deep breaths to recover and then grabbed the doorknob tightly, turning it. The readers in the knob unlocked the door and let me in.

There was no reason for the door to be locked. We didn't keep it locked when one of us was home. I dove into the house, not taking any chances, and rolled to a stop behind the couch. Nothing moved. Nothing at all.

"Shae!" I called out, trying to decide if I was being foolish or prudent. But I knew. I hadn't stayed alive by ignoring my gut on things like this. If I looked like an idiot later for my actions, so be it. But if I didn't...

Well, then, there I was.

There was no response to my shout. I stood, warily, and made my way to the kitchen. Two steaks lay out on the counter. They sat there, on a cutting board, nearing room temperature with every passing second. Damn it all. I couldn't piece it together, not quite.

I started to search the house. I moved methodically, if carefully. Flung doors open hard and waited, clear of the doorways. Switched on overheads as I went, casting the whole place in harsh, telling light. I stopped in the bedroom and tapped a section of the floor with my foot, hard. A panel swung down and I reached in, pulling out an old gun.

Projectile weaponry wasn't in common use anymore, wasteful and too dangerous aboard a ship, but I kept one around the house just in case. Most people armored against sonics and minor heat-based weaponry. They weren't up to a .45-caliber round in the chest. I enjoyed the edge it gave to home security.

But there was nothing to secure. I wandered the house and found it as silent as the night sky. Nothing obvious. Not a single damned thing. The place looked like Shae had simply walked off in the middle of preparing dinner and forgot to lock up behind herself. So sure, if I was crazy, it made perfect sense.

I wasn't crazy. Not yet. So I moved on to the weapons store, the room that no one, except us, could get into. We had tested the doors against all sorts of munitions, having to redo the walls of the bedroom several times due to the blast radium. There was no way through the door, or the walls surrounding it, if you even knew where it was.

I slid myself down the stairs and hit the lights. Shae had been here, but I couldn't tell how recently. Nothing seemed too disturbed, which meant she'd come here to take an inventory and think. Still, nothing seemed to be missing.

I checked the lockboxes that took up an entire corner of the room and saw they were still secure. I checked them anyway, my hand running over the ridged metal, tracing years of memory.

I pulled my hand away, growing frustrated with myself, and crossed the room to the small lab we kept. An atmospheric scanner, a heat residue monocle, and a jamming box found their way into my hands without much thought. As I left, I grabbed a small, red metal box and headed upstairs. Lights off and door secured, I went back to the kitchen.

The monocle showed me recent heat signatures, and I watched faded memories of my wife as she had moved around the room. Blurry and fading fast, there didn't seem to be anything abnormal. I followed her phantom out of the room.

The entranceway. Four other signatures leapt out at me, and by the brightly lit trails of their passage I could see a struggle. Shae's heat index rose as she took them on, but one of them was crystal: arm raised and unmoving. He fired something. A disrupter, sonics, or worse? I couldn't tell.

I could tell that whatever it was hadn't taken Shae out. The specter of her passing blurred off toward the bedroom. Of course, she was going for the exact gun that tugged my waistband down with its firm weight. She didn't get there. The four figures, their heat dropped noticeably, stood in the entranceway. I saw Shae's shape on the floor, heat dropped low.

The atmo scanner flicked to life at my command. I thumbed the controls and swept the entire place. Minimal traces of gas in the bedroom. Not enough left to bother me now - it had dissipated quickly, but would certainly have been enough to take her out.

My vision threatened to blur. Whoever they were, they had taken my wife. You don't do that and live. It's a simple equation. I studied the shape of the four figures as best I could, working only from their heat residue. Their shape, their armor and basic shape, seemed strange to me. Inhuman.

I thought back to Mills. He said the invaders were, if his reports were right, taking people. If they were smart, at all, they would have known the Government would call us. So why not head here and grab us. But if they didn't know everything— what if they were *just* loose enough in their research, coupled with being alien, that they thought Shae was me? Or that they figured taking her was good enough?

I grabbed the phone and dialed without looking. The code didn't change, that was certain. A voice answered, but I couldn't hold on to what it said. I didn't care.

"Get me Mills. This is Madison, Jonah. Calling on hot basis," I said in a simple monotone. I didn't trust myself to talk above that, not then. Not when they had Shae.

Mills came on quickly, asking me what was wrong, what had been done and pressed me for how he could help. I told him what I knew. He started to fuss and bother, offering suggestions and plans. I cut him off hard.

"Send a ship. You wanted me on this, I'm on it. I need a transport ship, within an hour."

"Of course, Captain Madison," he agreed quickly, "I'm sorry it—"

"Save it. Less talking, more getting it done. Jonah out."

I hung up the phone and stared at it. I wanted to crush it, to throw it through a window, something. Anything that would make me feel better. None of it would, so I put the phone back and went into the bedroom to change.

I grabbed my dress uniform from the closet and changed into it quickly. It felt like coming home, and I would have smiled if I wasn't so ready to kill. I strode back out and opened the red metal box.

I took out the two things in the box and pitched it back into the room over my shoulder. Stepping outside, I left the door open and stared into the darkened sky. Stars stared back. Soon I would be among them again. For all the wrong reasons.

I uncoiled the holster belt I had taken from the red box and belted it on tightly. Then I hefted my gun, my old friend; the gun that had blasted the foot off of Talkon-Galxos' President Alfonse, cut through the airlock on the Halgoron battle cruiser, and served me well in a thousand other moments. The gun that had saved my life for years on end.

I lifted the gun and pointed it directly at the North Star, sighting along the barrel. I flicked off the safety and checked the power levels. Satisfied, my thumb clicked the safety back on and I slammed the gun home, deep into its holster. The creak of the leather when the gun settled felt *right*.

"I'm coming for you, baby," I said to the stars.

I stood there, military straight, and waited. Nothing would move me again, except purpose. Right then, I had only one of those. I waited.

Chapter 6 – Jonah

AFTER A WHILE I thought better of just standing there and went back into the house to grab a few things. Not much: a decent-sized bag of personal items and clothes, a few equipment boxes, and the like. I got it all outside and locked the house down. I put all of its systems into sleep mode and rerouted the phone to my personal communicator. By the time I was finished, there was a ship landing on my front lawn.

Wide and solid, the thing was built like a brick. Extraction and personnel ships never did have style. Still, it shone in the night, gleaming like a dark promise. The thing settled down, lowering itself the last few feet on air jets. Running lights flashed from warning red to approachable green and the pilot hatch opened.

"Captain Madison?" the pilot asked, climbing down to greet me.

"Jonah," I said, and nodded.

"Spaceman first class Malik, sir. I—" he looked at the stack of boxes next to me, "well, sir, I'm not sure that all of that is allowable cargo."

"Malik? All of that has to go with me."

He nodded, caught between his conflicting duties, "No, I understand that, sir, but those three boxes were reading as high-grade cargo from the air. Regulations state—"

"That you can't transport them without proper paperwork, security, and authorization, right?" I asked.

He nodded. And there was his problem. His first job was to get me up to the command ship as soon as possible. His second job was to fly correctly, where "correctly" meant that he followed the rules and didn't endanger anyone through neglect. Letting my cargo onboard could constitute neglect if something went wrong, and that could cost him his flight status. I felt bad for him.

"Well Malik, I do understand your situation," I said, swallowing my impatience, "but you need to see the bigger picture. You were told this was a high priority recall, yes?"

"Yes, sir, Captain Madison—"

"Jonah," I corrected him.

"Jonah," he corrected smoothly, if uneasily, "but if my sweep readings were right, I can't take those crates."

"Look," I said, feeling the annoyance threaten to creep into my voice, "nothing is going to go wrong with these crates." I pulled out my blaster. "These things are built to withstand more firepower than either of us have. Hell, you could drop them from orbit and they wouldn't crack." I fired directly at one of the black crates and the surface shrugged it off, not even marring.

"Uhm," Malik said, raising an eyebrow, "is that an Acadian blaster?"

"Yeah," I said with a shrug. I holstered the gun and kicked a crate, "and see, the crates are fine. So why don't we load them up and go already?"

"Sir, Jonah, Acadian blasters are illegal. I can't transport that, either."

Which is when I lost my temper for a second. "Damn it all, you have your orders and you'll fulfill them! This stuff goes or I don't. Is that clear, Spaceman First Class?"

"Yes sir, sir!" he barked, on instinct. I outranked him and there was only so much he could push. "But we'll have to wait for—"

"I'll authorize it, and take full responsibility. I'm sure there are recorders on your ship that are picking this up, so there's your certified auth. Let's get this stuff on board."

Malik took a deep breath and held it, as if waiting for lighting to strike him down. None came, and he started to help me load the three matching crates into the ship, keeping silent. We finished quickly enough and I started for the passenger hatch. As much as I wanted to sit in the copilot seat, I knew it wouldn't be allowed and I didn't want to push my luck forcing the poor guy to break too many regulations.

"Sir," Malik said, in a tone of voice I was already familiar with. He had a problem.

"Yeah?" I asked, knowing what it was before I asked.

"The blaster, sir, Jonah, I can't. An illegal weapon, in a side holster? It isn't even locked down."

"The gun stays."

"On board, sir, you'll have to put it in a passenger safe lock."

"We'll see. Let's get going, all right?"

"Yes, sir."

He climbed back into the cockpit and I trundled up into the passenger area. This being a military transport ship, it wasn't exactly lush. Acceleration couches sat lining the walls, each one with a secure storage area under the seat.

The storage boxes were big enough for rifles, and really only designed for larger munitions then a handgun. My blaster would have rattled around in there, possibly doing some surface damage to it. Not that I would notice a few more scratches along the grip, but I saw no reason to bother.

So I thumbed the box open and then closed, knowing Malik couldn't see me but would register the lock cycle on his panel. As long as he thought I locked down the gun, he would be fine with it. What he didn't know wouldn't force me to consider hurting him.

The engines cycled on, lifting via air jet for the first few feet. Then the thrusters cut in, softly, and we rumbled to life. The ship vibrated and tilted as Malik changed our angle of attack, nosing up against the pull of gravity. I had no windows, no way to see what was going on outside, but I didn't need to. I knew takeoff like I knew the back of my hand.

I leaned back and closed my eyes, enjoying every second of it. The engines picked up and roared to full life. My body felt like it compressed, becoming paper thin as the vibrations increased, shattering my sense of self for an instant.

We broke clear of atmosphere cleanly. The engines settled for a minute, and I felt the lurch to weightlessness. I kept count in my head and ended up only a few seconds off. The engines cut back in and internal gravity settled over my body, dragging me back down.

The ship accelerated, providing that funny feeling that always accompanies travelers in artificial gravity. The pitch of the engines told me we were moving, speeding up, but inside the ship I could feel no actual sign of it. The gravity field cancelled out and kept us all at one Earth standard.

Maybe it was because I had spent so much time dealing with them, but artificial gravity fields *felt* artificial. There were subtle clues, if you knew what to look for. The fields just felt off, and it took me a second to settle into myself again.

Gravity fields, engines and all, had helped us expand out through space. But the bigger the ship, the less they could use them. You couldn't use gravity as a raw engine for anything bigger than the smallest of crafts, or the forces when you turned would rip a ship apart.

So medium-sized ships like this, able to carry twenty or less, only used them as environmental fields to keep passengers safe, and to help with higher acceleration. Bigger ships, like the command-class cruiser we headed toward, would use the fields the same way, not able to really let the engines incorporate the fields to push more than a smidge. Smaller, single-person fighters could engage gravity engines for a short push, but normally kept the interior gravity off unless the ship was making such a hard velocity shift that you needed the field to stay alive.

The command ship wasn't far beyond the moon and we made good time, Malik being a good pilot and keeping us on the closest course possible.

Before I grew fidgety we were docking, our gravity field snapping off so it wouldn't interfere with the larger ship's own doings.

Malik hit the doors and managed to meet me before I could climb out. He was good. I made a note of him in my head and gave him a nod as I passed. Normally I would've stopped and chatted, talked about the flight plan and whatnot. Not this time. Malik seemed to understand, at least, nodding back and standing at attention with his helmet under his arm.

There was a young kid waiting for me as I walked off the ship. Had to be Mills. He had the look, that nervous glance, the underlying steel just starting to form with experience.

"Captain Madison—" Mills started, but I cut him off with a shake of my head.

"Jonah."

"Jonah," he corrected, "we should go talk to the General."

"We should. Where is she? Where'd they take her?"

"The General can discuss that with you," Mills told me, turning sharply and starting to walk away.

I grabbed him arm and turned him back to me, being none too polite about it. I wasn't in the mood for games, protocol, or niceties.

"Mills," I told him, staring hard into his eyes, "you'll tell me what you know - what *you* know," I repeated clearly, "as we walk. Understood?"

"Yes, sir," he said softly. I let go of his arm and we walked off the flight deck and into the bowels of the ship.

CHAPTER 7 – JONAH

THE COMMAND BRIDGE surrounded me sleekly, convincing me my age would be a hindrance. I try not to get caught in the trap of "in my day," but I admit to having difficulty once the gleaming command nexus started curving in every direction. Had I really been out of the game long enough for them to redesign the major ships in the fleet - again?

I knew the answer to that question and also knew better than to ask it. Damn. Still, a bridge is a bridge. So what if I felt like I stood on a kid's toy? It worked, right?

"This place works, right?" I asked Mills. I gave him a small shrug to punctuate the question.

"Uhhh, yes sir?" he answered, hesitating. Great, now the kid was wondering whether senility had set in. Perfect. No, none of it mattered. I shoved everything out and only let Shae in. Focus.

The General came on deck not long after Mills and I. Hodges looked utterly in control as his men stood and saluted him. I knocked one out for him, too - after all, I stood in his house. He looked me up and down and noted the weapon at my belt with disdain.

"Captain Madison," he said, walking quickly over to me.

"Jonah, General, just Jonah. Now, where'd they take my wife?"

"Easy there, Captain," he said, stopping a foot or so away and facing me dead on. Hodges and I didn't have too much history - I'd heard of him while he came up the ranks but never bothered to really follow the man's career. I couldn't keep track of everyone. What I did know boiled down to him being mostly business with the occasional dumb risk to get things done. That all wrapped before he hit General, though. Since then we'd talked once or twice, but nothing critical or even memorable. I just knew I'd never grown warm to the man.

"Easy my ass. You wanted me here to stop some sort of invasion. Fine. I'm here to get my wife. Let's not misunderstand each other, General, sir," I told him. He didn't faze at all.

"And we'll get her back, Captain," he said, "but we also do have priorities. Yes, of course, getting your wife back is one of them, but working out what we're up against and then *stopping it* has to take precedence."

Not true, but no point in telling him that just then. Shrugging, I added a quick nod to keep us moving somewhere useful.

Mills redirected the conversation before I could, putting a hand to his ear and growing pale. "Sir," he addressed Hodges, "we have reports of the long-rage command group about to engage the invaders."

"Already?" Hodges looked surprised.

"Yes sir, General. Flight leader says that it's a small recon force."

"Perfect. Captain Madison, would you accompany me to the battle deck? This is exactly why I wanted your help." Hodges wasted no time, starting to move as soon as Mills mentioned the established contact. I liked that.

"Only if you call me Jonah," I said, already falling in step behind him.

"Jonah, then," he said over his shoulder, "this way."

Mills stayed right with us and the three of us left the command bridge, taking a lift down into the battle deck. Battle decks never changed, no matter how sleek they made the bridges. A battle deck was all function.

One large plotting area sat in the center of the large open space, a big table with a screen embedded in it to display whatever the field of combat happened to be. Markers for us and them sat along the edges, being moved into position silently by deck hands with earpieces, listening to navigation updates. All around the outer rim of the room, other people stood by: on communications, collating data, bringing the field reports in and handing them off to the deck hands who made them come to life on that table. That awful table.

I hated battle decks, even as I made sure not to blame the men and women who manned them for my distaste. No matter how you measured it, the problem came out the same: I couldn't deal with anyone who was so removed from what a fight felt like trying to help me fight one. I knew those were their jobs and they were good at them, but battle decks and I didn't see eye to eye. And now I stood on one, apparently expected to help them, somehow.

"You've had no contact with them before this?" I asked Hodges, who raised an eyebrow at me.

"We have had limited contact, but nothing definitive enough to consider telling. This is our first engagement."

"That's not what Mills told me."

"It's what Mills knew," Hodges said, resting his hands on the edges of the plotting area. "Let's get this board live!" he barked, and our discussion of how much anyone knew ended with a snap.

The plotting area flickered to life, stars and planets fuzzing into view. Deck hands quickly pushed markers into position. I looked around for Hodges' other battle advisors and realized that the three of us were the only ones who didn't live in this space.

"Hodges," I asked, ignoring chain of command and all of that. I didn't care and was sick of pretending. "Where's the rest of your battle crew?"

"That's General, Jonah," he corrected me, but not unkindly, "and we are the battle crew. This whole thing is being kept hush-hush, orders from above. It's why we needed you."

"Because you can't trust your own men? That doesn't wash, General."

"It's the truth, Jonah," he lied to me.

"Yeah, sure. It still doesn't wash."

"Listen, Captain Madison," he said, spitting out the words, "this whole operation is classified. We don't want to leak that we've had contact until we know more."

"No dice yet, General." I turned and looked around the room. We were still crewed, just not with actual advisors. Which meant that Hodges didn't want to hear anything other than his input, and mine.

It brought up a question of why he would want that: what was he trying to keep away from me? I could've assumed he wanted to keep information from his advisors, but really the variable in the room was me, which shifted things in my direction. I bit back a wave of old-standing paranoia and brushed away the feeling that the events unfolding were being faked for my benefit. The expense, uselessness, and sheer audacity of someone trying that didn't hold water. No, Hodges kept something from me, possibly multiple somethings, though I couldn't begin to tell what they were, and found himself willing to put his own men at risk for it. That pissed me off.

Shae still held the top spot in my focus, but if Hodges tossed his own men, good men, to the wolves just to play games...bile rose in my throat. Those men and women were all a Shae to someone waiting back home. The operation stood live, regardless, and my anger wouldn't do any good – and neither would leaving. All I could do was win this.

I gripped the edge of the table tight and took a deep breath. Hodges watched me, uncertain as to what thoughts roiled across my brain. Good. Let him wonder. I'd do my job and then explain to him exactly why he was a damned fool. Probably teaching him the lesson at the end of my fist.

The board sat, lit and waiting. Techs stood back, only reaching in when they found a marker to shift. I watched the angles unfold in front of me and turned, looking behind me.

"Get these markers off the board," I demanded.

The techs gaped at me and when I turned back, Hodges had the same look on his face. They were thinking like a battle group, which may have been right for what they normally did, but I couldn't think that way. I had no training, not in this state of the game, I keyed off of being in the battle, not watching it from afar and calling plays.

"Get me more star markers. Color code them for battle groups," I said quickly, "and throw them in the holographic field. I need all three dimensions, damn it!"

How anyone ever helped run a battle operation on a flat table when we piloted across an entire extra angle baffled me. I'd seen it done - I knew it could be done, obviously, otherwise no one would still do it - but it felt wrong.

The star field shifted and grew in size. Colors changed, mimicking the marker colors used previously. The board techs stayed away from the table, their job changing before their eyes. No markers to move meant no reason for them to stand there and help out. Instead they moved to the walls, shifting placement of the new "stars," my makeshift markers. I nodded at Hodges and watched tiny dots move around a field. Our men were outnumbered, but not too drastically.

"What's the goal, here, General?" I asked him, fighting to regain full composure, at least verbally.

"Take them out, but grab at least two prisoners in the process. We need to know more."

"Fair enough." I glanced behind me again. "Hey, can you rig up call signs to show with the battle group?" The techs nodded at me, and a short while later names popped into place.

The two groups closed toward visual range. We tensed in the room as, I'm sure, they did in the ships themselves.

Chapter 8 – Mud

I APPROACHED A CLOUD of debris and considered my options: around or through. Around would take longer, though not much, but going through could prove interesting. Harder to fly through, of course, but you didn't become a good pilot without learning how to fly through the hard stuff. Or a crazy pilot, for that matter. But being good and sometimes crazy had saved my life a few times. Through it would be.

I slid into the field, cutting the ship around what looked to be someone's cockpit. They didn't seem to need it anymore, at least. I slowed down, pinging out for any signs of life, electronic or otherwise. Nothing came back. A ship's central banks should be protected enough to survive the level of destruction I saw around me. But I got nothing back to let me know the banks were floating out there. That made me curious.

I slowed down, nudging closer to the wrecked cockpit. No blood stains on the seating, so whoever had flown her had also gotten out. No bodies floating nearby, so that theory held. For now.

The ship's data bank was normally kept in the back of the cockpit. Easily reachable for emergency measures, but not up front where it could be hit by simple crashes. Kept in a secure box, radiation blocked, extra thick, all the standards: each one was supposed to be able to withstand the destruction of the ship and keep pinging out for recovery.

Here I had a cockpit with nothing. No ping, no extraneous destruction. The thing hung there, spinning slowly in space, while I looked it over. The edges weren't especially scorched or melted, which tended toward a no-explosion explanation. So what had happened here? Was it calmly torn apart?

There was no good way to find out from inside my ship. Scans weren't telling me enough. I reset my goggles and slid on a helmet, locking it into place on my thinsuit. As a last thought before I cycled through the airlock, I routed all ship messages back to the ship instead of my suit. Distractions could mess with me out there, and I wanted the silence to think.

I leapt out into open space, harnessing a small compressed-gas backpack in place as I did, firing it to angle me toward the bulk of the wreckage. I came to a stop, bumping against a section of what seemed to be landing gear, and set myself into a slow spin along all three axes. I relaxed my neck and my eyes and just drank in the sights.

I often found that, though it could be time consuming, just letting the sights slide into my mind worked best for me. Problems would have answers, but sometimes I needed to let them come to me. The wreckage came into and out of view with an easy regularity. Part of my local scenery now, I let it become natural.

No visible burn marks, nothing notable at all about the ship. Except the fact that it was in pieces and the data banks seemed to be missing, as were any crew. So what did that leave me with? Not much.

Except. What could take a ship apart like this and not leave a trace of its work? Lasers, sonics, missiles, and disruptors all, well, disrupted. Brute force, on the other hand, wouldn't. I grabbed a section of hull about as large as my leg as I spun by and turned it around in my hands. The motion set my gentle spin into a warble, but I fought the urge to correct myself to something resembling normalized.

The hull section had a nice ragged lip to it. I peered at the edges, running a finger carefully over the hills and valleys of the rough metal. A gravity wave could do this, if aimed right. So could pinpoint magnetics. Modern ship hulls tended to be nonferrous, but what ship designers normally meant by "tended" only went as far as the engine blocks. Ships still needed to be docked, and there were enough magwebs in use that a fully resistant hull made no sense.

So all right, I assumed a magnetic weapon with incredible accuracy. Gravity bubbles would have scattered the ship far more than I saw. Magnetics won out by a nose. The problem was, no one had magnetic weaponry that could do this. I didn't like it. I shot myself back to my ship, grabbing another smaller hull section as I went.

Using the communications array would be one of the dumbest things I could do. Chances were that the Hurkz Reclaimer's beacon had gone out already, putting nearby landing points on alert for me.

I sat there, playing with two now-heavy pieces of metal, considering my options. Broadcasting this in to authorities would almost certainly give away my position, and I would need to state a name and shoot an ID beacon wave to get anyone to listen for a tic. Sitting on the whole affair left a bad taste in my mouth.

I thought, quickly, about calling the parents in. The idea found itself tossed away twice as fast as it came up, though. Keeping my wanted status from them for now meant no running to them with odd problems. Still, some sort of cavalry needed calling and I had to do it. My own problems loomed, but I couldn't just ignore this sort of thing because of a few personal issues.

I keyed the communicator array and pinged out a general distress. Leaving my ID in the ping would bring the Hurkz, but would also ensure that someone responded. Even they could be of some use here.

The array chirped with incoming and I thumbed the mic open. No video request with the incoming signal, which was nice, and I pushed up my goggles, relaxing back as I did.

"Signal received," the message loop started, "please stand by for connection. Your request for assistance is important to us." Well, good to know. I waited a while longer, probably less than five minutes, though it felt closer to fifty.

They came on the line and were all business. "Registered craft MA19-2, this is Emergency Response, how can we help?" I sighed in relief, quietly enough that they didn't hear it. First hurdle leapt clear, they didn't feel the need to bring up my status first thing.

"Emergency Response, this is MA19-2, I have a wreck out here. Location was in the ping."

"MA19-2, what is the nature of the wreckage?" Did you cause it, son?

"Emergency Response, craft MA19-2 was not involved, repeat not involved. No damage here, guys, just passing through and found a wreck. No recorder, no crew, this is a strange one. Sending scan and hull camera data supplemental. Request investigation and retrieval of other craft." I bundled up the extra data as promised and shot it to them. They would get it fast enough but take a few to sort through all of the information.

"MA19-2, supplemental data received. We will dispatch to your location. Can you hold for meet and brief? Records show MA19-2 as registered response-capable craft," yeah guys, I know, I'm licensed to help you, "and, ahhh, further questioning may be needed." The Hurkz.

"Negative Emergency Response, on another call," I lied to them, "and cannot remain in area. Will deploy markers around current state of wreckage for ease, and you guys have my data, all right?" I gave up on the formal patter and hoped they would, too. "Just send someone out to have a look and deal with it, I'm out-system bound."

"MA19-2 we may need to question you... regarding the wreckage." Her slight pause told me everything I needed to know.

"Negative, E.R., repeat negative. Look, like I said, I'm out-system bound, and I'm already late."

"Hey, MA19-2, we don't write this stuff, we just do what they tell us. Response ship has already deployed and will be at your location within an hour. Still, you need to remain—"

"Thanks, E.R.," I cut her off, "I'm sure they'll be fine. If you have any questions that can't be answered by the data I sent, leave me a message and I'll get back to you quick, promise."

"MA19-2! I am authorized to warn you that failure to remain on site will jeopardize your flight status."

"So will staying, E.R., but thanks for the warning. MA19-2 out."

And so much for staying off the radar. Still, something hit that ship, and whatever did it needed to be bundled up and found. Doing my duty, now don't mind me while I leave town right quick.

I plotted a course fast and hard, not really paying too much attention to where I ended up so long as it really would be close to out-system holdings. I thumbed the engines to life and shot away from the problem in the opposite direction from the incoming Emergency Response crew.

Banking, already a fair distance away, my internal gravity hit a tiny lag and I glanced down at the odd clanging sound from near my feet. The two pieces of wreckage I'd brought on board with me. Whoops.

CHAPTER 9 – JONAH

HODGES STOOD with his scowl aimed directly at me. I met and held his gaze. Most people, when they meet my gaze when I'm stressed, angry, and working, can't hold it. To his credit, Hodges could and did.

Wasn't a time for pissing contests, though. I wouldn't forget that Hodges was playing me. No, not at all. The flight group, showing up as tiny marked stars moving in a holographic field, needed my attention more. They were, even if they weren't aware of it, counting on me to help save their lives.

"Flight group, this is Jo…Captain Madison, requesting full group status," I said to the room. Mics picked up my speech and relayed it to the helmet of each pilot in the group.

"Acknowledged, Captain. This is Strike Leader, group status clean." As she spoke, her name flashed on the display. Captain Sarah Bushfield, call sign "Deep Water."

I scanned the board again and tracked her team's progress. They were in formation, spreading out slowly as they went. It was a solid move: spread out slowly enough and the enemy might not notice, focusing their plans on a much tighter group.

The enemy ships also flew in a formation. They were using a simple flying V to come in straight and fast, by the looks of it. That could be good. Even if they had darkened a few systems, they hadn't met serious resistance from the military, not yet.

Perhaps their tactics extended only to planetary movements and not to full-on space combat. Then again, if Hodges was keeping things from me, and I could tell he was, this may not have been their first meeting after all.

We had a numbers advantage, though: thirty of our best fighters to fifteen of theirs. But their ships and pilots were unknown, in terms of both capabilities and firepower. It wouldn't do to get cocky based on numbers.

"Flight group, you're almost in visual range. Deep Water, invert formation once visual range is achieved. Over."

"Sir, we don't know what *their* visual range is," Bushfield pointed out. Damn, she was right. I told her so and backed off.

The enemy group scattered a few seconds later, spreading out impossibly fast. They seemed to skitter across space, markers flickering to keep up. "Scatter!" Bushfield demanded over the radio. "They're too damn fast, find a target and take it out!"

"Deep Water, report, what do they look like?" I asked, seeing Hodges lean in over the board.

"Sending visual data now, sir," she said. I could hear the tightness in her voice. No one likes being asked to stop trying to stay alive long enough to send a picture back home. Intel was as crucial as anything this time out, though, and she knew it. She just didn't have to like it.

"Sir," some technician behind me said, and I turned to see a series of pictures lighting up along the wall. The ships were thin, coming down to a long nose cone that didn't quite seem practical.

Four wings sprouted, one every ninety degrees around the ship. I could see the engines, one at each wingtip.

"Enlarge that as best you can," I told the tech. He nodded and the image zoomed, losing quality as it did. There was enough detail that I could make out what looked like joint points under the engines. That's how they moved so blasted fast.

I didn't think I wanted to meet the pilots who could take that sort of G-force for the whip turns those ships looked designed for. Maybe they had gravity tech, too, but even then, gravity adjusters in a ship that small would have trouble adjusting fast enough to keep the pilots in one piece. Trying those moves in anything bigger than a pack would be deadly. I didn't know what we were looking at, or who.

"Deep Water, be advised, the ships' engines are on the wing tips. Take those out and..." I started to relay.

"Copy. We've *been* trying to get a target lock on one, but they're so damned fast," she said. She spoke quickly, distracted. I needed to shut up and let her do her job.

"Left wing, close in, try a three-sided box, Hammerhead, come over the top and let's do this. Engage, guys. Engage!" she yelled. I took half a step back, watching the formations of ships sweep and change, and just listened to the chatter.

"Cap'n, they're too damn fast..."

"Shut up, Tommy. Get in there."

"Yes, sir."

"Deep Water, this is Echo Chamber. I got one of these things on my tail. I can't shake him."

"I got Echo, Cap'n. Highball out."

I watched as Highball made a sharp cut - his engines must have screamed bloody murder at him for the move - as he shifted around to close in on Echo Chamber. I couldn't see the actual ships, but the way that the light indicating the enemy ship had just reversed, I could only begin to imagine how the engines must be able to rotate fully around and what kind of stress that would put not only on the pilot but on the ship itself.

Regardless of stress, the ship had reversed itself and took out Highball. I watched the light marking his position go out, listened to the cries of shock. Those cries were quickly followed by a stone-cold death confirmation by Deep Water. Bushfield was a pro. Of course she was. Same with the rest of her group.

As Highball died, hopefully quick enough that he didn't feel it, Echo Chamber turned around and started to fire. The enemy ship followed Highball to the grave. No one cheered.

"This is Deep Water to strike group. Reform and wedge. Repeat, reform on me."

"Deep Water, this is Captain Madison: don't do it."

"Repeat, Captain?"

"Don't form up, they're too fast for you to wedge through. Stay loose and pick them off."

"Sir," she told me, "they're swarming. Honest-to-God swarming. If we try a pick-off they'll weed us out. If we form up we can cover each other."

"Damn it, this is an order. Stay loose!"

"Negative, Deep Water out."

I looked at Hodges, who only scowled once again. "Hodges, damn it, they're going to suicide if they try this!"

"Captain Madison," he said, "you're here to advise, not demand."

"I'm here to make sure these kids don't die!"

"Stand down, Captain." And with that Hodge straightened, removing his hands from the edge of the table. I wanted to punch the wall. Or Hodges. Maybe both.

Instead I watched the board. The ships were forming up, quickly, as the enemy moved around them. If the enemy was following a pattern in their movements, it wasn't immediately apparent. I could sense something at the edges of it, though. Obvious pattern or not, the movements didn't look good.

"Hodges," I asked, keeping my voice cool, "what planet are they coming up on, anyway? How far out is this wave?"

"Trasker Four," he said, not bothering to look at me.

"That's a system and a half out," I said, "there's no way we'll get there in time to provide assistance to the strike group."

"They won't need it, Captain," Hodges said.

We went back to watching the board and listening in to the group's chatter. It didn't matter. What we were listening to, it became obvious, would be a live recording of their last moments alive. Boxed in, not able to re-scatter fast enough, they were being picked off by the enemy ships that outclassed them handily in speed and maneuverability.

I didn't want to watch, not from afar. I wanted to be in it, then maybe I could make a difference.

But from where I was, what good could I do? None, just hearing orders barked and radios squelch as they exploded. I tried to give advice, but my options were as limited as theirs. More so, really. I couldn't see. I couldn't see and I couldn't help and all I *could* do was try desperate attempts at second-handing a battle strategy against an enemy I didn't understand.

A muscle in the corner of my jaw twitched and I felt my anger rise again. Hodges. If he had given me all of his data, maybe this would have played out differently. His secrets, whatever his agenda was, were costing a lot of good men and women their lives. They also cost me time I could be looking for Shae. Unacceptable.

Hitting him just then wouldn't have solved anything, though. As much as I wished different. But something else might work.

"Deep Water, this is Madison. Do they follow you?"

"Are you...Yes, sir. They follow us." I knew she wouldn't like this next part.

"I need you to lead them away from Trasker Four. Can you force them along our vector?"

"While we have a few ships left, sir, I suppose so. But there's no way you can get us reinforcements in time."

"That's my problem. You have your orders." I started toward the door. Hodges called after me.

"Captain Madison! You can't leave the battle deck! What are you doing?"

"Saving who I can, General," I spat at him, "if I can. Court martial me later."

The door slid shut behind me and I knew it wouldn't be more than seconds before Hodges himself came for me or security found me in the halls. Nothing for it. I had a purpose.

Chapter 10 – Shae

MY HEAD THROBBED. It was a good throb, the kind that told me I was alive. I had that much going for me. Not much else. There was something blocking my eyes and muffing my hearing. My breathing was being stifled both in and out. A hood; had to be.

I tensed my arms and legs, joint by joint. Nothing felt broken or damaged, but someone had managed to secure me really well. My arms and legs were each strapped down to whatever platform pressed against my back. Other straps pulled tight across my chest and hips and knees. They'd left my neck free, not bothering to lay a strap across my forehead. They'd left me upright - I could tell by the ease with which I swallowed - and I didn't feel particularly drugged.

I strained to listen through my hood for any noises. A soft electrical hum cycled and an air scrubber clicked on and off slowly. I pegged it as a ship. Something big, too. Big enough to have space to leave one woman in an empty room. I couldn't, of course, tell how big the room was, not for certain. Still, the change in sound when I turned my head, even muffled, was enough to suggest an open space.

Using each limb in turn, I tensed and strained slowly, testing to see how secure the straps really were. Secure enough, it turned out, that nothing budged. I curled my fingers into my palms and tried, with my left hand, to then inch my fingers up under the wrist strap there. If I could get to my wrist, there was a tiny patch of skin under which lay an emergency beacon. A quick burst would let Jonah know where I was.

I turned my wrist around as much as I could and felt a bandage there. Hell, they might have done a passive scan and picked up the beacon. If they had, it would've been easy to remove. I took a deep breath, strained by the hood, and exhaled slowly. No choice but to wait for their next move, whoever I was waiting on. I knew everything I would get to know from where I was. Now it came down to a matter of time. They wouldn't leave me here to rot like this, too much work had gone into securing me. If they wanted me to go to waste in a box, they could have just dumped me in a box without lashing me to a table first.

The fact that they obviously wanted me alive, even for a little while, coupled with an educated guess that they knew who I was, helped. Removing that beacon was their mistake. It meant they probably thought my biggest threat came from my darling husband, the hero. They'd regret that, later.

My breathing filled my consciousness for about an hour, as I waited. Muscles relaxed, mind in a simple meditation loop. Random exertion wouldn't get me any closer to free. After that hour or so of waiting, I heard a door open. Smells hit me first, something not-human. A biological smell, one I couldn't quite place. Nothing I'd encountered enough to cleanly identify, at least. That left a wide-open field.

As they came closer, I could hear nails against the floor and a stride that spoke of long legs. The smell got closer, as did the sound, and soon enough I felt claws against my head. Gently, not trying to gouge chunks of skin off, the claws slid against me, gathering up some of the hood to drag it free. The fingers felt inexpert, almost clumsy.

I kept my eyes closed when the hood came off, not wanting to blind myself. I opened them slowly, letting the light stab my senses in a somewhat controlled fashion. I tried to look down first, assuming any lighting source would be above or in front of me. I caught sight of the feet that made the claw-like clicking noise and changed the word "claw" in my head to "talon." The feet were leathery and long-toed, each having two toes pointing forward and one pointing back: bird's feet.

Sure enough, as I let my gaze wander up the body of the alien in front of me I took in a bird's body: lightly feathered, long limbed and overall thin. Vestigial wings hung beneath the arms. A sharp bird's head stared back at me, the eyes to each side of the face, just forward enough to grant good line-of-sight vision.

There were four of the aliens, each taller, on average, than a human. They looked at me and then at each other, beaks opening to chirp and chitter away in some language I'd never heard. Which made sense, really; there was no record of a species like this. If they were our invaders, then they were also something brand new.

"What do you want?" I asked them four times in different standard languages. One of them, a standard trading language from out around the far-spun end of the galaxy, hit. I kept going: "Why am I here? What do you want from me, can we help you?"

I wasn't, honestly, a fan of that last question. Still, the polite thing often proved the most useful. Ask if they need help, if this is a misunderstanding, and then when it proves to be very intentional, blow someone to hell.

"We require information," it said to me, accent thick and slurring. Recent language acquisition, that beak had trouble with some of the sounds.

"Me too," I told him, her, or it, whatever this bird was. One major rule of being captured: don't act like you're inconvenienced. Present yourself as part of a conversation and sometimes, if they're new, you can get lucky. They get sloppy. Sloppy gets you free.

"You will tell us of your home system," the bird said.

I laughed. "I doubt it." I took a minute to glance around the room. Simple, standard room, sadly. No clues to be found: empty except for me and the flock in front of me, metal walls, recessed lighting in the ceiling. Any number of species from any number of systems could have built it. "Where are you from?" I asked, relaxing my head against the board I was secured to.

They didn't reply, choosing instead to look at each other and start chirping. I couldn't understand them, and couldn't count on inflection meaning the same things it did for humans, but if there were correlations, they were pissed. My refusing to play along must not have sat well.

"We will leave you to think and cooperate over time," the only bird to have spoken a language I could understand said to me.

I shrugged. "You can keep waiting, but it won't change anything," I told them, truthfully. I knew I could out-wait them.

The leader, or at least the one who had spoken to me, turned and the others followed him. The door slid open and they left. Amateurs. The hood was left off of me and the lights were left on. Not smart.

I scanned the room carefully once they had gone. Nothing looked like it could be recording me. That didn't mean much, really, but it gave me a bit of hope. Still, they could have tech I never dreamt of monitoring me. No clue.

Something still felt off, though. If they wanted real information, then this sort of interrogation was truly pathetic. And if they didn't need it, then why bother? Stalling made no sense, but it fit decently. Which begged question: why stall me, and from doing what, or knowing what? I wasn't sure, obviously, but I also didn't intend to stay that way.

Then I looked down. I craned my neck as best I could, trying to find a weak point in the board I was attached to. It stood up from the floor, tilted back maybe fifteen degrees. Making an L shape against the floor, the plate that secured the board to the floor itself shined, made of the same metal that the board was.

I was missing something and I knew it. Something in the room, in the aliens - the entire setup and sequence of events didn't ring true for me. I didn't know what I was missing, though. So I relaxed again, shut my eyes, and thought. They'd be back, but by then I'd know what was bothering me. I hoped it'd be enough to change the odds.

CHAPTER 11 – JONAH

I ONLY HAD a few seconds before someone found me and tried to stop me. Would've been easier with Shae by my side. Together there wasn't much we couldn't deal with, but no, I stood alone. I didn't want a fight, not with these guys. They were on my side, and I was trying to save some of their own friends. Still, they'd be following orders to stop me. Put me in a small bind.

I stopped a pilot on her way by. A hand on the shoulder, a concerned, honest-type look, and she raised an eyebrow at me.

"Hey, do you know where Mills is," I asked, "or a pilot named Malik?"

She looked at my dress uniform and name tag, trying to place me. "Uhhh, Malik?"

"Yeah, nice guy. He was my transpo up here. Left something on his ship, just need to ask him where it is."

"Malik left on another dirtside run. Any non-perm cargo would be routed to storage B, I'd check there," she said. She added a shrug for emphasis.

"Thanks." I stood there another second and looked around.

She laughed - Hanley, her name tag said - and pointed. "Down this corridor to the access drop, down two levels and sternward from there," she said helpfully.

"Thanks again, Captain," I told her, already starting to move. Breaking into a run would be suspicious. Also not recommended, in case my knee went. Instead, I walked briskly, and kept my chin up. I really didn't want a fight, but I also didn't plan on being stopped.

I made the lift, and as I got in I saw security round the turn behind me. Not long now. They'd use the access shafts instead and beat me to the next level. Nothing for it. I tensed as the doors opened.

Two security guards came up to me, only a few steps away, as I exited the lift. "Captain Madison, please, stop where you are. General Hodges' orders, sir." They must have been asked to be gentle. Hodges knew what I planned to do, at least loosely, and hadn't ordered them to stun on sight. Interesting.

"Hodges told you to ask all nice, huh?" I kept walking away from them, slowly.

"We have our orders, sir," he told me.

"I'm afraid I can't stop, boys. I need to go save your friends. Hodges and I disagree about this, but seriously, just let me go, all right?" I knew they wouldn't - couldn't, really - but nothing was lost by giving them the truth, either.

"Lieutenant Mills said you'd tell us that," the second guard said, "but Captain, we can't let you..."

"Mills gave you your orders?" I asked.

"Direct from General Hodges, sir."

And then the hands-off approach made sense. Mills decided to tone back the good General's orders a bit. Nice work, kid. I saw the turn I needed and ran the odds. I could keep them from stopping me physically until I got to storage B, but getting in and grabbing my equipment (and all that entailed) wouldn't be possible at all. I needed to talk them down or take them out.

Twenty years ago - hell, ten - I would've broken orders flat and punched them both out. The bodies would've fit in a closet and I could've gotten everything done and worried about consequences at the end of the mission. The idea still appealed to me, but these guys were in the prime of their lives, in great shape and ready for a fight. I felt old.

That sat heavily on my chest and annoyed me. I didn't want to feel old. No one did, I reckoned. I pulled my gun from its holster and leveled it at the two security goons. "This, in case you don't recognize it, is an Acadian blaster. Got that?" I flashed them a grin and watched as their faces told me that they knew exactly what the weapon was. "Good. Now, you two are going to lose any weapons you have, and any comm units."

"Sir, Captain Madison, this is—"

"Sure it is, kid," I cut him off, "don't care. I'd rather save some lives." I gestured with the gun and they laid down their weapons and took off their comm units. I found the nearest storage room and shoved them in.

Now, would they have backup comms or something else? Of course. I didn't frisk them or check close. It was enough to get the obvious stuff and leave them a way to free themselves, after I had left. The door closed and I used the blaster to melt the bulkhead and door together with one seamless, ugly weld.

From there it was into storage B and signing out one of the cases that Malik had carried up to the ship with me. I dragged it off into a private room and opened it. Retinal, fingerprint, and voice scans all registered correct before the top of the case hissed as the interior sucked air into what had been its interior vacuum.

I grabbed up a bunch of old, familiar items and smirked at them. My dress uniform came off quickly, and I shoved it inside the box. I tugged on my old battle thinsuit - it still fit perfectly. I stopped and slapped on a pressurized knee brace to prevent strange maneuvers from causing havoc with the joint. I stood there and looked at myself in the warped reflection of the case's remaining object.

The suit was a solid black with dark blue patches that ran from the outer half of the boots up the outside side of each leg. The blue ended at the belt and then picked up again halfway up the back, where it ran up to cover my shoulders with a bit of color and then scooped down over part of my chest in a loose curve.

The old team insignia sat over the left breast, five arrows in an upside down V, and JONAH in block letters under it. I belted my holster around the suit and grabbed the GravPack, which made a crap mirror anyway, and slid it on, securing the straps around my shoulders and belting it at my waist above the holster. It looked like a large silver bullet and extended from just below my neck down to my ass. I could sit while wearing it, but only just. I grabbed up and strapped a bunch of extra O2 mini-tanks around my calves, activating the first. Enough air for a month the way these things worked.

I grabbed a last tiny bag and closed the case, securing it. I dragged it back to the storage clerk, who looked rather surprised to see me dressed for combat. He took the case anyway.

Back out into the hallway, I opened the small bag as I walked. The contact lenses were still fine in their case, and I put them in with years of distracted practice. Five timed blinks to activate them and an overlay popped to life, floating there in my field of vision.

A combination of a gesture system in my gloves and line-of-sight selections let me pull the specs for the ship and float a map. There was an emergency hatch just down the hall from where I stood. Perfect.

Less perfect was the second security group that came up on me as I headed there. These guys weren't planning on asking nicely for me to stop. Their weapons already sat in their hands as they started to hurry toward me, shouting variations on the concept of "stop." Too close and no time for a fight, then. I grabbed my blaster and set it on high, pressing it against the hull before I pulled the trigger.

With my free hand I activated my forcehood, a tiny, double-sided gravity field that would keep my air in and anything aimed at my head out. My lenses compensated for the vision distortion and I yelled back at the security guards, "You might want to hold on!"

The hull gave and I got pushed out of the ship. I knew the self-seal would engage before anyone else was badly hurt, so long as the guards realized what was going on fast enough. They did. Good.

A series of quick blinks and the bullet on my back hummed to life. Gravity engines were hell on ships - the bigger the ship, the worse the effect. But a single-man pack, that worked wonders.

I called up star charts and worked out where the strike team had fought, relative to my position. If I pushed the GravPack as hard as it could go I could catch them as they came toward our vector. Nothing else out here could catch me, either. GravPacks, going full bore, had a way of moving too fast to catch. Universal forces don't like to be outclassed.

I signaled the strike team. "Deep Water, this is Jonah. You still out there?"

"Copy that, Captain Madison."

"Jonah. I'll intercept your current vector, meet you in a few. You stay alive, copy?"

"There's no way you could get here fast enough to—"

"I'll meet you in a few. Copy?"

"Copy that Captain...Jonah. But *how*?"

"Leave that to me. Jonah out."

I stared at the stars surrounding me, the ships nearby, and the galaxy as a whole, all waiting for me to do what I used to do best. I just had to be up to it. To hell with it. I locked the GravPack on target and pinned the throttle to max. I'd have to be good enough.

And once I got out there, I'd also be a step closer to Shae. All I had to do now was survive. My specialty.

CHAPTER 12 – MEANWHILE

TRASKER FOUR WAS OBLIVIOUS to the battle that raged on above them. No civil defense mounted up and no government warnings were issued. The citizens went about their lives the same as they had a week before, and a week before that.

No one on Trasker Four looked up. They seldom did. Even if they cast their gaze skyward, all they would see would be the endless gray of smog and clouds, with the occasional clear patch of sky full of enough reflected light to still obscure the stars from the city below. For Trasker Four was, at this point, one giant city.

The central artificial intelligence, Squire, ran everything - including the government, for all intents and purposes. It was not, Squire reasoned, in Squire's best interest to allow the population to look up. Instead, let them produce and live their lives productively.

Not that the people of Trasker Four thought of their lives that way. They wandered the giant city - the Archives of Buul, Northern Region of Transport, the darkened maze ways lit only by aging neon, King's Hospitality Range, and the tree laden Oxygen Creation and Preservation Zones - thinking their lives like any other.

They knew technology as a means to an end, any end, but only used cast-offs and hand-me-downs from generations past. Straight progress, with the exception of devices for the betterment of Squire, had stopped. Adaptation of existing technology into new and unheard-of uses was the order of the day.

The black markets ruled the lowest levels of Trasker Four. The so-called middle class bought their goods from people reselling stolen items, the serial numbers and ID chips sanded off, and thought themselves honest. Upper-class families, with money enough to live in estates built high enough to escape the worst of the pollution, didn't care about ID chips, and bought items directly from the black market - when they weren't trying to sell to the same. Slowly, everything on the planet, in the vast city, revolved around and around, growing ever more hodge-podge.

And still no one looked up.

Once, a generation or two ago, Trasker Four traded with other nearby planets. Their spaceports were as busy as one would expect from a fully formed and modern planet, and pilots were what children longed to be.

Squire, however, had different ideas. In its quest to better its own functions, Squire decided to lock the planet down. By controlling who worked with what technology, Squire managed to shut down the people who would have served it best had it wanted any kind of progression.

The city aesthetic, for lack of a better term, tended toward large black buildings that rose high into the muddy air and created narrow, sunless streets. People left their buildings only when they had to - often working, eating and sleeping in the same sky tower. Entertainment, then, was the best and sometimes only reason to venture out onto the streets. The loud, endless engines, exhaust fans, and other machinery temporarily deafened people who forgot their noise-cancellers.

Most citizens decided that the entertainment proved worth the bother. Dogs fighting dogs, people fighting dogs, people fighting people - if you wanted to see bloody, unsupervised combat, it's what Trasker Four provided best. Sex, illegal organ trade, and biomechanical implants all ran a close second.

Regardless, the citizens of Trasker Four considered themselves good and just people, on the whole, and lived life as it was handed them, as did many other people across many other planets. They were neither overly religious nor anti-so, and many gave voice to wanting to improve the smaller aspects of their lives and thus their own status.

In general, the city of Trasker Four, known simply as The City, found itself both as content, and as generally malcontent, as any other human urban environment. It was merely much, much bigger. But its citizens didn't look up.

Above Trasker Four, a battle still raged. Ships fired at ships and lives were lost and won by inches. Squire tracked all of it and listened in, illegally, on the military channels. It knew of the threat and weighed its options.

Warning the population would lead to panic and work stopping. Keeping silent could mean an invasion and destruction of that same workforce. Squire's planetary defenses were quite capable, but even it could not predict to a reasonable degree the chances for success in fending off the wave of enemy destruction, especially should the larger, galactic military be unable to prevent it.

The lost time working toward its own goals was not, in Squire's opinion, worth the risk. The military existed for just this sort of event. Should they prove unable to defend Trasker Four themselves, Squire decided that it could save enough critical technicians to keep up appearances through the invasion. That number should also prove sufficient to repopulate the planet.

So Squire waited, and kept silent. The population of Trasker Four continued about its day, oblivious. Life went on, as it always did - full of smog and neon and buildings that obscured the sky.

CHAPTER 13 – JONAH

I HURTLED TOWARD Trasker Four at speeds that were probably impossible. That was the enduring problem with GravPacks - they made physicists nervous. Use a small gravity field to reduce inertia, keep passengers on the deck of a ship, ease takeoff, or help contain some of the stranger materials used to power conventional engines and everyone was all right with the idea.

Strap a gravity generator to your back and give it a computer good enough to help you chart a course and avoid accidently hitting a planet and everyone got nervous. The contact lenses' HUD let me select a destination and starting point so the computer could map out a line from A to B that didn't intersect with anything large. The auto-selector could lock onto multiple targets, generate a gravity field, and attract or repel to it across vast distances.

A small repelling field, five feet or so, kept small rocks and other debris from smashing into my body. Then the entire process came down to being able to survive a trip of the length selected. The field didn't care, nor did the navigational systems. They simply moved your body as fast as possible. Sometimes that brushed against conventional ideas of space and time dilation, which is when the physicists started to tear their hair out thinking about what you were doing.

It took Shae's father, Doctor Williams, the bulk of his career to realize and convince them that the application of gravity fields curved space/time in a way that seemed to, well, make it not care what you were doing. No one knew how it worked, not on a deep level, but Doctor Williams proved it could work and that it didn't leave you with bad time dilation problems. Of course, he could also show you math that proved he was wrong.

So I rode through space at speeds truly insane, with an impossible silver bullet strapped to my back, and refused to worry about it. I'd logged more flight hours with a GravPack over the years than anyone else still alive. After a while you just trusted the thing.

Still, the travel wasn't instantaneous. I raced the clock, even as space shifted by me. Deep Water and her strike group, what was left of it, couldn't be doing great. Going full throttle I couldn't use my comms, one drawback of going too fast. Instead I borrowed a trick from Shae's book and let my mind empty.

She knew when to relax and when to move. Not an easy thing to do, for me. Still, I tried to focus on the trip instead of guessing what lay at the other end. My mind wouldn't empty, though, even with years of practice. Meditating while in a tight spot had never quite agreed with me.

Instead I ran through my systems and checked myself on the GravPack controls. The few years since I'd taken it for a spin had left my reflexes rusty and I knew it. A blink brought the HUD online and I studied my destination charts. Trasker Four didn't have many satellites around it, and if the strike group was heading out along the vector I was rushing in on there wouldn't be much in the way, locally.

In combat, the GravPack could select multiple targets to both attract to and repel from, picking localized spots near them and moving those spots a slaved distance from the actual target. I didn't want to lock directly onto a ship in case I dragged it back to me by mistake.

Those targets were used to describe arcs and paths that continually shifted. Combat in a GravPack was half dance, half jumping off a building, and half sheer madness. Back when my own strike team was still around, we were all great at it, from formation whips to multiple target switching. This time it was only me and whatever handful of ships remained.

I ran a second systems check and then a third, trying to make absolutely sure that I felt ready to drop into combat. In my head I wasn't, not quite. Down below that, though, my body sang out at being pushed and responded by craving more.

System alerts rang out in my earpiece and I slowed down as I got close to the action. I dropped into the middle of a battlefield like a bullet that lacked a target. Better than dropping down to a dead stop, I reminded myself as I had to fast-switch target points and avoid a missile.

"Deep Water, this is Jonah, do you read?" I said as I tried to drink in my surroundings at speed.

"Where the hell are you, how'd you get here so fast, what the—" she came back with quickly.

"GravPack. Pop a low blinder for me to spot you."

A few seconds later, one of the ships, one of the human ships, lit up brightly before banking hard. I switched to target it and closed in quickly. From our starting numbers of thirty we were down to, at my quick count, only five ships. The enemy counted something like twelve. Not good. Not good at all.

I tucked myself in under Bushfield's ship and watched the fight for a minute. Seeing lights on a board didn't work for me, I needed the full picture. And once I had it, I saw the problem.

Not only were the enemy ships faster and far more maneuverable than our ships, but they didn't seem to use a consistent flight pattern, choosing to regroup and scatter at strange intervals. There was math behind it somewhere, but I couldn't get a lock on it.

"What the hell are you doing with a GravPack?" Bushfield asked.

"With this I have a shot at being faster than they are, that's what," I answered, "and I think it'll work." I outlined a quick plan and she agreed.

Taking off toward one of the enemy ships at speed, she played chicken with it, heading right in. Both ships opened fire, though neither looked ready to break off. Little did they know.

She broke hard, relative up to the cockpit of the enemy, and I split off, selecting its underbelly as my new attractor. I blinked quickly, selecting my options and wishing I could wipe my forehead. No sweat. Just one of those desires that hit in the middle of a firefight.

This guy didn't know what to do with me. He thought I was a missile at first and did the normal flare-and-chaff scatter response. So I closed my eyes and trusted that my proximity field would keep the crap off me. I lowered it from five feet to a suicidal two. I wanted close and personal.

He cut tight, and I wasn't sure if even my GravPack could keep up with him. Turned out that it could. The selector shifted clean and I targeted his upper wing. As I came up on him, I let the proximity field stop me two feet out and then cut it out of the loop. My fingers grabbed around the wing and I kept my head out of the sweep of his engine.

With my free hand, I grabbed my gun and put it right against the wing. Pulled the trigger and couldn't help but grin. Not many people got to ride a fighter by just holding on in deep space. Perk of my life.

Time for basking later. I sliced through his wing, slower than I wanted, and cut the engine free while he tried to shake me. The first roll wasn't a big deal but with the second I set my GravPack to slave to his ship. He couldn't toss me off no matter what he tried, after that.

I let go of the wing, not needing a handhold once I was slaved to his ship, and used my now-free hand to grab the engine before it flew off. It'd need to cool before I stored it - the raw edge where I'd cut was bleeding heat and light. But it wouldn't disable him badly, much less take out his ship.

For that I decided to go the easy - if messy - route. A few blinks and I selected an attractor field around his cockpit. Not just near - around his actual cockpit. Then I stood and waited. Slightly showy and wasteful of time, but it would tell me a lot about how well the ships were made.

The seals on the cockpit gave, and I cut the attractor and ducked as it ripped free. It flew past my head cleanly. Fine. The seals were no better than ours. That was good to know. Engines they knew, clearly. Some things were evenly matched, though.

The pilot wore his gear and kept trying to shake me off even after losing his cockpit. I couldn't clearly make out what he looked like. Bipedal, his helmet was elongated, but otherwise he was just a life form in a cockpit. A life form flipping a switch and glancing back at me.

Crap.

I took a chance, a lifetime of instinct kicking in. I was rusty, but I wasn't that far gone. I undid my lock to his ship, reversing it to repel myself far and fast. Good timing, too, as he self-destructed. All right, they'd rather die than get caught. Got it.

"Jonah, come in, did you get clear?"

"Roger that. Also, have an artifact for you to get back to HQ on the quick. Who can you spare?"

"Spare?" Bushfield asked, incredulous. "No one!"

"Wrong answer. Who?"

I picked another target and slaved myself to it, dragging myself in despite his attempts at ditching me. No one these days was used to GravPack combat, and these guys didn't seem like they'd ever even heard of the concept.

"Frogger, this is Deep Water, respond," came over the radio.

"Yeah, boss?"

"Jonah here has a gift for you. Quick march to HQ with it."

"Jonah?" Frogger asked.

"He'll come to you. On a GravPack."

"Deep Water, we can't spare me, I don't care who..."

I pulled up a HUD display keyed to the strike group's frequency and got call signs over layered over the ships. Much better. I focused over toward Frogger and grabbed onto the underside of his ship. Luckily for me, ships still had storage doors on a separate airlock, just for this kind of problem. Need to grab a friend, or a bit of evidence while on the fly, just tuck it into the hold.

Except the hold didn't open. I noticed the chatter stopped, but guessed he has switched to a private channel to argue with his flight leader in private. We didn't have time for that. I said as much over the main channel and the bay door opened. I tossed the engine inside and hit the manual close, snatching my hand back before the door cut it off.

"This is Deep Water," the radio cut in, "When Frogger breaks, press the attack. Don't let him get tailed. Copy?" Everyone, myself included, copied her on her order.

Frogger cut out and the rest of us circled the wagons. The enemy, damn them, didn't care. They regrouped long enough to wedge toward us and then scattered with enough speed that it reminded me of a group on GravPack. And maybe that was the answer. Fight them like they were a GravPack strike team. It couldn't work *worse*.

I radioed my idea to Bushfield who admitted she didn't know the tactics - they basically didn't teach them much anymore, and no one drilled the few bits that were still mentioned. So I trusted in her ability to get her team together and explained as fast as I could.

We had to funnel them through and take their maneuverability and speed away from them. It wouldn't be easy with slower ships and fewer numbers, but it was, at least, possible.

I started toward another enemy ship and it fired some kind of missile at me. My display lit up with warnings that I cancelled as quick as possible. I could see the blasted thing, I didn't need to be told where it was.

I hit it with a repel angle, keeping my lock on the ship that fired it. I had to jack-knife my body to keep up and felt my knee pop from the stress of it. I lost focus for half a second as the pain flared. It'd be fine. Just hurt like a bitch.

I knew I'd made a mistake, I needed a third field set-up to pull the maneuver off, and my knee pop distracted me just enough. I'd just started to switch all fields onto that missile when it exploded. Bushfield's ship cut sharp between me and my target, a passing black blur.

"Thanks," I radioed.

"I'm your squad leader, that's my job," she said, "now finish him off, huh?"

I grinned to myself and hit my pack's systems harder. I came in on top of the ship, flipped over and came to rest near the cockpit. Gun out, I cut through the cockpit quick and grabbed at the pilot. He hit the self-destruct before I could pull him clear and I had to bail. That was two, but I wasn't satisfied. We needed to grab one alive.

The rest of the strike group tried to box the remaining ten ships, to not-great success. We were down to four ships, and me on top of that, but still. Then Bushfield had an idea. "Guys," she came on over the radio, "everyone but Jonah, launch half of all remaining missiles on my mark. Target blank

95

space near the enemy but not on top of them. Let them have room to scatter. Set fifteen-second fuses when you launch."

It was a great plan. I felt stupid for not seeing it earlier, and I'm sure she did as well. The strike group readied itself and launched. The enemy scattered, as expected. The missiles went off and the bursting explosions were fairly random, but covered enough area to do the job.

Some of the ships wobbled in their patterns, slowing down, two got caught square and exploded. Eight to five felt much better. And most of that eight was now dinged up enough to be fightable.

I came in at another ship, Blue Water on my tail. Bushfield was sticking close to me. Either she was worried I'd screw up again or she felt flying my vector gave her a chance to peel off and deal with something else if need be without worry. Couldn't tell.

I popped an enemy ship from a distance, my gun managing to wobble the engine a fair bit. The ship spun and started to bank without intent, and Bushfield nailed it with her nose guns.

I was stupid. Too close to the explosion, still locked on. I got sucked into the heat of it before I could retarget, my own combat rust playing its hand. My GravPack spazzed out and the HUD went offline for a reboot. While it did, I couldn't do anything but float. Dead in the water - which is when I realized that my comms were out, too. Damn.

I floated there while Bushfield drove past me at speed, not concerned yet, or, frankly, noticing. I had at least ten seconds before the system rebooted enough to get me somewhere. Another enemy ship came in and fired a missile at me.

At least there were no useless warnings, with the controls dead. Eight seconds and the missile was only about seven seconds out. Ten if I were lucky. Turned out to be around nine. I hit a quick lock on the largest thing around, Trasker Four itself, and tried to drag myself out of the way. The missile was too close and went up near me. Too near.

Systems went critical, but caught as they were coming up, somehow managed to not go down fully a second time. Sheer luck. I was stuck, however, in Trasker Four's gravity well. I went down toward the planet, flames and bits of debris following me, fast.

Nothing for it but to ride it down and land, hoping I could get back off planet quick. If the GravPack was fine, it wouldn't be too big a problem, but if it was toasted...I tried to remember everything I knew about Trasker Four and not worry about landing.

If nothing else, the GravPack should have been functional enough to save me from hitting the planet hard. That was the plan, anyway.

Chapter 14 – Shae

I SCANNED THE FLOOR again and caught it. A bolt. That was all. A simple bolt with a perfectly ordinary hex-shaped head. The bolt sat on top of the plate that held the plank I was tied to. And that clicked in my head loudly, like a gunshot.

The clawed hands of the bird aliens wouldn't work with hex bolts. I'd met more than my share of aliens, overall, and everyone used slightly different shapes for their fasteners. But hex bolts, those were human in design. The bird-aliens' hands wouldn't stand a chance working them. Oh, sure, they could have tools that made the bolts work fine, but why would they have built a bolt like that in first place?

Following that chain of logic took me to a place where the aliens weren't real. Which meant I was being held in a human ship. Suddenly, far less made sense. The "waiting around and collecting data" phase ended right there.

Instead I focused on getting myself free before they came back. I tensed my right shoulder and started to raise it, inch by inch, pressing it against my side. I may have been strapped down at the wrist and across the upper arm, but there was still enough slack if I shifted myself right. It hurt along my arm and ribcage, but freedom was worth some pain.

The wrist shackle would be the worst part. My thumb popped as I dislocated it and I bit my own lip hard enough to draw blood. Once I got my right arm free, the rest proved simple enough. My thumb clicked back into place with no more pain than the dislocation itself.

I wanted to throw up. More than that, I wanted to use a few grenades on people. I held that desire close. I let it blot out the pain, but also allowed myself a ten count to lean against the platform and wait for my legs to get steady again. Freed, I did a quick scan for cameras again, knowing I wouldn't find any. They couldn't afford to tape me being imprisoned, not if it got out. No, then they'd have to deny everything.

The door stood between me and getting out of the cell. I studied the palm scanner, but made sure not to touch it. The last thing I wanted was to find out that the system logged and alarmed unknown prints trying to access the system. I had no tools, nothing to break the panel open with or to access the system once I had. The door sat locked and I considered my options.

Option one: Wait for them to come back, try and surprise them and make a break for it. I loved it, except I didn't know where I was or what I was up against yet. So that made it a fool's move.

Option two: Get the door open. Much better for stealth, except the lack of tools, a key, or explosives. All right, the explosives wouldn't help with stealth anyway.

I studied the door and its access panel again. Assuming these were humans after all, then the tech could only go so far up the ladder. All I had to do was find the right way to outsmart the higher-end, military-grade stuff and work my way down.

I kicked the wall twice out of frustration but, strangely, it didn't result in the door opening. There was, however a seam. There was always a seam, even if it sat recessed into the wall. That would be a weak point. Wait, I was an idiot. The door slid open from my right to my left. Which meant the wall to the left would be hollow for the door to slide into.

I went back to the plank they had tied me down to and tore one of the straps free. Bending the buckle back was work but I managed it after I braced it against the floor with a foot. Five minutes counted off in my head as I worked the edge of the bent metal buckle into the seam to the left of the door. Bending back bits of the edge of the door frame let me see the retraction mechanism for the door itself.

The fact was that there should have been a safety release on the inside of the door, but they were easy enough to "forget" installing to make rooms secure. A little-known addition to that fact, though - the interior mechanism always had a security retract, just in case. Almost never used and generally impossible to access, they weren't worth a damn until they suddenly were.

I saw the trigger for the release and tried to reach it with the buckle, but even bent flat it would be too short. I'd have to resort to using my fingers. The metal of the door frame, now badly bent and worn, sliced my pinky open, but the blood lubricated my way and made flipping the emergency release easier.

The door hissed as the release caught and I pushed the thing open, staying behind it while I did. No way to know what was on the other side.

As the hallway beyond came into view, I felt my jaw go slack.

This was military. This was *us*. What the holy hell was happening? I didn't even want to guess. Instead, I slid out into the hallway. I kept to the walls, ducking into doorways when anyone came by. So far, so good.

Strange situation or not, there were two things I needed to do: let the family know I was all right and get out of here. The first proved fairly easy. I came across one of the many backup comm rooms any decent sized ship had. You never knew when sending a message would be important, and enemies targeted main communications hubs as a matter of course.

I closed the door behind me and took a deep breath. Time would be running short. Even if no one had come to check on me, someone would notice the open door and have trouble closing it. Security would find out quick and be looking for me. Hallways were decently monitored in general so I wouldn't be hard to find.

Keeping that mind, I jotted out a quick message to Mud and Jonah and sent it. I didn't bother to look up my location, just tagged the message with a normal location packet so they could find the source. That's all they'd need. I wiped the message, thought again, and smashed in the comm deck. They definitely wouldn't work out what I had sent who.

The door slid open and a sonic blast hummed through the air, catching me in the leg. Guess security had worked out where I was. They wouldn't take me easy. No need to hurt any of them badly, not yet

- I didn't know the score and they might innocently think I should have been a prisoner.

I kicked one of the guys in the faceplate and grabbed his sonic rifle. Two quick shots took care of the second security thug. I dove for the ground as the third and fourth spilled into the room. They laid down suppressing sonic fire and I winced as the walls of the room rebounded the effects back at me, catching me square. The world started to go black but I fought it, getting off another shot.

Pretty sure I hit one of the security goons, but the blackness swam fully over my eyes and I gave in, passing out.

Chapter 15 – Mud

AN ALARM WOKE ME from a nap. I rolled off my bunk and slapped at the control panel on the hull nearby until it played back. It was from Mom, sent to me and Dad. The entirety of the message was "Held by Gov, no ws, n ext." No location code or anything.

The fact the message itself was in plain, unencoded text, coupled with the hurried shorthand, worried me. Expanded out it told me she was being held by the Government, and with no other indication as to which Gov, she meant Earth's. Tossed in for extra fun was the fact she didn't know where she was, why she was being held, or anything else at all. That "need extraction" at the end didn't create a thrilling cap to the message, either.

I send a few packets to Dad, figuring he would be on this already, and wondering why he wasn't. For her to send to both of us meant one of two things - She thought they'd need help, the two of them, or she was out and alone, not knowing where he was. Chances were with the latter, but chances could get someone killed.

I grabbed up a cup of something warm and took a deep breath of the moist, hot air in the cabin. Time to get to work on this. On my way to the cockpit's hot seat I kicked the metal slab again. Still don't know what happened there. No time now. I tossed it into a storage locker and then sat down heavily in the pilot's chair.

No location on the message. But the headers looked complete. That meant there would be standard codes embedded. I could translate them and backtrack from there. Shouldn't prove too hard. I loaded the file into my system and took it apart. The message ID would be embedded at the top, the station info at the bottom. Strip out the coding for the body of the message itself and toss it. The message ID would prove useful if I could get another message from the same relay point. The IDs increment, and that'd give me a decent time lock. Margin of error, of course, based on how many messages they sent, but I could guess that once I knew what sent it in the first place. Which meant the station ident.

Easy enough to grab out, but a pain to decode. Gov equipment doesn't like to tell you who it is unless you're reading the message on authorized Gov equipment. My ship most certainly wasn't that. Fine, enough of why this sucked, more doing it regardless.

Dad had shown me how a few years ago, just in case: one of his paranoid moments. What if, he reasoned, I worked for the Gov and my transmitter broke and I had to rely on non-spec stuff. How would I know where to go? Heh. Good old Dad.

I ran a few tools against the encryption, betting they'd upgraded. They had. Still, I knew what markings to look for in the code and was able to get enough of a match to run that against a database of known bases. I came up empty so I switched to larger ships. That got me a few matches. Which meant Mom was certainly on a ship somewhere.

The class was full-compliment battle cruiser, and only six of those were active currently. Narrowed it down more for me. I grabbed the registry numbers for all six and crossed them against the code snips I had. Narrowed the field down to two ships: the *Kingsburg* and the *Dozier*. *Kingsburg* was a bigger ship, but *Dozier* sat closer to Earth, normally.

I tried to find some information on where either ship sat currently and got nowhere fast. Well, they didn't tend to publicize that sort of thing. Fine. But even military class ships are required to post trajectories and flight plans, they just don't have to give a public ident. Troublesome, but not if you knew where a ship launched from.

I ran a simulation for all flight plans that matched both the *Kingsburg* and *Dozier* launch points for the previous month. With us not at war with anyone, the chances grew small that either of them wouldn't have hit a home berth in that time. I pegged the *Dozier* easily, actually. They weren't trying to hide, and why should they?

The *Dozier* fit. It fit good enough that I felt confident they were holding Mom. So I sent them a routine ping to grab a message ID. The number of the message I got back fell right in line with my theory.

Now I knew where she was. I checked the console for any other incoming messages, but Dad hadn't replied. Bad on bad. I was a bit farspun from where the *Dozier* should be. I set two courses, one submitted and the other real, just in case, and took off at a full burn toward a large rock that the *Dozier* would be approaching at around the time I could get to it.

After that? All I'd have to do is break into a Gov battle cruiser, find one person, and escape again. It took my mind off being hunted myself, at least. I left the ship to fly itself for a while and went to count my ammo stores.

Chapter 16 – Jonah

I GAINED CONTROL of my rapid descent with about thirty feet to spare. As the ground rushed up to greet me, my HUD came up and I quickly selected a stop and hang, equalizing my own mass against all the large fields near me. With a planet under me, the GravPack switched itself automatically to planetary views. At least I wouldn't have the planet itself being the only attractor.

I floated down to a soft landing, coming to rest in the middle of a street. It wasn't subtle. With an invasion on my heels, I didn't see the point of subtle. People stared and they stared hard. A guy no more than half my age, with a shoulder-length shock of purple hair, walked right up to me, trailed by some friends.

"Hey, you for real, hombre?" he asked, turning to his friends and laughing. They all laughed after half a beat. If they hadn't looked quite so hung out to dry I would've considered them a gang.

"Pretty much," I said, ignoring his tone, "wanna tell me where to find the local enforcement around here?"

That got me another laugh. "You want *us* to ring up the Badges?"

"That gonna be a problem?" I asked. I didn't have time for a pissing match. I knew it. He just annoyed me.

"Is it gonna be a...oh *man*," another laugh, followed by his right hand sliding into his pocket. "Walk away, man, just walk away."

I shook my head at him and his friends. I really didn't have time, but then, I didn't think they'd take much of my dwindling supply anyway. We locked eyes, me and the laughing fool. Then his hand whipped out of his pocket. The snap of a wrist and a knife blossomed there, in his fist. I grinned but didn't make a move.

He took a swipe at me, which I dodged just by leaning back a bit. As I leaned, I brought both my arms up fast. I grabbed his knife arm at the wrist with my own right hand, pulling him in and yanking his arm across his body. My left hand came up, palm out, and smashed into his elbow, bending it the wrong way hard enough to pop it out of joint.

He howled in pain, dropping the knife even as his knees gave out from under him. I still stood there, shifting my gaze from him to his friends. "I'll ask again. One of you know where to find anyone who works for the Government, maybe? Some, uhh, Badges?"

They looked at me blankly, like they weren't sure what to do. No. Time. I pulled my gun and let it hang heavy in my hand, pointed at the ground. I didn't speak, just let the menace of the gun say everything for me. I could see they wanted to try attacking, all at once, but were thinking better of it.

Turned out I didn't need their help after all. Sirens rang out instead. Above me. I glanced up and saw the cruisers circling, ready to descend. I went up to them instead. The mini-gang watched me rise and ran in to grab their fallen leader.

108

"REMAIN WHERE YOU ARE." I winced a bit at the volume but stopped my ascent and looked at the police cruisers. There were three of them, each one venting smoke as they hovered there, their lights flashing. At least they cut out the sirens. "RETURN TO THE GROUND," they told me, at the same ear-splitting volume.

So I did. They followed. When they landed and got out of their vehicles I remained standing, holding my hands out, palms up, my gun securely in its holster. "I need to talk to someone in charge," I told them.

"Yeah, yeah, you'll see a judge eventually," one of the four cops said to me. Great, these guys seemed as helpful as the gang did. Still, I had to try.

"My name is Jonah Madison. I'm with the Gov. There's a battle raging in your planetary vicinity. Invasion is imminent. *Let me speak to someone who can deal with this.*"

All that little rant got me was guns drawn. I kept my own holstered. Zip ties came out and the cops approached me, warily. "I think we got a nutter, here," one of them said. They were, to me, just nameless uniforms. I knew they had a job to do, but so did I. Mine would save their lives, theirs would help ensure they died. No choice.

I blinked to call up my HUD again and selected the tallest towers I could see. I knew there would be no way for these guys to keep up with me, so I took off as fast as I could manage, setting my personal field to a nice three feet. That'd be enough to keep me from hitting a building and also make sure no local flying wildlife made things too interesting for me.

Before I could firmly process it, I left the cops behind in a blur of motion. Not smart, though. I knew it to be a dumb move, even as buildings rushed by. Sirens sounded below me and I cut a hard turn, selecting buildings at random and trying to think. But I wound up just cursing myself out long and hard while I ran.

Ten seconds on a new planet and I'd managed to push for a fight and get on the wrong side of the local law. I wanted to think maybe I set a new record – that would at least have made me feel productive - but I knew that dumber had been done. By me.

More sirens sounded behind me. What they lacked in speed they tried to make up for with numbers. Great. Nowhere to run. So I went higher, shooting straight up. Clear of the buildings, squirting out from the overabundance of the city, I flipped over and pointed myself back at the street. Ten cruisers drove after me, climbing as best they could, sirens and flashers going. Gravity reclaimed me and I fell, letting myself go.

I tucked my arms against my side and dove straight as an arrow. The cops couldn't react in time and I turned myself, like a spinning arrow, winding through their cruisers. Wind screamed past me and the ground promised me a deep kiss. I denied it, selecting a target at random and pushing off at the last second, my body flipping horizontal just inches above pavement.

Sirens squelched closer, and there was no need to look back and see that they were still giving chase. No need to check if they were being cautious or not as they followed, either. They were - nothing on this planet could turn like me, and they didn't want to slam into anything. The chase stopped interesting me, however, once I realized what else I could see.

The gang members stood and watched, whooping with glee, unsure of who to root for but screaming their damn fool heads off regardless. No officials tried to stop them, fine they were busy with me, but the thing of it was that the gang members didn't seem to have given running a thought, not seriously. They didn't care if the cops hung around. No fear, no flinching, these gang kids looked immune.

Admittedly, they could've just been too dumb to think, but their posture suggested different to me. And that told me who really sat in charge around these parts. Oh, hooray. Still, you go where the power sits if you want to get things done.

Flying low to the ground, still able to reach out and trail a hand along pavement if I wished, a plan blossomed in my mind's eye. A tight loop brought me back along the other way. Right back at the cops. More importantly, right back at the gang members who still watched, ducking as cop cruisers flew close over them. Their hair caught in the wind and wash from the cruisers, and the gang kids closed their eyes and laughed. They loved watching this.

As I went by them, I dropped my field for a second and grabbed the guy who'd been about to try and start a fight. Hooked him around his waist and started to climb. He loved watching this all - I wondered if he'd love being in the thick of it. His screams told me he did not. I bit back a laugh and poured on the speed for real, extending my personal field to ten feet. Too close to a building and the field forced a turn. We pinballed through the city at uncomfortable speeds.

"Stop screaming," I told my new best friend as I gripped him tighter. "You won't die unless I screw up, and I won't screw up if you stop screaming in my damn ear."

He managed to clamp his mouth closed. Good boy. We kept moving, the city a blur. I doubled back, flew around a few different blocks, and otherwise tried to make sure we couldn't be followed. Somewhere about two minutes into it, he threw up. Luckily he was still facing down when he did. The last thing I needed was this kid's vomit on my thinsuit.

"You're gonna have to do me a favor, kid," I told him. "I need to speak to the grand poobah, all right? Whoever signs your checks. You lead me to him and this joyride stops."

I looked at him, taking my eyes off our course and trusting my field to keep us alive without attention for a few. He shook with fear, and I saw he really was just a kid. A kid shaking with raw terror. I could've felt bad for him, if he hadn't threatened me for asking a question earlier.

I gave him a hard rattle. "Come on, we don't have all damn day. Where am I going?"

"Man," he said weakly, "I don't even know where we are." Well, that posed a problem. I didn't want to slow down enough for him to get his bearings yet, and I didn't want to climb high enough for us to be easily seen by the cops, either. Well, maybe if I pulled off another climb and dive it would be all right.

I climbed again, pushing against the planet hard. The kid screamed, probably because he thought I was going to drop him, and didn't stop until I rattled him again. We stopped once, high enough for a pretty view. As pretty as I bet things got around here, smoke and buildings and a general dank air about the entire city.

"Now, find a landmark and get your bearings. We're going down, and fast, in about ten seconds," I said. "Once we get back to street level you need to give me directions, good ones and fast ones, or," I jangled him, "I'll have no need for you. Got it?"

His body went stiff as a board, except for his head, which nodded like it sat attached to a spring. He got it. Good.

I turned off all connecting fields and let us drop with the force of gravity, turning myself and clutching him hard to my side. My arm ached. He was heavy. No, he wasn't all that heavy, I was just old. You never think about how hard it can be to carry another human under one arm for an extended period of time until you have no option to drop them. Used to be no problem, I could lug guys like him around all day. Now my shoulder ached with the force of history and injury.

"Where are we going, kid?" I asked as I stopped us once more, only a few inches above the ground. "Come on!"

"L-left," he said, and threw up again. Kids. But I listened and moved as quick as possible. Slower than I wanted, but he needed time to tell me my next turn. Not used to high-speed maneuvers, this one.

I doubled back a few times, looping whole blocks, warning him before I did so he wouldn't lose his bearing again and force us to start over. He got better as we went, I admit, and pretty soon he started threatening me again.

"Why you wanna go and find the Boss, man?" he asked. "He just gonna kill you, like I shoulda done," he said, adding, "left, then the first right."

"Don't make me give in and drop you."

"Ha! You can't, can you? Then you'll never find the Boss! You need me, old man." He laughed again and sighed. He was right, of course, but that didn't do anything other than make me want to drop him more. But no, I hung on, arm burning with the stress of it, and kept flying. I picked up a bit more speed with every other turn, letting him get used to it.

Soon enough, and yet after what felt like years, he told me to pull up short - we were there. I stopped and set us down on the ground, feet first. "If you're lying..."

"Why would I lie? You wanted in, you'll get in. I want to see you die. This will be where you die. Get it?"

"Oh yeah, I get it," I said. I didn't bother to keep the contempt and boredom out of my voice. I worked my shoulder, carefully so he couldn't see, trying to ease the pain some. No use in letting him know I hurt. "Then again," I said, moving behind him and drawing my weapon, "I have a fast trigger on this. So let's just go, all right?"

I let him lead the way, keeping far enough back that he couldn't grab or slam into me quickly. Their security was - as expected, frankly - sad and small. But he treated it huge, which told me all sorts of things. The prospects for how great their leader was shrank by the second. Also, as a nagging voice in my head wouldn't stop reminding me: I had no time. None. A fleet grew closer to the planet by the second and once they got here, nothing else would

114

matter. We'd all be dead equally, and Shae would be alone, wherever she was.

We walked past guards who didn't know any better than to laugh at the situation their friend had got himself into, happy to leave him being frog marched by me. So secure that nothing would ever take them on and win, they only took care to mock their friend being held hostage by an outsider. These guys seemed to be idiots. The fact that they were also the idiots in charge didn't escape me. Something was keeping this place down and until I took that out, I couldn't save the people.

Carefully and silently, I switched my gun to the lowest possible setting. Not often I did that, but I didn't want to kill anyone and if my guess was right, a good hard stun from this baby would do as well as death for my purposes.

"All right, old man, we're here," my Sherpa told me. He shoved open a thick metal door and entered a room that, at best, could be described as *less* squalid. They'd done it up like what they imagined a throne room to be. Dank, greasy rugs hung along the walls and flickering lights set into long poles cast shadows around the room. A few guys stood around giving the air of being guards, but I could tell they had no formation and no training. They looked as though they had rushed to their places when the door started to open, not that they had been standing guard all day.

At the head of the room sat a slightly raised stage with a starliner's command chair bolted to the center of it. A throne fit for a child. And a child sat there, no more than twenty-five. He commanded his domain with an eye toward cruelty. His eyes swam with it, lank hair drifting into his line of sight and hanging there like crappy curtains. This was a man I was supposed to respect, who the rest of these chumps actually did.

I didn't even wait to get his name. I called up my HUD display, selected the ceiling and the edge of the stage in a tight sequence, and turned my pack on. I shot into the room like missile. Up and then down in a short arc, leaping over everything between myself and the boy in charge. I landed on the edge of the stage and watched his eyes grow wide.

Yeah, he must have been the smartest guy around because he saw me for what I was: hurried and not in the mood. His fear brushed by me, not anything to relish or dwell on, just another factor as I raised my gun and fired on him. He slumped in his seat and went dead limp. I shoved him out of his chair and sat down.

"Now, who's smart enough to tell me what's going on here? We don't have much time," I said airily.

They stood there, gaping at me. Brilliant. "Listen! We don't have much time. Bring me the bright folks who can speak, or I'll shoot the rest of you and call it a day!" That got them to move. They didn't know who I might be, but they respected power and anger well enough.

One of the guards who ran out of the room calling for help and screaming about the situation must've gotten the attention of someone who gave a damn because a bunch of kids ran into the room, armed. They saw their leader, looking dead, which he'd go on looking for an hour or so at least, and stopped. I just sighed.

116

"There is, right now, an invasion force coming to wipe out this planet," I said, not caring if they all followed or not - I knew someone in the crowd was bound to understand. "I need ships, I need to restore off-world communications, and I need all of this right now!"

One guy in the back worked his way through the crowd. "We don't have ships," he said glancing toward the ceiling as if, by saying it, a ship would land right there in the room. No such luck.

"Who does, kid?" I asked, waving him forward. They were just buying my bid for power. I had hoped they would, but there are days you don't think things will go according to plan until after they have. "And how do we warn the planet?"

"We—well, we don't," he told me. "Off-world communications and transportation are forbidden by the Council. Wait, but then who are you?" Oh, a smart one indeed.

I grinned at him, "Exactly. I didn't just - well, no, actually I did just fall out of the sky. And now I need to get back up there and take as many of you as possible."

"But we're at war with the Red Blood," he told me. The crowd murmured agreement, tinged with anger.

"And you're...the..." I dragged out, feeling my way.

"Stone Hammer!" the room shouted. Stone Hammer and Red Blood, sure, why not. Little gangs fighting over control of a world that didn't even know it was already dead.

"Wonderful. Well, Stone Hammer, you make me proud today. Why, when I came to this world I knew I had a choice between Red Blood and

117

Stone Hammer, and I can see I chose correctly," I lied happily. "But now I need you to prove me right one more time. We need to make the Council understand the invasion is real, and I need a ship to get off-planet."

They muttered amongst themselves for a moment and I let it drag out. As they came to the realization that their new leader might just be serious, I added the capper. "And I need it all done inside two hours."

That part they really didn't like.

CHAPTER 17 – SHAE

I WOKE UP GROGGILY. Sonic blasts give me a hangover, I swear, though Jonah thinks that isn't possible. It is, because I get them. I tried to not move my head - and kept my eyes closed, opening them would only make me hurt more - and took in my surroundings by feel.

They'd decided to tie me down better this time, I'll give them that. I was seated and secured at the wrists and elbows, as well as across my chest, hips, knees, and ankles. The chair itself felt bolted to the floor, of course. I gave in and moved my head a bit, wincing, and found they'd left my neck and head free. If they knew about the hangovers I got from sonics I would have thought them right cruel for that oversight, but they couldn't have.

I opened my eyes and silently thanked whoever had locked me in here. The room sat pitch dark. Bad for escaping - I couldn't see a damn thing - but great for my head. Light would've been anything but helpful.

What were my options, really? Sitting and waiting could work. I'd sent off family alerts after all, and though I didn't know where either Mud or Jonah were, one of them (if not both) were bound to come get me. It made sense, just wait it out and stay alive.

The other option, of course, was to escape again. No tools, they knew I would try it again, they were prepared for it, and, worse, they knew that I knew they were human now. They - and I still had no clue

119

who they were - had every reason to have secured me properly this time. Which all, really, made it far more fun for me. I also don't do damsel in distress really well.

Never did, either. Back when Jonah and I first met, there were a few too many times his enemies used me against him. They all decided I must be helpless, an easy tool to use to stop him. It didn't take long before I learned how to fight, found a love of explosives, and took to getting myself out of messes on my own. Why stop now? No reason I could think of.

I listened, holding my breath while I did. Nothing to hear, outside of my own heartbeat, so I could assume there weren't guards waiting just out of reach in the dark. Good. Next I flexed everything I could think of, and heard the straps creak softly. Not much, but it meant they weren't made of metal and had give and flex. Good again. Well, good for me, bad for them.

My captors were our own military, which meant everything would be milspec. I knew milspec possibly better than they did. The bolts securing the chair would be single thread and hardened, the chair itself a rigid, no-flex metal blend. The straps would be attached inside the chair with bolts and welding, so I couldn't rip them out.

The weak point would be the buckles themselves. Secure but designed for emergency release in case of depressurization: you didn't leave captives to die, and if you had to free them in a large pressure suit, that's what you did. It meant that if I could reach the buckles, chances were I could undo them eventually.

That was why the wrist straps were tighter than the others. I couldn't rotate my hands to get them palm up at all. Palm down, I could only grip the arms of the chair. With my elbows secured and pressed against the back of the chair, I couldn't pull the same trick as last time; they'd learned that much.

What I could count on them not learning was to do a dual-mix explosive search on me. No one ever did. Last time I escaped I hadn't gone for it because it's the sort of thing you save for the last minute, but now I couldn't see an alternative. Also, this would hurt far worse than the thumb trick had.

Against my collarbone, one on either side, were two tiny capsules that produced a nice bang when mixed. That's the sort of thing you sometimes leave under your skin for later. Or maybe that's just me. I'm perfectly all right with it just being me.

By not securing my head they'd given me a tiny window of opportunity. I'd take it. I bent my head to the right and started to gnaw at my own skin. Hurts like the devil, biting through your own flesh. A few minutes and some careful work later, I had one capsule in my mouth.

I spit it out and aimed for my hand. My fingers bent enough for me to catch it, just barely, except I missed. The capsule brushed my fingertips and dropped onto the floor, next to my right foot. I took a deep breath and lowered my head again, stretching to bite into my other collarbone. I wanted to scream, that or gag on the blood filling my mouth. Also, my head still hurt fiercely. I knew the headache had thrown my aim off last time, so I took a deep breath with the second capsule in my teeth and thought about this.

The best I could hope for would be for the two capsules to hit on the floor. They would explode and, if they were close enough, blow one of the straps with little enough noise that I wouldn't be noticed. If it had been at my wrist I could predict it, but the first capsule was lost in the darkness somewhere by my foot. I moved my boot around and felt it on the floor. Taking a second slow, deep breath, I spit the second capsule out toward the first and heard it plink delicately on the floor.

I had to escape soon, now, or I would risk bleeding out. The ragged holes on my shoulders weren't going to close by themselves. They at least needed bandages of some kind. Time would be short.

Nudging first one capsule and then the other between my boots, I picked them up and rolled them onto the top of my right boot. It took every inch of painful extension I could manage to get my toes to touch that way, but I did it. In the process of getting them both on my foot I smashed them together, starting the reaction.

With both on top of my right boot, fizzing audibly, I flicked my foot up as best I could and felt the mashed-up capsules roll down my leg and hitch against the strap across my right ankle. This wouldn't be pleasant - all I could hope for would be that it wouldn't take my foot off when it blew.

My boot and the strap took the brunt of the small explosion, but I knew that my right ankle wouldn't be a happy place to visit, either. I bled freely from three points now, and my time ticked away. Then again, my right leg could move freely. The strap broke nicely. I wormed out of my boot and moved my right leg over to my left. The straps, like I thought, were designed to be worked by a thick-gloved hand, which meant my toes would do fine.

Except they were also slippery with blood, so it took a few seconds longer than I would've liked, but then both legs were free. Now it came down to a question of flexibility. Yoga, stretching - I might have gotten older as the years went by, but that was no reason to slack off. Taking a deep breath, I slowly moved my right leg up until it could work on the strap holding down my left wrist.

With a hand free, the rest proved easy enough. I sat there, in the chair, and thought for a second or two longer than necessary. The blood loss wasn't trivial. Nothing for it, though. A few strips of outfit here and there and I stopped most of it, enough to count, at any rate. Then I managed to get my mangled boot back on my torn-up foot without screaming.

On the bright side, I really didn't notice the headache anymore.

Now I just needed to get out of this room, off this ship, and work out what the hell was going on. Not necessarily in that order, mind. Except the room should come first. Moving in the dark meant going slow and searching for light. The door sealed fully, so I wouldn't have to worry about light showing from under it - none showed from outside, and I could bet they hadn't darkened a whole lot of the ship just for me.

Of course they could still have windows into the room, one-way jobs that wouldn't show light from the outside. I had no way of knowing how observed

I was except for the fact that no one had come in to get me yet. I limped around the room twice, memorizing it, and decided to not bother with finding a light after all. I found the door, and a dark open room would be far better to fight from than a well-lit one.

Assuming I could get the door open. The trick I'd used last time wouldn't work twice, I had to assume that they'd be looking for it. Then again, I also knew whose doors stood in my way this time. Advantage about even, really. I didn't have any more implanted explosives, either, or any good way to keep bandaging myself even if I had. No, I'd have to pick the lock.

Not easy to do when the lock in question is a biometric scanner. My prints wouldn't work on it, and I didn't have anyone else's hand lying around to try. Instead I took my left boot off (the boot still in one piece) and used it to beat the casing off the door scanner. Wires I could deal with.

With access to the system, I could get the door open easy enough. I could also, I realized with a muffled laugh, short half the ship's systems. The leftover remains of an old design flaw in the doors, one Jonah and I had pointed out to them years before. Why they wouldn't have fixed it I could imagine all too well. They took the problem to committee and review, realized we were right, and pushed out the fix to all new designs, planning to implement it in the older systems when they got their standard upgrades. Those upgrades could be decades between installations for things like this and, it seemed, in this case literally had been.

One wire over here, another over there, and a few quick twists. That's it. Now the next time anyone opened a door on this side of the level I was on, the whole system would unlock, switch states, and then lock down until they worked out what had happened. That would give me practically no time at all to slip through the door.

About two seconds later, the door opened. On any big ship there's always someone going somewhere. Perfect. I slid through the door as it opened, getting clear before everything clanged shut and locked.

Of course, that meant I stood in a brightly lit hallway, ragged and bleeding, bandages made from bits of my own clothes wound around me, and a right boot that flapped because half of it wasn't there anymore. I stood there in the middle of a ship that seemed to want me locked up, weaponless, alone, a bit woozy, and in pain. I smiled.

There'd been worse. Now for the next step.

Chapter 18 – Jonah

MY NEWFOUND MINIONS scurried around, trying to do the impossible. The problem was, I knew there couldn't be a way to find a ship, convince the ruling council, gather the population, and evacuate a planet in the time left. I knew it. I just didn't want to believe it.

There's losing and then there's never having a chance. We were deep into the no-chance zone and spiraling down. I was playing King of the Hill without a real point. At best I could save myself and a few of the folks closest here. That would be it. But how could I explain that to them? The answer to that escaped me, and always had. I didn't like to lose. I liked this even less.

I stood up and kicked over the makeshift throne I'd inherited. Time to cut loses. Damn it. How could an entire operation go this far south this fast? Something didn't gel right in my mind. I'd have to work it out along the way.

I stood there, feeling every inch of my age. I was a stupid old man who had gotten in the way of something far bigger than he'd suspected. I still had no idea where Shae was, I stood on a planet with a timer running down quickly, and something about the entire thing didn't add up. I'm sure it could've looked worse to me, but I couldn't see how.

"Hey, you two!" I called out, stopping a few of the Stone Hammer kids who were milling around trying to work out how to do anything I'd asked for.

"Let's focus on the ship, all right, what've you got for me?"

I leapt down off the little stage and smiled a false smile at them. They smiled back nervously and just as falsely. Great.

"Nothing, Boss. Off-planet is forbidden, there are no ships," a kid told me, his shiny shaved head glinting a bit in the flickering light of the hall.

"Not good enough, since when do Stone Hammers listen to the cops? To the Council? No, someone here has a ship and we need to find it."

Baldy nodded, his face grim, and ran off to talk to a few other people. As he did, a shy girl inched around, her feet shuffling and nervous. She wore a torn-up jumpsuit and had a rag tied around her head. She looked, honestly, like half the nerve-wracked techs I'd worked with. The ones who had answers but didn't want to tell you because they weren't the right answers.

"Tell me," I said, moving to stand directly in front of her.

"Oh, Boss," a tall, reedy guy interrupted, "you don't want to listen to Bee. She's not right, you know?"

"Thanks for that," I told him, "but I'll take my chances." I smiled at the woman, "Bee?"

She looked at me and nodded. I could see courage deep in her eyes, but around here, around here she was the kook. No matter how good her info might be, it wouldn't improve her standing with the group. She knew it as well as I did.

"Bee, if you got something," I said, "open your mouth and get it out. If you don't, stop staring and keep moving."

"The junkyard," she managed to get out, "might have something we can use."

A bunch of people nearby laughed and started to repeat what she said, causing ripples of startled laughter. Me and Bee weren't joining in. "Might? What kind of might are we talking here, kid?"

"There's an old hull and some engines out there," she said, staring at me hard, trying to will me to believe her, not knowing I already did. "We can maybe make them work if we had enough people who tinker..."

I sprang to life. "You heard her, people! We're headed to the junkyard." I thought about it a second. "Bee, how big is the hull?"

"Could hold ten or so, probably."

Ten. Maybe ten people would be all that I could save. Ten people out of an entire planet. Though if I got off with them, once I was back in contact with the rest of the fleet there stood a slim chance of a miracle. Ten it would have to be.

"You find eight people, Bee," I told her, "folks who can lift this stuff and folks who can fix it, along with you. You can fix it, can't you?"

She smiled at that and nodded. "We've been keeping the rust out of all the best pieces. I once got all the lights to turn on in the hull," she whispered like it was a great source of pride for her and a secret she wanted to keep.

"Go find us a crew, Bee," I told her, and I turned to address everyone else. "You will all listen to Bee. I don't care what you think, but she's deciding a crew right now to head out to the junkyard and get us off this rock. Disobeying her is like disobeying me, and you saw what happened to your *old* leader, right?"

128

Actually I'd had to stun him again when no one was looking, just to make sure they continued thinking he was dead. I might be sentencing him to death anyway with this plan, but hopefully he'd wake up, take control again, and have a long life of being a miserable, tiny gang leader to look forward to.

I prodded Bee to round up folks faster and we were off to the junkyard. She led the way, still not used to being in charge of anything at all. We grabbed a few of their vehicles to get there - old, beaten-down things with four huge tires to get over obstacles. There were, of course, plenty of those, but we arrived at the junkyard fast enough, I suppose, considering we didn't have any time at all.

The place looked like any junkyard I'd ever seen. Piles and piles of rusting metal and despair, lumped together to make a monument to waste. Bee and two others leapt from the transport and ran off, shouting at each other to keep up and giving directions to the rest. I told the convoy to follow them as best we could. Chances were, the parts of our vehicles would be needed. It wasn't like we were coming back for them.

The techs - well, at least the folks Bee felt were techs - crawled over an old hull that had a small, reverent, junk-free area cleared around it. A quick glance at it didn't fill me with confidence. The metal tube didn't look like something that could be made airtight with a month's worth of work, much less a few hours.

"Are you sure this'll work?" I asked Bee, nodding at the wreck.

"No," she said, "but it's the only hull I've ever found around here." Honesty. It'd have to do.

"Right then!" I yelled. "We don't have much time so let's get to work! Bee's in charge."

"Uhm," she said low, "wouldn't you rather be in charge? You've been in these before."

"In them, yeah, built them from the ground up? Not so often. Just do your best, I'll be right alongside."

And I was. I used my Acadian blaster at mid-power, close range, to spot-weld the hull together and repair breaks. We pulled engines from the wheeled transports and mounted them to the inside of the hull. They would power life support and electrics inside.

Bee and her crew split off to find the larger engines they'd toyed with when they were pretty sure no one was watching. I got called over to help drag them back to the hull and mount them. We test fired them, one after the other, more to check whether the batteries worked and make sure the hookups weren't backward than to see if they would generate enough lift. One of the hookups was reversed, actually, and it almost cost us the engine. We also lost one of our heavy lifting crew in the explosion. We didn't, thankfully, lose the engine itself.

They were smart kids, all mechanics and tech-heads with obvious affection for what they kept calling antiques, which was fair enough. Soon, the crap old hull started to look like a very old, run-down ship of sorts. The transport engines gave us lights and heat and worked at filling the air tanks. The batteries on the lifting engines had enough charge to get us up with (hopefully) enough left over to move us around decently. My own suit could handle radio communications.

I ran down a mental checklist and it ended up not bad. We might even get to win this one. Spot welds were almost finished and we were loading some cargo, extra bits of machinery just in case, when the screaming began. I stopped work and looked around.

People were pointing up and my heart sank. I followed their points into the sky, where everything flashed red and yellow and white. The invasion had started while we sat on the ground helpless. It also meant that even if we launched, we'd have to go through an invasion fleet that could out-turn and out-pace cutting-edge ships. That cut launch time from somewhere in the next few hours to somewhere in the next five minutes, max.

"Guys, we gotta go!" I yelled, zipping down with my GravPack to find Bee. "They're here. We gotta go and go now, or we won't make it."

"We might not make it anyway, Boss," she said, full of fear.

"Call me Jonah," I said without thinking, and added, "We'll make it."

"How can we? The ship isn't ready, we aren't ready, how can we possibly—"

"Bee, we'll make it because if we don't, a lot more planets are going to die this way. We'll make it because my wife is out there and…you know what, this isn't the time for speeches. Get everyone on board, I'll do an outside check and we're taking off!"

Bee grabbed her tool bag and ran for the hatch, stopping long enough to physically shove each crew member toward the opening as well. I flew around the hull and realized the ready lines hadn't been disconnected. I started to grab them and rip them free, getting bucked off the hull intermittently by Bee starting a full systems check and launch sequence. Good. She was smart. Even if I didn't make it inside, she knew enough to take off without me.

The last hose pulled free and I did a final scan, pulling out my blaster to do one last quick weld where I could see the metal bending a bit as the hull pressurized. We'd have to hope it'd all hold. With that, I opened the hatch and dove inside.

Bee and her second, a kid named Kem with a large shock of black hair that stuck up every which way, sat at the controls. I came up behind them and kicked Kem out of his seat, forcing Bee into it as I sat in the pilot's chair. He pouted a bit, but moved.

"I can do it," he insisted, hanging around behind Bee.

"I'm sure you can, kid, but let an old man have his kicks." I wasn't so sure this ship would even fly, and I didn't want them at the controls solo if something blew.

The ship rumbled to life and I started a countdown to liftoff when Bee hit my shoulder. "What is it?" I asked, thinking she saw something hurtling toward us.

"The ship doesn't have a name! It needs a name, isn't it bad luck to fly without one?" she asked, perfectly serious.

I wanted to laugh but the hell with it, the kid needed something to reassure her. "She thing, Bee, sure. Let's call her the Don't Crash."

"That's a terrible name!" she insisted. I kept readying for takeoff, and asking her for data as I went, but the name issue was keeping her calm and I think we both knew it.

"How about Rust Bucket?" I offered.

"Don't insult the ship, it's our only hope."

"She's our only hope," I corrected. "All ships are 'she,' just the way it is."

"Fine, then she shouldn't be insulted. Why don't we call her—"

But I cut Bee off as the engines sprang to life beneath us. "Hang on!"

"That'll do for a name!" she shouted back at me.

"It wasn't a name, it was an order!" I yelled back, the engines deafening us.

"Well, it's her name now," Bee told me before turning around to look at everyone else. "Hang on to something!" she shouted at them.

The ship, apparently now named *Hang On*, lifted out of the junkyard slowly but with determination. Bee and her crew had done it. The question now was whether we would break orbit. We got higher and higher with no worries, and then the invasion force started to show up around us. They didn't attack right away, unsure of what the hell we could be, I guessed.

Our luck didn't hold for long, though. The sky around us turned to black, orbit was close enough I could taste it, and the ship lurched as one of the bird ships fired at us. We couldn't take much of that, maybe not even a second hit. One of our lift engines cut out and the ship started to spiral off to one side. We'd miss an orbit break if we didn't correct for it, but a correcting course would have to be clean and unhindered.

I rolled the ship around to shift the force and started to correct us when I saw we were aimed right at one of the invading ships. Fine, they could turn fast enough, let him get out of our way. Except he didn't. The collision didn't do us any favors, and the dent in the front of the ship was visible from where I sat. It also knocked us back and killed some of our momentum.

"I can reroute our internals to the blown engine and get at least one burst," Kem shouted in my ear.

"Do it!" I told him. He was a good choice on Bee's part.

"If he does, what will we breathe?" Bee asked, adding, "We'll also freeze to death!"

She had a point, but if we didn't try it, we would fall from the sky like a stone - if we weren't blown up on the way down. Six of one, might as well try for orbit.

Kem shouted that he had managed it and for us to try the second engine again. It caught and we lifted, straining for the black.

CHAPTER 19 – MEANWHILE

Bercuser drifted, as was its wont. No one knew, off of a chart, what its orbit truly was, or where the planet thought it might be. Not that anyone thought the planet was conscious. Not really. Planets are not conscious beings. Still, if there was one that would be the exception to the rule, that would have to be Bercuser.

Folks not from the planet, those who knew of the planet as more than a legend, told stories of a strange history involving a number of highly questionable scientific experiments. They said, often in hushed tones, that one of the experiments went horribly awry and that the planet itself broke off from reality as a result.

Others thought Bercuser to be one of the lost and fabled Wandering Planets. The first group insisted that the second group agreed with them, even if they didn't know it, and that those tales were all examples of the same fate that had befallen Bercuser.

No one knew what really had happened. This was, in part, because many maps omitted Bercuser and the stories were told as legends. However, even the military, which did know about Bercuser, held its tongue about why the planet seemed to vanish from one system and appear in another with no obvious pattern.

What no one did was ask the people of Bercuser for a reason. Travel to the planet, when it appeared, was illegal, owing to the fact that no one knew how to get there or where they would be leaving from. There had been military incursions, peaceful and fact finding, throughout the years, but they could only discern two things.

The first, that Bercuser didn't wander nearly as much as previously thought. How or why it wandered they didn't understand, but they found only three different places where the planet would appear. People claimed to see the planet all across the galaxy, but truth be told, the planet had three separate orbits it could claim as its own. All three were near each other, system-wise, and though their orbits weren't fully predictable, they were at least somewhat understood.

The second thing that the military learned was that the people of Bercuser didn't care one bit about the supposed problems with their planet. They were content to treat the stars above their heads changing in perfectly unaccountable ways as one of life's mysteries.

The people of Bercuser didn't try to solve mysteries, in general. They rather enjoyed them. The more obscure the better. On Bercuser, the natives wandered from city to city and continent to continent in a state of openness toward life being a mystery. And by solving life you left yourself with nothing, they figured, so why should you risk solving any mystery much bigger than "Where did I leave my keys?"

Life on Bercuser was not, however, as strange as the classified reports made it seem. People lived and died, ate and slept, and lived as people do. Industry and culture, art and music and writing all, flourished on the planet outside the majority of galactic influence, creating things that no one else did.

Bercusans, as they called themselves, knew of space travel and dabbled in it, but they didn't care for it overall. Their expeditions had a habit of never returning. This was not, of course, due to their own personal shortcomings. It was wholly due to the planet moving around and the expeditions becoming lost. And so such projects were scarce.

The strange tri-orbit of the planet also affected its weather. No one could predict it decently, and the weather in most areas of Bercuser changed as often as night and day, which were also of varied lengths.

No organized religion existed on Bercuser, the last of them having died out a generation back. Their sense of spirituality, on the other hand, was something that each Bercusan held close. Though they wouldn't use the term mystics, they often behaved in ways that would be appropriate for the label. They drifted in their lives, accepting what came to them and ascribing many things to the unexplainable without spending much effort to explaining them. Many would predict the future (a few predicting the past instead) using the strange fogs that blanketed most of the planet. The fogs themselves were the result of the oceans being subject to things oceans are not often subject to: the weather, orbit shifting, and everything else about the planet.

Trapping The Fogs was the most popular ways of working out the past, present, and future of

Bercuser, and it would be fair to say that every household had at least one Fogger per generation.

They were fairly decent at predicting the future, with a success rate good enough to worry some of the larger Galactic Government, though they also proved to be bizarrely bad about predicting the past.

A number of people on Bercuser started to predict doom around the same time, which worried many of the citizens. Others took it as one of life's mysteries and waited. No one expected the planet to pop out into one of its orbits in the path of an invasion force. Luckily for them, the invasion force was busy with a different planet just then. Unluckily, the orbit that the planet drifted along would make it too easy a target to pass up. Bercuser's days were numbered. A few of the citizens knew it. Some of the officials on the planet believed those few and contacted the wider Bercusan Government for assistance, only to find that they were already dealing with the problem to the best of their ability.

Bercuser readied itself for invasion and considered evacuation. They didn't posses enough ships to get even a noticeable minority of its people off-planet. They also didn't have weapons of the sort of quantity to fight off a full-scale invasion. Almost no planet did. Planets did not, after all, get invaded, as a general rule.

And so Bercuser found itself simply waiting. Foggers sought to see the future as accurately as possible, and everyone else walked about nervously, watching the skies.

CHAPTER 20 – JONAH

WE BROKE ORBIT before the engines died or the hull blew apart. The ship didn't have artificial gravity, but I gave it a hard spin to let the newcomers enjoy something close enough. I needed them focused, not throwing up in free-fall.

Our biggest problem turned out to not be breaking orbit. Getting there had been a rough path, but staying there looked to be even worse. We popped up in the middle of a battlefield. I knew any second we would be attacked by everything out here, and that meant a lot of guns pointed our way. Then I remembered my thinsuit radio would work again.

"Deep Water, this is Jonah, come back," I said, holding a hand up to Bee to shush her. "Repeat, Deep Water, this is Jonah, come back. You out there, Bushfield?"

"Jonah?" her voice sang in my ear. Oh beautiful, she was still out here raising hell. "Where have you been? I tracked you falling to the planet. But then—"

"But then. Yeah, I get that. Listen—"

"Hey, where are you?" she cut in. "Listen, intercept that big bucket of rust coming out of orbit, will you, it might be a bomb or something."

"Shows what you know, Deep Water, that rust bucket is me. Long story." I yanked on the yoke hard and managed to avoid colliding with ships moving fast enough to blur. "Put the call out, ship's call sign is Hang On, repeat, call sign Hang On. We'd like to not be blown up, thanks. Also, maybe a rescue?"

"Have you looked out a window recently? We'd all like a rescue." She broke off for a second as, I assumed, the battle took her concentration. I waited while the crew of the Hang On stared at me, hearing only half a conversation. "I'll get you a quick escort out of the line of fire, but after that you better be able to suck air a while in that thing."

"It'll have to do, and hey, Bushfield, thanks."

"Thank me when we're on something soft and solid. Frogger's on return vector, close enough, and will escort. He'll vector from your right," she said.

"I won't shoot him, no worry," I said with a laugh.

"Shoot him? I'm worried you'll run into him by mistake."

I turned in my seat to explain what was going on and what would be happening to everyone else. They were, almost to a person, too scared to listen. None of them had ever been in space before, much less in the middle of a firefight. Not the best introduction to the wide world of interplanetary travel.

Frogger showed up a few seconds later and started to clear a path for us. I grabbed up my GravPack and gave it a decent once-over. The pack had performed fine on Trasker Four and I knew I put it through its paces, but I wanted to make sure it wouldn't loop-crash me into a planet again. Nothing on board seemed to indicate a problem with the pack at all, which meant the planet fall was what it seemed like. I got too close, I got sucked in. Fine. Better to check now that I had a moment than to find an error with the selector array or something the next time I ducked out.

I considered ducking out to help Frogger escort us, but a look around told me this crew would panic if I left. Not all of them, but enough to overwhelm the few who wouldn't. They were on edge, and losing the one guy who knew what he was doing, and who could actually talk to anyone outside the ship, would shove them right over.

So I stayed where I was and piloted. Frogger kept us on a straight vector, leading us right out of the fray, except the bird ships didn't seem to like that.

"Frogger, there's—"

"I got it, Jonah," he cut in, peeling off to go deal with a ship that had turned after us. He had sensors, we didn't. I was flying pretty much blind. Then again, the blindness worked to my advantage as well. All we could do was look out the window, which meant everyone else wasn't busy freaking out about the size and speed of the fight.

I took a deep breath and tried to find some sort of calm center. I wanted to be out there. A second deep breath. The staleness of the canned air in the ship started to annoy me as well. Sweat mixed into it, and with no air cleaners installed we weren't going to enjoy this trip one bit.

I also couldn't afford to call in to base until we were clear, so I had no way of knowing if there were any updates on Shae. I needed to leave my radio open to the fight. I hated this. I flipped the ship end over end to get a decent view of the field while Frogger was busy. Off to the far right I caught sight of a planet. There shouldn't have been a planet in orbit this close to Trasker Four. It sat at the outer

141

end of our range, and if we could make it there we might be able to land safe. But what was it?

"Deep Water, this is Jonah," I called.

"Go, Jonah," Bushfield replied, sounding harried. Not a surprise.

"I got a planet out here, might be in range for us. Once Frogger gets back I think we'll head for it."

"Roger that, Jonah, but wait, what planet?"

"Scope it," I told her and fired off truly rough coordinates based on some guesswork. She didn't get back to me for a bit, so I took the time to explain to the crew what my hopeful plan was.

"Another planet?" Kem asked, "Will we be able to breathe?"

"That's one of the things they're finding out for us right now."

"We'll be aliens!" insisted one of Bee's lifting squad, a guy with no neck who liked to be called Steelbox.

"Well, sure," I answered, "but that won't matter, I'm sure. Listen, most other planets get visitors, they're part of the galaxy. It'll be...hold on," I blinked and shook my head, not sure about what just came over my comm. "Repeat that?"

"Jonah, they took out Squire! Trasker Four is defenseless."

"Well, crap."

"To put it mildly. I can't spare Frogger any more." She sighed and spoke softer, "And listen, don't head for that planet. It's Bercuser, Jonah, you can't land there."

"Sure I can," I fought down a chuckle, "I have before."

"No one is allowed to land on Bercuser, Jonah! No one."

"Now, sure. But how do you think we got the information on it?" I asked her. "Listen, I'll tell you all about it when this is over. I'm headed there, no good choice. You keep the fleet alive, will you?"

"Roger," she said angrily, "spot you at base, you buy."

"Over."

I explained the situation to the crew and, as I did, I had an idea. If I could convince the people of Bercuser, they might be able to send some of their ships out to Trasker Four and save a few folks. Without Squire, nothing should be preventing ships from landing on the planet. That meant the invasion as well as a rescue convoy, but the theory held.

All I had to do now was pilot us to a contender for the strangest planet in the galaxy, through the edge of a fight. In a ship with no weapons or sensors. And a crew that couldn't have had less experience if it'd tried. And then land a ship that shouldn't have realistically broken orbit to begin with.

I felt alive. Young again. My mission sat in front of me, part of a larger goal, and it invigorated me. The stale air in the ship, the constant low hum of the quickly patched-together electronics, none of it bothered me anymore. I smiled out the scarred viewport and turned the ship hard.

"Listen, I'm gonna stop this roll, so get ready for zero G for a minute," I warned them. We came out of the turn and headed slightly away from the planet, looking like we were basically trying to limp out of the field of fire.

It worked for a few minutes, and we were well on our way until one of the bird ships fired at us from behind. I had to assume it was them, not one of our guys going crazy. Didn't matter, in the end, because they managed to tear a small hole in the hull. We started to lose air, and fast.

"Shove something into that hole, will you?" I called out.

Steelbox launched himself from his seat toward the hole and got sucked up against it. Then he started to scream.

"I'm gonna get sucked out!"

"You won't get sucked out," I told him, "it doesn't work that way. It'll hurt, maybe, but you'll be fine and the air will stay in. Don't worry about it. You don't have to be there long. Just take off your jacket it and shove that in there instead, all right?"

I didn't want to tell him he'd be fine so long as they didn't shoot at us again. Standing against the hull when they could pierce it was not a recipe for a long life. Still, it wasn't as if we had a patch kit.

I hit the engines, hard, and we lurched forward unsteadily. That second engine wasn't working quite right and gave us a list to port. I kept them both at full burn. A bit of gravity settled the ship as we hit speed. Of course, the gravity wasn't oriented the same way as we were, and most of the crew turned slightly green upon realizing that their up and down had shifted yet again.

I knew that bird ship wouldn't give up after only one shot so I started to take basic evasive maneuvers. Nothing fancy, the *Hang On* couldn't do fancy - it could hardly do simple.

144

Another shot rocked the ship, this time along the starboard side, which meant they'd noticed one of our engines struggling and had decided to help it along to its demise. I started to roll us again and kept weaving as best I could.

I wondered about my GravPack. It was rated for a one-man field, and could extend to maybe three times that if it had to, but could I wire it so it would extend the field to the entire ship? Probably not. And if I didn't get the whole ship, we'd be torn in two. Then again, maybe not.

"Bee," I said, looking over at her. Her face showed me no fear, only determination. Somewhere in there she'd gone from scared, mousy woman, afraid of the other members of her own gang, to someone who wanted to live badly enough to do what it took. Perfect. "I need you to pilot for a few minutes. Just a few."

"I can't fly the ship," she said simply.

"You've been watching me. Just keep doing things like I've been doing and it'll be fine. I'm going for a walk."

Kem cried out, "You've leaving us?"

"Not going far," I told him. "I think I have a way to save us, but it's dicey and requires me to do it from outside the ship."

"How will we know if it works?" Bee asked.

"If we suddenly speed up, and I mean way up," I said as I adjusted my helmet, "let go of the yoke and trust me. I'll be steering from out there."

"What? How?" I didn't see who asked, it was someone on the crew of nine people who I didn't know. How did I not even know all of their names? Shameful. I'd apologize when we landed.

"I'll explain on the ground, just trust me."

Bee shifted into my seat and started to steer, "What if it doesn't work?"

"Don't worry about that," I said, refusing to add the reason why: if this didn't work, we'd be dead.

I left the airlock, hoping the pressure would hold since we hadn't tested it, and found myself in space again. Home. I moved to the top of the ship, pulling forward until I was almost at the viewport. Landing on the ship proved easy enough, and I pulled my blaster and fired behind me at the bird ship I knew was out there. At any sort of real range I couldn't harm it, but maybe it didn't know that.

I extended the field of my GravPack as far as it wanted to go normally and then pushed it. The HUD lit up red with warnings and I pushed the field farther. I inched back along the ship and got the field aligned over the entire hull, with maybe a centimeter to spare.

My GravPack would need a bit of work after this, but I'd at least be alive to fix it. Grabbing my blaster again, I burned two handholds for myself and holstered the weapon so I could grab on. Then I selected my target - the planet - and pushed the GravPack into action. It whined, I could feel the vibration along my back. They weren't supposed to do that. I didn't even know they could. I wondered how long before it exploded and what I would feel when it did.

No time for that. I had a ship to accelerate. Bee stopped fighting my direction quickly and I gave it everything I had. Steering wouldn't be pretty, no finesse, but all I had to do was get us into orbit and get back inside the ship.

The engines whined, giving thrust uselessly, but we'd need them going and hot when I turned off the field. So long as they didn't burn out. Come on, Bee, come on, think of it. Turn the engines down but not off. Come on, I chanted to myself for a full three minutes until the engines died down to a steady hum.

Bercuser came up far too quickly. We were approaching it at impossible speeds and I'd have to bring us back down to the speed the ship had been going in order to give it a chance of landing. I knew the GravPack wouldn't hold on through a landing, which meant the ship had to be going slow enough to stop itself. It would stop, regardless, but I preferred one piece to splattered face first into the ground.

I spun the ship so we faced away, engines pointed at Bercuser, and took us down low enough for the planet's gravity to tug. Cutting the gravfield, I took a good look, mapping our relative position in my HUD - once I got back inside, I would be flying literally blind to our destination for a while.

Back inside the ship, everyone was trying to not panic except Bee. She sat there, still determined, trying to project it to everyone else. They seemed happy enough to see me.

"Miss me?" I asked Bee as she moved over and let me grab the controls. "Nice work on cutting back the engines."

"Sorry it took me so long to think of it," she said.

"No, I should've mentioned. Look, doesn't matter, if we land."

"We'll land either way, won't we?" she whispered to me.

I laughed and nodded, knowing everyone else would be wondering what could possibly be funny. Bee shook her head reproachfully at me but couldn't hide her own grin. She'd picked up a taste for this madness fast.

We went down into the gravity well, ass first and blind. My HUD gave me approximate distances based on my earlier readings and I flipped us back around, hoping I was guessing right.

Close to right, at least. A little too low and way too fast, the ground rushed at us. We hadn't built this bucket to fly in atmo at all. Never thought of having to land it on a planet, I figured the worst we'd have to do would involve a space docking.

I aimed for water and came in low, hoping to skip us to a stop and beach us before we kept going into whatever lay past. We hit with a bone-rattling thump and soared - thump, glide, thump, glide - until we hit land hard. Everyone, myself included, got thrown from where we were. Not from our seats, we were still strapped in: the seats themselves ripped free from the floor.

It hurt like hell, but we stopped moving. We had landed.

CHAPTER 21 – MUD

THE *DOZIER* LOOMED at the edge of my scanners. I didn't want to get much closer without a fully formed plan. Their sensors outstripped mine, so if I could see them, even just barely, they could pinpoint me without breathing hard.

The best bet would be to go in presenting something much smaller than my ship. I hated GravPacks, didn't carry one (though Dad wanted me to, and made sure I'd been trained on them), so that was right out. I did have a standard EVA suit, and they had small pressure jets but worked best short range. No, I needed a diversion.

Then it hit me. A diversion, my EVA suit, and a few munitions. Easy. I set myself a course in the other direction, looking for a few big rocks. Nudging them back toward the direction of the *Dozier* rattled my seat a bit but worked fine.

The rocks drifted off and would reach the shield range of the *Dozier* in about a day. Not fast enough by half. But before I tried to speed them up I'd have to be outside. My ship sat outside of their scan range, so I put it in a hold-and-wait pattern. The power would be on minimum but hot enough to leap to a full burn in seconds if I whistled.

My EVA suit was clumsy and annoying, but a thinsuit didn't have any propulsion to it. Once in the EVA, I had to find a way to secure my bags in such a way that they wouldn't tear free. Sadly, with only one person this proved to be the hardest part of the plan to date. Couldn't leave the bag, though, even if it would've made life easier. Assuming Mom and/or Dad was being held by the Gov against their will, chances were high there would be some blowing up of things to be done. Can't do that with no munitions. So they came with me in two bags strapped to my body.

The bags hung badly and got in my way, but I couldn't throw them onto my back because I'd need to put the pressure jets there. I holstered one sonic pistol on the inside of the EVA suit, and a second along the leg of the suit itself. The outside one had a much larger stock-and-trigger-assembly, built for the clumsy, or those with pressure-gloved hands.

I kept the helmet of the suit kinked so I wouldn't start running down my air. This was all routine stuff, annoying but easy enough. The rest of the plan got worse as it went. I did a final systems check on the ship and then on my bags. The rocks drifted the right way, the ship felt steady, nothing left but to do it.

My helmet hissed and flooded with slightly less humid air than I liked. I didn't need my goggles yet, but a half-step down in atmo mix would make it last longer. I sniffed deeply to get used to the annoying tang this suit produced. I'd have to strip down the whole suit to fix it and never found the time. One of those problems that's only noticeable on the rare occasions I used the suit. Easy to forget. Until I was in the suit, and then it became a priority. Probably a hose seal somewhere, nothing life threatening, just annoying.

I realized I was stalling. To hell with that. The airlock cycled around me and I checked my readings. The armband on my EVA suit read fine, I could control the ship on a limited basis from it. Enough to get this job done.

Outside the ship, I hit the pressure jets and floated quickly over to the rocks. I grabbed one and used the jets to start turning it. Over-rotated and I had to maneuver it back a bit. There we go. I faced my body away from my ship with the rock between us.

I hit the remote trigger and closed my eyes. No noise, of course, but a flash of light and I was set spinning and hurtling toward the *Dozier*. A few more flashes and there were a lot more rocks, all of them smaller now, speeding more or less the same way. I hoped my impromptu meteor shower worked.

At least for part of the trip, clinging to a rock would get me a bit of the way in unnoticed, but the *Dozier* would have shields that these rocks would dust against. The rest of the way, I'd have to manage it alone. Assuming I could get past the shields myself.

My EVA suit had a Gov tag on it, legal and everything, so the shields should part for me, but they'd also log my entrance. I could bet on that being strange enough that they'd investigate quickly. So I had to ditch the tag. Which is where phase three of my plan came in.

As the rocks and I got closer to the *Dozier*, the pressure jets on my EVA suit fired, changing course for the rock I clung to and bumping against others along the way. Then I stripped out of my EVA suit, reslung my equipment bags across my chest, and proceeded to rip the bulky suit and smash it as best

I could with rocks I found. My thinsuit kept me fine, and the backup remote for my ship came online fine. Systems still checked. We were just heading out of my ship's scanner range, but while it could still see my rock garden, I had my ship relay data on us. Everything was drifting right where I wanted it.

Everything approached the shield limit of the *Dozier*. I held my breath as the leading rocks turned to dust against those invisible shields. Me, the rock I clung to, and the EVA suit, ruined and held tight, slid right by. In that second the *Dozier* logged our approach. I kicked off the rock hard, leaving the EVA suit on it.

If everything went as planned, they would soon get a rock hard against their hull. It wouldn't do any damage, but they'd wonder how it got there, go check, and find the suit. That'd match the log. Then they'd waste a few hours checking and rechecking where the suit came from and where the person in it had vanished to. The suit's condition should make them assume the worst.

By the time they straightened it out it would be too late. If everything else went right. That felt like a mighty big "if" as I drifted toward a side hatch on the ship. I couldn't just blow the hatch or the entrance scanner. Either one would bring everyone in the ship with a weapon running right for me. I had to be sneaky.

I reached the hatch and grabbed it tight, looking over the scanner. It'd take an ID tag at close range or an input security code. Both would be logged, of course, and I needed to come inside in a way they couldn't trace back to me. So I detached the scanner plate itself and let it sit there, wires stretched like umbilicals.

A few tools from one of my bags and I rerouted power to bypass this plate. They wouldn't notice the shunt for a while, long enough for me to work. Once the plate sat lifeless, nothing stopped me from grabbing the wires that fed the data channel back to the server that would do checks against the plate input and allow the door to open or not. I put those input wires into my own scanner and fed it a bit of test data. Routine stuff that wouldn't be noticed. Everything came back green.

Perfect. They weren't in a heightened security setting. Grabbing the door wires instead, I sent current through them. Too much and the doors would detect a problem and go into full lockdown. Too little and they'd try to alarm the doors with a malfunction flag. I tried to remember the exact settings for Gov hatch charges. I knew it was one of two numbers and took a stab in the dark.

I sent the current and waited a second. Then another. Nothing, not a twitch. That was bad. Over or under? Under. The door would flag a malfunction the second I hooked it back up. But I had to hook it back up or they'd notice that, too, the same as a malfunction flag. I'd screwed myself.

I sent another power burst and the doors twitched and the hatch cycled open. I hooked the scanner pad back up, taking care to leave one of the power couplings frayed and loose. Just loose enough so it shouldn't engage. They'd notice, but with the EVA suit causing them mysteries, they might not notice for a while.

The inner airlock was much easier to bypass. It assumed you'd gotten in by normal means. A quick rewire and power shunt and the air cycled and hatch opened. As it did, I suddenly wondered if anyone would be on the other side at the wrong second.

Too late to worry, and thankfully no one was there. I retracted my thinsuit's helmet and put my goggles on to keep my eyes moist. I hated this air mix, but I was pretty sure someone would notice if I changed it.

I was inside one of the Gov's bigger battle cruisers, unnoticed for now. I felt like it shouldn't be that easy. I stood there and looked around, finding a dark corner to crouch in. My thinsuit blended colors with the wall, as did my face. The needles hurt, but the needles always hurt.

Something felt off. Sure my intrusion was smooth, but this really did feel too smooth. I hid and considered my options. Now that I'd managed to get inside I had to locate Mom at least. I would also need a map of the ship. Both these things would be in the same place: any decent-sized communications room. Which were all, of course, staffed and secure.

Getting in kept proving to be the easy part. Though I couldn't work out why everything felt off. The hallways seemed too deserted for a ship this big out of dock. What could be causing that, when no alert was ringing?

Oh. Right. Mom. Or Dad, or both. If they'd escaped, then the ship wouldn't want to go to high alert and give them the chaos as a cover. By staying at normal running mode, except for shifting personnel out of the way, they could hope to lull them into a false sense of security.

I loved that anyone thought that idea would work. But it really was how the Gov thought this stuff through. Didn't mean I was right, though. The theory held water for now, but I'd need proof. Easiest way to get proof would be to find my parents.

Which took me right back to finding a comm room. That wasn't exactly hard. Any ship this size is required to have at least one comm room per level, if not two. I grabbed my sonic pistol and slapped the access plate with my other hand.

My entire plan was to go in shooting and lock down the room. I could secure it on the way out and go from there. Messy but it'd get the job done, and I felt like I was wasting time doing anything else.

The door opened and I raised the gun, aiming it into the room. My finger twitched against the trigger and I felt the sonics go off, rumbling into the open space. Right into the sonic-shielded plate of the guards posted inside.

Didn't expect that, but it confirmed that at least one parent was out and about. They'd try for the comm room, Mom had done it once. So they must've staffed them with guards, hoping to catch her. They weren't expecting me. Not sure if that's good or bad.

Sonics wouldn't work and now I had to secure the room, and fast, before they could radio me in. Best way would be to leap right at them. So I did. Tackled one of the guards, shoving him down into the other. A sonic shot going off right against his helmet seam blew it open and rattled his brains enough to take him down. Which left his friend and the comm techs.

The techs were easy, two shots and they were out. My arm started to feel rubbery from the bits of bounce back the sonic pistol gave off. The second guard got a good whack in and my head bounced off the desk. I cursed and punched him in the helmet, which hurt me more than him.

Changing tactics, I grabbed his helmet and smashed it against the desk a few times until it cracked open. Then I tried punching him again. Much better. He dropped and I brought myself up into a crouch. They were all out, but not for long.

I slapped the door panel and shut myself in with them. I started to play with the comm panel. Not long now until I could find what I was after.

CHAPTER 22 – JONAH

I GOT EVERYONE out of the ship as fast as possible. Not very fast, truthfully, considering we needed to roll our chairs over with us in them and then fight broken straps. The hatch, too, gave us trouble, bent and snarled, but I cut it open with my blaster and we could taste fresh air again.

Bercuser. The fog drifted around us and I remembered the first - and only - time I'd stood on this planet. Years ago, not long after we had adopted the Newt, Shae and I pulled a mission to "The Strangest Planet in the System," as they'd dubbed it. No one had understood an ounce of what went on here, no one dared to land and find out. So they sent us. Turned out they were a nice bunch of folk, once you got used to them. Pretty much like any other.

I tried to remember the place and kept coming up blank on finer details. Too many worlds, too many years spent dealing with problems just like this one, and everything started to both run together and shuffle to the back.

Albertoth. The name surfaced at last. Albertoth - the guy in charge, last time I stood around on these hills. He was old then and certainly not in charge now, but it'd be a place to start.

Bee, Kem, and the rest were standing around, whispering to each other and pointing at things. I gathered them up and started walking. Instantly, they wanted to know where we were going. I just pointed and kept moving. We needed to find a native and build from that.

We came across someone soon enough and he took us up the chain, knowing who Albertoth was, if not knowing the man personally. He had a friend who knew someone who knew someone, and so on up the ladder. An hour or so later we got out of an old, underused transport and stood at the door to Albertoth's old office. I remembered the doors fondly. Large things, made of metal and etched to resemble the fog itself.

I had taken the time to catch up on things, as much as possible, while we went. Albertoth had retired as leader. Amusing to me, since all the leader of Bercuser seemed to do was listen to other people who told him the future, and a few who tried to predict the past, and wrangle sense out of them. I suppose the work bore out to be far more frustrating than it looked.

He'd been replaced by a guy named Tonth. They told me Tonth judged very similar to Albertoth, but I would have to see for myself. Everyone I talked to, it also seemed, knew there was an invasion coming. They weren't scared, though. No, they were waiting to see what happened, with the calm certainty that an answer would be found and would reveal itself as events unfolded. I'd have liked to have had their confidence.

Instead, I had a growing lump of worry in my gut that we were wasting time. I didn't share it with anyone. I couldn't see how it would help. I followed our guide up into Tonth's office. Tonth, unlike his predecessor, preferred a shine of glamour. Ornate carvings littered the wall, his desk, and his chair.

Lights sparkled and bowls of fog glimmered on various flat surfaces.

Tonth himself had an air of nobility about him. This was a man used to being listened to. I hoped he was also used to listening. I bowed, the standard formal greeting on Bercuser, and Tonth nodded, gesturing with an open hand for me to speak.

"Head Seer Tonth," I addressed him, "I am Jonah Madison. In the older days I spoke at length with Albertoth, a wise and gentle man, truly great, and today I come before you, seeking—"

He cut me off with a grim smile and a nod. "You come to tell us to flee, do you not?"

"I do, Head Seer, truly your powers are great."

"It does not," he said, warming up, "take great power to look up, Mister Madison."

"Please," I said, giving him another bow, "call me Jonah."

"Sit then, Jonah," he said. More chairs were brought in and shoved around and we all sat, the office growing cramped with both furniture and people. "Now, tell me how you intend to save our people."

"Uhm, well, Head Seer—"

"Tonth, please. We shall be friends and consider each other equals."

I nodded at him and continued, "I'm not sure there is a plan. Do you have enough ships to evacuate the planet?"

"No, of course not."

"No," I agreed, "not many do. Can you make Bercuser shift orbits again, or do you know if it will do so soon?"

"None of us," he told me, a stern edge creeping into his voice, "can predict such things."

"I was afraid of that," I admitted.

"However," he continued, "that doesn't mean that some do not try."

"Does that mean you can or you can't?" I asked, not sure where he was going but trying to follow along.

"It means that some claim to be able to. They are not right as often as they wish, but nor are they always wrong."

"So, they guess, and at times they're lucky and right?"

"You cast doubts on all our abilities with your reductive speech," Tonth said, growing cold again.

"Your forgiveness," I said hurriedly, "I only meant to express disappointment."

"Disappointment that we are not perfect?" he asked. "We never claimed to be so. It is others who see us as charlatans and feel that we should we should be perfect lest we reveal ourselves as frauds. They accept no margin into their lives, no belief, no wisdom. We only—"

"Tonth," I said, interrupting him. It was a risky move if I wanted to stay in his good graces, but I couldn't sit and listen to him make speeches. "We don't have time. Honestly. We don't. Can we discuss a plan?"

"Yes," he said with an air of seriousness, "of course. A plan. We have many ships, though not enough to evacuate the planet, as I said."

"Which is fine, I wasn't thinking of evacuating this planet. If your seers think there is a reasonable chance the planet will orbit shift in a few days, then we should use that."

"And simply wait? Is that wise?" I couldn't tell if he was joking or not. A minute ago he'd seemed all about trusting the predictions.

"Not really, but it's the choice we have. I do, however, want to use your ships." And here was the gamble.

"For?"

"I want to send them to Trasker Four to evacuate as many people from there as possible. If you land them here and the orbit shift happens, they'll be safe, as will the people of Bercuser."

"To take in such refugees, they would not know our customs. However, we have long felt a time would come when our lands would need sharing. This must be why. Yes, we have lands set aside for a group of outsiders."

"You do?"

"Our seers," he said with a small grin, "are not kept just for show. There were some who thought the invasion and the refugee problem would be linked. They were right. Some thought the invaders themselves would be the refugees. I see now they were wrong in the details."

"Happens to the best of us," I said quickly, pushing on. "Now, with enough ships we can evacuate some folk and bring them here."

"How will we get to a planet that you are telling me is being invaded as we speak?"

"Landing will be the tricky part, yeah." I admitted. "But I can let the military know and they can protect your ships going in and out of orbit, and direct you to land where it's clear. This isn't a great plan, and there will be a lot of good people lost, but it's the only plan I have."

"And you will lead these forces yourself?" Tonth looked at me as if he knew something. Then again, maybe he did. Even if he didn't, he could claim to later. I didn't put much stock in seeing the future, and maybe he was right: maybe I failed to look at the big picture the way he did. I had my own way of seeing the future, though, with plans and strategy.

"Not quite." Two words and the whole room burst into babble. The kids I brought with me started to yell, as did Tonth's advisors in the room. Everyone who shouldn't have been talking was. The two of us who actually needed to be talking sat silent and looked at each other. I turned and looked at my guys. I gave them the same hard glare I used to give my team when they knew better then to be doing something stupid. Same as back then, people shut up.

"Some of my people will be with me. The rest will go with your ships to help guide them and collect their planet-mates," I told Tonth. He nodded.

"I expected as much," he said.

"Of course," I inclined my head to show respect, and then got down to brass tacks. "How many ships do you have and how many people can they hold?"

The rest of the meeting was simple planning. We managed to work out a decent number of cargo ships, each capable of holding a thousand people if they weren't too comfortable. They'd survive the trip, and that remained the important part. Work began as soon as possible on launching those ships, knowing no one had much time at all. They weren't the fastest ships, and if the planet was going to orbit

162

shift in two days - never mind that an invasion that could wipe out the planet was already attacking them - we'd need every minute we could scrape up.

I pulled Bee aside and told her she wasn't going back to Trasker Four, she was staying with me. A curt nod was all that she allowed herself, but I could tell she'd hoped it would be that way. Steelbox came over and asked me the same thing.

"I wanna stick with you," he said, his lack of neck robbing him of the ability to nod well.

"Yeah, well, uhm, Steelbox? Do you have a real name, kid? Steelbox is a bit—"

"Steve Bokonski," he said with a shrug. "So, you know."

"Steelbox. Right. Sure," I told him, "the thing is, I need you going with the others. We don't have many people from your world to help and we need you to show them where to land and convince people to get in and go."

"I think they'll be willing to go even if none of us try to convince them. If your planet was getting blown up around you, how much talkin' would it take to get you to leave to safety?"

Damn it, he had a good point. I just didn't want to drag too many people into this mess. Bee would come with me and I had planned on getting Kem as well. Two tech heads never hurt anyone, and they'd be more use to me than to the Bercusans, who had their own tech teams.

I just couldn't think of a good reason to say no to Steelbox. I shrugged at him and told him I'd think about it. Really, I decided to ask Bee her thoughts. She knew him, they had been in the same gang.

As I approached her, a tall, reedy guy came up to us. His eyes seemed to refocus and he started intensely at me.

"Can I help you?" I asked, knowing he must be a Bercusan Seer.

"I must go with you," he said, his voice solemn.

"Yeah, the rescue ships are over there. This isn't one of them," I told him, and I patted our new loaner ship with one hand. Bee and Kem had been familiarizing themselves with it. They were both now stopped, watching with interest. "I need to get back to work, but good of you to help."

"You misunderstand me," he said. I was afraid of that. "I need to come with you, specifically. I have foreseen it."

"Can I ask why?"

"So that you may die." This guy didn't know how to sell himself at all.

"So if you don't come with me I won't die?" I asked. "Because that isn't a great reason to bring you along, I hope you realize."

"But you must. I have seen it. You must die, and I must be along."

"I really don't think this is going to work out. Now, if you'll excuse me…" I turned back to Bee and started to ask about Steelbox when my new best friend grabbed my shoulder.

"Truly, Mister Madison, I need to accompany you and your crew," he said with all the inflection of a corpse.

"Jonah. Call me Jonah. Or Captain Madison. Never Mister. And my answer was no, and it was final." I turned back to Bee and Kem. Kem nodded when I

164

mouthed a question at him, asking if the guy had gone.

That done, I put the idea of Steelbox joining the crew to them. They didn't mind so I gave in, deciding they needed more faces from home. They also promised to ensure that he'd keep in line. Kem seemed to think Steelbox would make a fine addition for reasons he couldn't quite put into words.

That settled, I left them to finish the preparations and went around to check how the rescue ships were going. Everything seemed to be moving smoothly. It took a while, but soon enough they were ready to go.

Now all I needed was a plan for us. I'd get there, though. I felt confident about that. We'd get back into the void and then go for Shae. Stopping the invasion along the way would be icing.

I headed back to our ship and saw Bee, Kem, and Steelbox waiting for me. Stowing my gear quickly, I sat in the pilot's seat and prepared us for liftoff. I brought the engines to life and we rattled and rumbled our way toward leaving the gravity well. Just before we launched ourselves up and through the atmosphere, I heard a door close. I turned my head and there was the stranger from earlier, sitting quickly in a seat and buckling himself in.

"Bee?" I asked, jerking my head back toward our new guest.

"He came back with a letter from Tonth saying we had to take him. Says his name is Olivet."

"Great. Thanks for the warning," I told her as I kept goosing the engines to life.

"Hey, you weren't here and he had official documents demanding his inclusion," she snapped at me.

"No, you're right. You made the right choice. I just don't like him." I ignored the presence of Olivet as best I could and concentrated on takeoff. The engines roared to full heat and we started to lift. As always, my body felt compressed back in my seat and I wanted to close my eyes and whoop it up. I loved this. I always had and always would.

We broke out of the sky and into the deep, straight and true.

Chapter 23 – Mud

I SLID ALONG the corridor, matching its color and feel as best I could. Locating the section they held Mom in (no sign of, or word from, Dad) proved easy enough once I had the room quiet. I had disabled the room and the door's ability to open, and had taken all the communication equipment the guards and staff carried, but I still knew it wouldn't be long before the rest of the ship knew I was there.

And of course, they'd put her pretty far from where I stood. Which meant I had a lot of ground to cover if I intended to help. I considered, briefly, dressing as a security officer, but as the only Hurkz around I'd still stick out pretty bad unless I wore a full helmet.

It wasn't often security wore a full helmet inside without a problem to respond to, and one officer never responds alone. Even if I could think of a good reason to pull that much off and get away with it, the security armor tended to have locators on it. Which meant the second anyone knew what I had done, they'd have me on a big map. A lone red dot trailing through their ship as obvious as could be.

No, I'd have to be better than that. Air ducts were right out, of course. Too small and rigged with security anyway. Maintenance passageways should do, for a while at least. There would still be security but less of it. Also less people in general. Just some engineering staff and a few drones.

I would've focused security on those passageways, personally, seeing as how they're off the beaten path. They're not a bad place to hide. Except that if you get caught in them, maintenance halls are far quicker to go into airless lockdown. Since they tend to be where people burn and cut things, you want a faster response time. Also, since people don't roam them quite as freely, you have to count on the ability to just deadlock a passageway from everything else on the ship and secure it.

So they'd be my best bet, but far from simple should I be noticed. Getting into the passageways wasn't as simple as a doorknob, either. Normal staff weren't allowed in them. You didn't give everyone keys to the backdoor.

A secure ID would've been nice, but I didn't have one. Big shock. I did have full access to my finer tools now that I was in atmo. I fished them out of my thinsuit and got to work on a hatchway. I triggered the auto-release without the door sensor noticing and slipped inside. At least a few things were going my way.

The hallway on the other side felt like it belonged to another ship. Instead of the nicely lit, smooth-paneled passage, the maintenance shafts were dimmer and had exposed pipes. The sort of thing you might expect from an area where people needed to work, and fast, to fix problems. Nice place to sneak around a ship in but I wouldn't want to live there.

I got through the first corridor fine, only a security drone to avoid. The drone looked one way, I went the other, no problem. Those drones tend to scan in a three-hundred-and-sixty–degree sweep pattern, but they can't look in every direction at the same time. You just had to not be where it looked when it looked and keep that up until it moved out of range.

My first instinct told me to blast the thing right in the comm relay and take it out, but leaving behind bits of drone would give me away. More work to avoid them in the short term, but worth it. Not hardly as satisfying, though.

But this wasn't about me. This was about Mom. I took a ladder up an access shaft and got onto the right level for where they were keeping her. I heard shuffling in front of my position and slowed to a creep. Back to the wall, I activated the suit's camouflage and sucked air in quietly as the needles bit. Crouching, I continued to slink forward, inch by inch.

The lights flickered, casting the passage into darkness. Must be a tech ahead, sent to fix them. I could sneak by him but it might be too risky. Taking him out would be just as risky, of course. No good answer ahead.

I decided to continue to sneak, taking the safe road over the easy again. I got past the tech easy enough; I couldn't even see him that well. Not clearly, at any rate. Enough to tell he faced away from me. Then I heard a soft "huft!" and the next thing I knew I was on the ground with the tech kneeling on my chest.

I grabbed his shoulders and started to roll on my side in an attempt to get leverage, but as I did I caught a fist to the face, hard.

"Mud?" the tech said, in my mother's voice.

Wait. I laughed and grabbed Mom close, laughing. "I came to free you," I told her, letting go and standing up.

"Well, dear, I appreciate it," she said, standing as well. I noticed bits of cloth tied around her shoulders and left foot. They didn't look good.

"Mom? What happened? You're—"

"Fine, I'm fine, dear. Now. Where's your father? Is he with you?" As we talked, we slid against the wall, hiding in the dark and whispering. We both kept an ear and eye out for trouble.

"No, I thought he had been captured along with you," I told her, "but I couldn't find him when I checked the comm rooms."

"I haven't heard from him, either," she said, "and if he isn't with you—"

"He's probably on the way, separately. Though I tried contacting him on my way over so we could meet up."

"And you heard nothing back, correct?"

"Right."

"Which means he's in something deep and it isn't this," she said. I could hear a level of exasperation in her voice.

"How can you be sure he wasn't captured as well?" I asked her.

"Not enough explosions," she said with a smirk.

"You're the one I would have expected explosions from, Mom."

"You've never seen your father get taken prisoner. He doesn't tend to be sneaky about escaping." She smiled at me, and I knew there would be a story or three. Later, after we were clear of this.

"So what do we do now, then?"

"Well, I was going to escape, find you, and that's two down right there, and then find your father and probably blow up a lot of people for something they did that I'm not clear on yet. What were you thinking?"

"Find you both and get clear. Less blowing things up, more getting clear."

"You're your father's son," she said. I could hear the tiniest edge of disappointment in her voice. It'd always been like this. If I went his way she sounded a bit put out, and if I followed her lead he would grimace. I tried to go my own way, which often ended up a mix of the two, and that made neither of them overtly pleased, but neither of them could pout for long, either.

They'd gotten better about it as I grew up, of course, but hearing that my plan seemed the opposite of hers annoyed Mom to no end, I knew. So I tossed her a small smile and took box out of my thinsuit's leg pouch.

"Not that I'm not prepared to blow up half the ship if I have to. Always know where your blast cores are, right?" It got the return smile I'd hoped for. "Now let me look at that foot and those...what happened to your shoulders, anyway?"

"Had to dig out my implanted charges," she said, wincing as she yanked her boot off.

"Implanted...Mother!"

"Shhh! What, without them I wouldn't be here," she said indignantly.

"I'm guessing that's what happened to your foot, too? Did the charges drop?" I grabbed some antiseptic gel and a thin roll of pressure bandages from my belt pouch and cleaned the foot wound as best I could. Yeah, this was an explosive charge mishap.

"Small price to get out of there," she said, rolling her eyes at me.

"Fair. Still, it isn't as if no one was coming for you."

"Oh, you'd be content to sit and wait for a rescue? Your mother is so bad at this she needed to just twiddle her thumbs all day? I'm an old woman now?"

I had to laugh. "Mom, you could still kick my ass all around the ship and we both know it. But I don't like seeing you injured."

"Fine. So what's the plan?"

"You're asking me?"

"Sitting here forever won't do. You got in this far, what's your extraction point?"

"My, uhm, well. My ship is just out of scanner range."

"And how are we getting there?" she asked pointedly.

"We could steal an escape pod," I suggested.

"Let's work out where your father is first, and why the Government felt it prudent to capture me. Then we can bail. Up two levels and we'll be able to start finding answers. Then again, down three and we'll have access to the battle room. Let's try answers first."

"Why did you ask me what my plan was if you already had one?"

"It's good to see what you have worked out, too."

"Mom, stop treating me like I'm a kid," I sighed, and I packed away the rest of the pressure bandages, her shoulders cleaned and patched as best as I could manage.

"You're right. I'm sorry." She smiled at me and stood, looking both ways. "You take the lead."

I stood next to her and considered. If we were headed up, we'd need a different access shaft. I held a hand up and slid away for a second. When I got back, I pointed and started to sneak off. I checked behind me to make sure Mom followed. Damn, she was quiet when she wanted to be.

Chapter 24 – Jonah

I ROLLED THE SHIP hard as we broke atmo, flipping comm dials to get back in touch with the fleet. My hand stopped above the cut-in switch as my display rolled and we hit a heading. I could see the battle from here.

That shouldn't have been the case. They were still converging on Trasker Four, no way the invasion could have reached Bercuser so soon. Hell, Bercuser wasn't even in the right direction for where the Gov forces had vectored from.

I watched my readings long enough to see the other Bercuser ships hit a different path than ours - headed right for Trasker Four, as planned. At least that looked right. I keyed the mic with a thumb.

"Deep Water, this is Jonah, come back." The silence lasted a bit too long for my tastes and I almost sent out another call for Frogger.

"Jonah, you're back," she said, just before I keyed out again.

"I told you I would be. What's going on, Bushfield? Is it me or have you guys multiplied like rabbits?"

"The *Washburne*, Jonah—"

"They sent in the *Washburne*? Great news," I told her. "That old warhorse can shrug off most anything."

"The *Washburne* went down, Jonah. It caught a bad hop into the system, fighters dispatched and they didn't realize they'd been swarmed before it was too late."

"What!"

"You heard me. Now why do I have unregistered ships heading for Trasker Four? They match your ship in spec, what's going on?"

I explained the evacuation plan to Bushfield, who sighed. I knew why before she told me. If the battle was going as badly as it seemed—Lord, the *Washburne*—then she couldn't spare fighters for escort. And yet, saving those people would be her number-one concern. Which meant sparing the fighters.

There was a small part of me truly glad I wasn't in charge. Bushfield was good, though, and did her job. She split off a few fighters and restructured the rest with minimal grumbling.

"So the *Washburne*, it's truly down?" I asked her, once we'd decided what everyone else was doing.

"On the way to it. It's between us and you," she told me. I checked my scanners and, sure enough, there sat a ship big enough to be the *Washburne*. It wasn't the biggest ship in the fleet, far from it, but even so. It commanded respect, having made it through the Sharp Wars and then some. If its full compliment of fighters had gotten clear, that would minimize casualties. Enough life pods added to that number and hopefully not many lives had been lost, all told.

"So the invaders split off a prong of their attack to loop out this way? Can you get a sense of why?" I asked, checking my own scanners and plotting a course to take us past the *Washburne*.

"No idea, they may just be scouting the way for the invasion's next move."

"We're headed that way. I'll let you know."

I sighed and flexed my shoulder. Stiff. I asked Steelbox to find me a med kit and grab me some kind of painkiller. No point in mentioning why. These kids looked at me as if I was indestructible, dropping some meds alone would bring me back down to human. Admitting the pain was fairly constant would make me old. They needed that confidence in me. Hell, to be honest, I needed them to have that confidence in me. Not something to be proud of, but once you hit a certain age, that's all right too.

At a full burn, we wouldn't intersect the *Washburne* for a while yet. Nothing to do but double-check everything and get a plan ready. I set the scanners to max and told them to scream like banshees if they caught anything that might even possibly be a problem. Then I slapped the autopilot on and turned around, tapping Bee on the shoulder as I did.

"All right, gang, let's talk shop," I said.

"Yes, for actions will be required," Olivet said. He leaned forward in his seat, eyes bright with attention.

"Good plan, vapor head," Steelbox shot back at him. He handed me my pills and sat back down.

"Let's all play nice," I said softly, "the five of us are all we have out here. We can fight amongst ourselves and die or work together and, hopefully, not."

"That's it?" Kem asked, "The best you have is that we might not die?"

"Kid," I laughed, "anyone who promises you that you'll make it out of a war alive is setting you up as fodder. Now, any other comments?" Silence

176

answered me. "Good. Here's what we know. Bercuser is being invaded and the invaders are already sending what seems to be a scouting party this way. They were intercepted, accidently it looks like, by the *Washburne*."

"It seems? " Steelbox asked. "Accidently?"

"You know what I know. Firm data in the middle of this will be hard to piece together."

"You wanna get out and ask the invasion force how it went?" Bee asked him.

I nodded. "She has a point. We go on what we got and adjust as we need to. The *Washburne* is not a small ship, guys. Heavy cruiser-class vessel. If the invaders took her down, they did it with surprise on their side. No other way. That much I can say with certainty."

"How do you know?" Olivet asked.

"Ship that size, that well armed, well - if they could knock her down easily whenever they wanted, this fight would've been over long before now. No, it was horrible luck that did the *Washburne* in. The problem is, they stand between us and the main force."

"Wait," Bee asked, putting a hand on my shoulder, "you meant us to fly into the fight? Jonah, we're not remotely well armed and can't hope to outfly them. What use would we be in the middle of that fight? Didn't we flee it once?"

"We did," I admitted, "but that was because we had no weapons, little air and half a working engine. This is different. Even if we used the ship as a search-and-rescue it'd be worth it. But that's not the point."

"Can we search-and-rescue the *Washburne* crew?" Kem asked.

"You know," I said, a smile growing as I spoke, "maybe we can. They'll have too many crew for us to take them all, but if enough were in the fighters that launched and most of the rest got into pods... we can help out some. Good idea."

"What do we do with them once we have them on board?" Bee wanted to know.

"Get orders and follow them. This fight isn't over, and if the Gov is sending in the *Washburne*, they'll be sending in other ships as well. There'll be a drop point and med ships out here soon enough."

"Why didn't they send them out in the first wave?" Kem asked.

"No clue," I told him, and I realized it was true. This whole battle had felt off from the start, back when Hodges first brought me in. As if the invasions were being kept secret from the people fighting.

In my experience, that meant one of two things: Hodges was in on it or had blown something critical in regards to the handling of the matter already and wanted to cover his ass. Either would get people killed – hell, they already were. I tabled that thought in my head for later.

"What you need," Olivet said, "is a way to talk to the invaders firsthand. Blowing each other out of the sky will never reveal the truth of the matter to us. Until we know that..." he trailed off, and I fought the urge to gloss over his words.

"Yeah, you're right," I said, thinking about it, "so how do we get to them? Let's think. We know they've gone to planets and grabbed people before invading. They send scouts out early for their next

178

planetfall locations. They're careful. We also haven't seen any sort of docking ship yet."

"Would we, if they're as fast as they look to be?" Bee asked.

"They are that fast," I told her, "I've fought them. So sure, put their docking ship out of range of the fight, so it's safe. Hide it. Where do you hide something that big?"

"Cloak it?" Kem asked.

"Cloaking is," I thought about the best way to describe it, "a lot harder than you might think." Not great, but it'd do. "Cloaking something as big as that ship'd have to be would take a lot more energy than they'd have, unless they're carrying their own sun with them. And they're not. We'd notice that."

"Do they even have to hide?" asked Steelbox.

Damn it, he was right. I nodded at him, "Good call, no, you're right. Space is big. Really big. Even if their ships were the size of a moon it'd be hard to spot them. Given that their ships have an unknown range and fly faster than almost anything we have..."

"They have gravity drives?" Bee asked.

"Nope, but they also don't have anything like what we do. Which means we can't track it, because we don't even know what it emits. No, I don't know what it emits. If the Gov does, they haven't told me, but either way it isn't something I've ever seen and I've seen every form of propulsion humanity's come up with."

"So they're just somewhere out there?" Kem didn't look like he enjoyed the concept.

"Pretty much. So now we...what?" I put the question out there and fell silent, thinking about it myself. Olivet had a great point: I wanted to talk to the folks doing this myself. I wanted to look them in the eye and ask them why. Then I wanted to slam their collective heads into a wall until they told me where they'd kept Shae. But that meant finding a way in. A way into a place we couldn't find.

Then I remembered something Olivet had said earlier. I had to die. The strange, future-seeing head case was right after all. I had to die. The plan was simple. "Simple plan," I said out loud. "I do what Olivet said - I die."

Everyone except Olivet erupted instantly with questions and confusion. I held up a hand for silence. "Not literally. We go in close to the *Washburne*. I get out. You guys continue on, with survivors, and join up with Deep Water. Do what she tells you and you'll stay alive, she's a good one."

"And you?" Bee asked.

"I'll play dead and hitch a ride."

CHAPTER 25 – JONAH

I BAILED ON THE SHIP and put my pack on an intercept course right for the *Washburne*. Right into a place I didn't want to be. I'd made my short speech out to sound heroic because it was called for. Didn't mean I had to like the situation.

I homed in on the ship, letting it pull me to it as straight and fast as I could risk. Pretty fast, all told. Almost too fast. I had to shut down the field sharper than I would've liked and the GravPack grew hot against my back. I'd been pushing it pretty hard for the last day or so without a recharge. Time to pay for that mistake.

Cursing, I checked my thigh pouches for recharge packs and came up empty. Stupid old man, bad prep gets you killed. I'd said it to enough people that to have it happen to me was simply insulting.

Stopping early was necessary because the space near the ship spun wild with shrapnel. Bits of rock and metal competed for room around the *Washburne*. Even the deflector field that my pack generated would've given up had I collided with this mess at a normal speed. High enough and I could've torn through it, but that was all tactical, and I distracted myself thinking about it so that my mind could take in the rest of the debris.

I hated myself for calling people debris. That's what they were, though, by then. The fallen, the hundred or more people who had served on the *Washburne* and died trying to get off her to safety or, more often, ensuring others could make their escape.

They wouldn't have died in vain, I told myself. Not if I could help it. My ability to help it might be questionable, I knew, but even so. I'd try, just like they'd tried.

I considered how, exactly, I intended to make this plan work. The first part was to seem just as dead as anyone else here. Pulling close to one of the bodies with a bad suit rip, I said my whispered apologies and stripped the outer suit off the guy. I tore it open wider, allowing me to slip it around myself loosely.

My gun would have to remain inside the ripped suit, making it harder to check up on later, so I gave the charge indicator a quick glance - about half a charge left. I really wasn't smart enough to still be alive, I reckoned. Holstering the gun again, I settled into the suit and looked around.

Engine burn sparked visible and growing, ships headed my way. The burn patterns weren't ours, so I'd guessed right about that, at least. They intended to send ships in close to make sure the *Washburne* lay dead. Smart tactical move, but I still bristled at it.

Their move spoke of the callousness one needed to wage war, just one of the things I wanted to put behind me. I fought with it and it fought back, as memories are wont to do. The Calaysian Wars had left a mark on my soul that wouldn't be brushed out with all the polish in the universe. Those days were gone, however, and what remained was only scar tissue, aching with the emotions of the past.

If they scanned for life signs my cover would be blown instantly, but if they only did a visual check

I'd be fine. I decided to increase my odds and drifted near one of the larger spinning rocks, grabbing it and matching my spin to its own.

The first of the ships caught up with the *Washburne*, and suddenly the scene of destruction was lit by harsh, probing lights. A second ship showed up, I assumed, by the second set of lights sweeping through the field. They moved slowly, doing a visual inspection. Not being able to scan for life signs, or not being willing to, told me a bit more about the enemy.

They didn't think their scanners would be compatible with our biology. Sure, they might not have scanners for life signs at all, but most races that were able to hit spaceflight also knew enough about themselves to be able to adapt scanners to seek their own kind out. It made complicated rescue missions far easier, and in space, those seconds mattered. A third and fourth ship joined the first two, probably because of the size of the *Washburne*.

A ball of blood, floating in the way liquids do in space, drifted by and smashed limply into the rock I perched against. I grimaced and kept waiting. Half a weapon's charge, about the same in my pack, and no one around to help me if I botched this.

Light swept close and I closed my eyes and held my breath. Back against a rock, the bulge of my pack wouldn't be visible, and I hoped the rip in my suit hung open enough to be convincing and closed enough to hide my thinsuit underneath. I saw red behind my eyes as the light passed over me, but I kept still, letting my breath out in the slowest hiss I could, sucking in fresh air just as slowly.

The light passed over me again, quicker this time. A third time and I would worry, but the second hopefully indicated nothing more than a passing turn. So far so good, except now I had to do something other than hide: I had to use the situation to my advantage.

The idea was crazy, but insane felt about as good as it'd get. Shae was still out there and these were the guys who knew where. A ship full of unready, gang-pressed recruits was running around on my say-so, trying to save lives they couldn't be expected to save. Bushfield and Frogger and the rest were somehow surviving an impossible fight just because they had to. Entire planets were at stake. I couldn't do less.

Unsure whether these brightly painted ships could detect gravity engines - we knew so little - I twitched on my GravPack on the lowest setting. Like taking a strong, controlled jump. The ships each sported four engines in a cross pattern, but the connecting point was empty. No engines, no lights, and no visible sensors.

My GravPack couldn't change vectors enough to keep up with this sort of design, even if I pushed the pack to max on a full battery. I shed the torn outer suit I'd been wearing and watched the ships.

I snuck up on one of them as they seemed to prepare to leave the *Washburne* to history, and I grabbed hold. My pack cancelled any addition to gravity I might have made if the ships had an artificial field of their own, but I didn't detect one while clutching tight.

This would only work if the ships flew in formation, with my hitched ride in the back, and if

184

no other ship got behind us. Basically, it wouldn't work well at all. Still, it was all I had.

We left the wreckage and started to sweep up, a vector taking us over the field of battle. There were three dimensions out here to use and any good pilot learned to use them all as a matter of course, but even so, battles only range so far. Most of them end up looking elliptical while they're in full swing, many of them approximating a three-dimensional sphere with the shape of the orbit of Earth, actually. I wasn't sure if that was significant or meant anything at all other than that the universe is a strange place, but I'd noticed it years ago.

These are the sort of things you think about while holding on to the back of a speeding space fighter. Well, that and Shae. Every second I hung on was a second I grew closer to finding her. I lost myself in thoughts of her, like a stupid old man, just long enough to almost miss another ship coming up behind us.

I let go, dropping off my hitched ride, and let myself drift off their vector a bit, decreasing my visibility. My target screen blinked online and I lashed myself to the new ship, just to keep up. If all my thinking was right, their base ship shouldn't be too far. These smaller fighters couldn't have the fuel to go that far on their own.

All my communications had to remain off so no signal would give me away. I set my life support on down to the lowest sustainable setting and let myself get towed by an invisible strand of gravity. Where they went, I would go. Napping was out of the question, though vaguely tempting.

How many times had I been in a situation like this before? Not exactly like, of course, but set and drifting with nothing to do but wait. Too many. You learned to take cat naps when you could afford them, to store up needed energy. Except I couldn't afford to this time. If the ship I was following broke off I'd have to be aware of it, and I still needed to get closer onto one of them before they docked, to try and work out how I could possibly get inside whatever they decided to dock with.

Not every maneuver in a fight is exciting. Some of them are just holding on tight and hoping. This was one of those. The fifth ship, the one that had joined us along the way, started to peel off. I caught a whiff of the vector adjustment before it happened, a wiggle in the gravity, more than enough time to switch ships again. I relashed my GravPack to the ship I had first held onto and snuck back up on it.

I reeled in and held onto the rear cross of my original ride. I could see, on my display, a large gravity mass coming up on us, just out of plane with our flight vector. Too small to be a planet or moon, and with the teardrop shape of a ship. Engines weighed more - even with gravity buffering, they warped a ship's profile. They definitely had some kind of gravity-based shielding, just enough to make life on their ship manageable, but no more than that. The signals were too weak for anything else.

The formation cut hard, realigning their vector, and sped up. They cut away, going anywhere other than their obvious landing point, making impossible turns. I got confused for a minute until I realized they were on a last ditch effort to lose any automatic sensors trailing them. No need to ever lead anything to their ship. They worried about it that much.

I started to wonder exactly how badly they worried when the lights came on. Blinding, startling lights, from drones I hadn't been able to spot, all glared at me, making a show of the human barnacle.

Well, that answered the question of whether or not they would spot me. I was bust, and out of moves. Even with a full tank and extra charges for my gun I wouldn't have stood a chance against a fleet of this size and speed, much less their mother ship, much less both at once.

Sighing, I flipped on my communications array and let go of my stolen ride. Floating there, visually pinned and tracked by lights, I wondered if they would shoot first or be smart enough to want to know exactly who else knew where they were.

A burst of green light washed over me. I felt like my blood had been replaced by fire. I screamed, not from the pain, but from rage that I wouldn't get to see Shae again if this beam killed me on the spot. Then the world sunk into black, fast enough it couldn't even make a sound.

Chapter 26 – Mud

A GLANCE BEHIND ME to make sure Mom still followed. Of course she did, the perfect distance away, too. Close enough to touch me with half a lunge, but far enough away that if something took me out it wouldn't get her as well, not with the first shot.

We needed to get into a vertical shaft and head up a few levels, but the problem so far had been finding one we could access. Which is to say the hallway we snuck down flashed red constantly. They knew that Mom had escaped. Or they knew I'd snuck on board. Possibly both. Probably both, if I wanted to be honest about it. And they'd stopped caring who knew it.

Not the best at this, really. I mean, I wasn't horrible, easily in the top few percent, but when it came to sneaking in and out of Government battleships, near the top didn't help much. You had to be the best, and I wasn't. My mother, however, was.

"Mom," I whispered, "we can't stay out in the open like this." It was true. There were security patrols scanning the whole ship and camera feeds being actively watched. We had only minutes, at a max, before we found ourselves spotted and grabbed. But the access shaft we needed wasn't close enough to just make a break for it and hope.

"Unless we make sure they can't get to us," she replied, drawing close enough to touch my elbow.

Turning to look at her, I raised an eyebrow. "That'd tell them right where we are," I said.

"But not," she said, "where we're going. We just have to make it look like we're headed somewhere else."

"So we blow the security cameras, wreck the hall, and make it look like we went down?"

"Pretty much," she agreed.

"But don't we want to go down, later?"

"That's later. We can worry about later when it's right in front of us, but we won't even get that far unless we focus on the right-this-second."

"Seems a bit slapdash, Mom." I loved her and knew she'd done this sort of thing a million more times than I had, but she was the planner. Dad would rush in and work things out as he went, not her. She always worked out her angles before making the first move. Which meant, I guess, the angles weren't workable just yet. So she fell back on Dad's playbook.

We kept moving along the hallway until we came to a door. Mom touched my shoulder to stop me. She opened the door. I'm not sure how, actually - she did something to the lock I couldn't see. I wondered how she'd overridden the handprint lock so fast but dropped the thought when she yanked me into the dark room and shut the door behind us.

"What do you have, explosive-wise?" she asked.

"Four blast cores, three handfuls of exploding paste, highgrade. Past that, some charges for a standard sonic gun." I mentally ran through the inventory of each pocket as I spoke, making sure I didn't miss anything. Then I touched each pocket as well, to make sure I hadn't forgotten to pack anything I thought I had. Nope, my count was right.

"All right," Mom said. "Now, they'll track for prints and heat residue, as well as for the usual signs, to tell where we went. So if we bring the corridor down around us and leave a big hole leading down, then we can go up."

"Wait, how will we go up at all? We have to get to an access shaft, and that's past this hallway. If we bring it down while we're standing here, we can't just waltz right through."

Mom laughed. "Well I'm hoping they'll think the same," she said. "Here's the thing of it. They know I escaped."

"Right."

"And you're not sure if they know about your break-in as well."

"Of course," I said, "no way to know that, so I'm assuming they do."

"I'm guessing the same thing. But they also don't know who you are or what you've done since. You're not bad at this, Mud. You're actually really good. So all they know is that someone cycled an airlock, at best."

"All right, then let's assume that."

"Which means they can try and track you and me and assume a lot of things, but right now they don't know anything much for certain outside of an airlock cycle nowhere near me and that I escaped and left some blood and ash behind."

"So we blow the corridor and convince them you're alone?"

"Exactly. We spread the paste along the ceiling, and a joint of the wall that faces the maintenance shaft, then some extra on the floor."

"We blow it in order and they think you went down."

"Sure, but that isn't enough to fool them and make them think it was only me."

"What will, then?"

"Blood."

"Mom!"

"I'm bleeding, Mud, it happens, and we can use it. Now. Go spread paste and get ready to run."

I sighed and left the closet alone, pulling a wad of explosive pastes from a pocket. I couldn't reach the ceiling without jumping and must have looked completely ridiculous leaping and smearing my hand along the ceiling as I went. Skipping down the hallway, I suppose. Not very stealthy, but we were out of time.

I spread it down along the wall as well and then stuck in two blast cores, one at each end. As I spread a half-handful on the floor in a pattern, Mom snuck out of the closet. I'm not sure why she bothered to leave sneakily - if my antics hadn't gotten us caught yet, she certainly wouldn't have tipped the balance, but old habits die hard, I guess.

She pulled back the bandage around one shoulder and pressed it into the wound, wincing. I pulled her over to where we could hopefully stand safely and nodded at her, offering her the detonator with my free hand. She shook her head at me. Fine. I'd press it.

Sound stopped having meaning, standing that close to the explosion of the ceiling and wall. The pressure wave from it flung debris at us with speed, ripping and slicing open clothing and skin. My ears rang, my eyes stung, and my skin ached.

I hit the second detonation anyway. Smaller, but still painful, added to the first. Sure did make a good-sized hole in the floor, even as it sent the debris from the ceiling bouncing again. I took a chunk to the shoulder and spun around from the force of it.

Mom was moving forward as fast as she could, the dust still settling. She rubbed the bandage along part of the edge of the hole in the floor and then dropped it down. "That should convince them I'm alone and gone down that way."

"Won't they still wonder about the airlock cycle?" I asked as we ducked into the now-open maintenance shaft for a bit and started to move again. I wasn't sure if I screamed or whispered, my ears still full of bells.

"They'll assume it was a short circuit from my messing with the lock in my cell."

"You hope."

"I hope," she said.

We ducked out of the maintenance shaft and took off down the hallway as fast as we could. Everyone would be deploying toward the explosion, and though some might pass us, it was a risk we'd have to take.

We almost made it to the access shaft we needed to go up before security came directly at us. They were surprised, and surprised people don't always think fast enough. As the one in front keyed his mic to let command know he'd spotted us, not only Mom but me, which would have blown every plan and made exploding a hallway with ourselves in it a worthless gesture, I pounced.

We went down, landing with my elbow braced against his face. I felt something crunch and rolled forward, intending to come up directly into the next guy's solar plexus. Luckily I managed to stop myself short when I caught sight of my mother's bandaged foot going by the corner of my eye.

The second security goon crumpled and Mom put him down for a while with a short jab to the temple. She grabbed his helmet fully off his head, from where she winged it sidearm at the third guard. He ducked, bringing up his sonic sidearm - the thought of letting command know about us all forgotten. I let him get his gun out but not raised before I tangled myself in his legs, shouldering him in the inside of his hip joint. I felt a wet pop and Mom had his face covered before he could scream.

We both stood and started to move, without a word. We hit the access shaft door and grabbed the ladder, climbing without discussing it. We'd been rumbled, and even if they didn't get discovered quickly they would be eventually, and that'd let the whole ship know we weren't down levels, but had been heading away from the explosion.

They would also, fairly easily, guess Mom wasn't alone after all. No, we'd been made, and now it was only a matter of time before we got pinned down somewhere. Outnumbered by hundreds, possessing a handful and a half of explosive paste and three full sonic gun charges wouldn't even begin to twitch our odds toward acceptable.

Our best bet would be to go up an extra few levels and confuse them, and then fight and sneak our way back down to the navigation backup rooms that would tell us everything we needed to know. From there we could, hopefully, find a communications room as well and work out what had happened to Dad. Mom didn't seem worried, but I edged that way, myself.

For now, though. It was ladders and quickness, and trying to not bleed all over the place. I also longed for my ears to stop ringing. Made it a lot harder to hear anyone coming up on us like this.

I glanced down to make sure Mom was still behind me. Of course she was. I could be sure of that, and her slight manic grin reassured me. This had turned sideways in almost every way possible and she was starting to enjoy herself. Which, history told me, meant there would be a lot more explosions coming, and sooner than I might like.

Chapter 27 – Meanwhile

ONE SMALL SHIP dodged and spun in the blackness. It drifted between the wreckage of the *Washburne* and the ongoing battle approaching Trasker Four. The acting ship's pilot worked to keep as clear of everything going on as she could.

Her navigator spotted the life pods that shot out of the *Washburne* before they'd even showed up. He would spot them and find coordinates for Bee. She would maneuver the ship as best she could, the controls never quite feeling comfortable under her hands, and pull up alongside them.

The non-specialized crew would manage the airlock matching and pull people from the escape pod into ship, then seal everything up again so they could continue on their way, looking for the next pod.

They focused on the damaged units first. There was no way, they each knew, that they could hope to hold everyone. So they prioritized as best they could, without proper, full scans, and saved who they could.

They did their best. Not only for themselves, so they could sleep at night and not see the demons of dead, the floating bodies dancing before their eyes, but for their leader, though he wasn't present. He'd brought them together and treated them as a compliment under his command, as a team, and they wanted to live up to that.

The last thing any of the four wanted was for him to return and be disappointed in their progress, considering how hard he had worked himself to save what they held dear. So they flew carefully, trying to stay off the sensor arrays of anyone on either side at first, and picked up the people they could.

None of their rescues went as planned, of course. They considered themselves a team but did not act like one. Worse yet, they knew it, and saw the gulf between what they expected and were doing, letting the frustration gnaw at them.

Their inability to work together combined with their inability to work with a defined military presence and protocol. The frustration levels rose, and rose yet again until in-fighting broke out amongst the crew. That lasted exactly as long as it took for them to find another pod that needed their help. The work centered them and reminded them of who they were and what they were doing.

Through it all, the saved crew members of the *Washburne* stood watching, silent. They'd been surprised by the attack and subsequent destruction of their ship, their home while on duty. Adding emotional insult to injury was the rescue from damaged escape pods by a ship full of non-combatants, who were also utterly unequipped to handle the ship they flew. So the tattered remnants of the *Washburne* crew found themselves incapable of doing anything to help or hinder. Confusion made them mute, and shock made them not care about the confusion.

All told, this strange, underpowered, and under-coordinated ship made a difference despite itself. Its crew, as well, made a difference to each other, and by the time the military envoys contacted them to take them out of active rescue duty, they had become something of the team they thought they could be. Not proven in many ways, but established in their heads and instincts as a unit of people who could work together and gave a damn.

They retreated, following orders, along a vector to allow them visual inspection of the edge of the battle, where they could relay data to the fighter squadron. They knew, instantly, the job was busy work to keep them out of danger but was also necessary. They would each help, as best they could, and ready themselves for whatever might come.

CHAPTER 28 – JONAH

I CAME TO IN A CELL - hardly the first time that's happened. Each and every time, I still feel it's better than being dead. So that was a point in my favor. Alive I could escape, fight, change the outcome. I was exactly where I wanted to be.

They'd left my thinsuit on me, but emptied all my pockets and taken my GravPack and gun. Fair enough as far as it went. The cell itself was an odd brown, not the normal flat grays of the metals humans tend to use. The walls felt like a metal, though, and hummed with the ever-present motion of the engines.

I'd come to on a cot, one far longer than a normal human would use. These guys must range tall. The bars along the front of the cell (bars seemed to be a universal truth of jails) were spaced slimmer than most. So tall and thin, check. I could at least use my time here to learn about them.

The room beyond my cell turned colors as it went. Starting with the browns of my cell interior, the floor and walls faded to brighter colors as the room went on. Everything was fresh and lush, visually. These weren't a people who wanted to live in a drab ship. Like the exterior of their fighters, they'd gone for something festive. No, that didn't feel like the right answer. It clicked when the guards came into view.

Tall and thin, as the cell suggested, they wore helmets with long beaks and a line of feathers along the crest. Bird people. The walls weren't festive - they were a form of plumage. For someone of their species, the color patterns must signal something primal, a power and purpose.

Their boots were shaped to conform to the feet of a bird, with three clawed toes forward and one back for grabbing and rending. I couldn't tell what the boots were made of, but it appeared to be something sturdy, as did the rest of their outfits: brightly colored pants and jackets, with what looked like protective sheathing over small underarm wings, connecting the arm below the elbow to the upper chest.

Bird people. I'd never even heard of bird people, not really. You hear stories, in the service, but there was no extant race of them around. Except, it would seem, these guys.

"Hey," I called out, hoping they had translators of some sort. If you're going to attack countless planets, it helped to be able to understand when they yelled out for backup.

One of the two guards that stood at the other side of the room looked over. The eye pieces of his helmet glowed red. The beak was fixed, closed, and came to a deadly sharp point on the downturn.

He studied me for a few and then turned back to his friend and they talked, softly. Too soft for me to hear. I tried again, "Listen, guys, take me to your leader?" Nothing. Or so I thought at first. One of the guards left and the other turned and kept me in his sight line.

So I stood still, facing him, arms at my side, refusing to be threatening. I wanted out. If it took playing nice to get them to let me out, that'd be far easier than breaking out, and worth a shot.

The first guard, or at least, I think it was him - hard to tell with the head-to-toe getup - came back. He conferred with the second and then they both came over to me. I took a respectful, slow step back from the bars and waited.

The second guard started to fiddle with a part of my cell door, and, as they unlocked it, I realized I had a good chance here. They didn't know who I was or what I could do. But they'd know humans, some. That's why they'd been picking people up - for study, to see what we were and how best to deal with us - on every planet they'd attacked.

Which meant they knew my age, from the sight of me, or at least that I was older than many. I decided to play up my bad knee for them. I limped as I walked forward, following their gesture. Not a bad limp, but enough to make them think I wasn't too steady on my feet. I wanted a look under one of those helmets: I wanted to look one of them in the eye before this went further.

Call it stupid, but I feel I can gain a lot from looking into the eyes of an enemy, and that's what these guys were - my enemy. They'd taken Shae, killed whole planets, and cost a lot of good soldiers their lives. I'd play the beaten and supple prisoner for them for a little while, but I never intended to forget exactly what they'd done.

We started down a long hallway, one guard in front and one behind me. They didn't prod me when I kept the limp up, allowing me to go at a speed that worked for my leg. Perfect, they'd bought it. Now for the second, harder part. The floor was smooth and even, but with my supposed limp to help, I stumbled and flailed. The guard behind me caught me and helped me upright again, not hurting me or even threatening to.

We turned a corner and I stumbled again, further this time, flailing like a mad man until I caught the guard in front in his back. He stumbled with me and I wrapped an arm around his helmet, hooking my elbow under the beak, careful to not slice myself open, and let my weight torque us over, ripping the mask free.

I expected to see a bird face glaring at me, as we laid on the floor for the three seconds before the second guard helped me back up, less gentle this time. Instead I saw green and brown scales, slit eyes, and flat nostrils. These weren't birds, they were lizards. I tried to not let my surprise show, to not give anything away, but that took shutting my now-slack jaw.

When we started to move again, the rear guard kept a clawed hand on my shoulder. Fine, I'd learned something and that'd do for now. I walked, easing off the fake limp but not dropping it completely - why throw away a good advantage?

We came to a large set of doors with guards posted outside. The door guards conferred with their compatriots and opened the set of doors slowly. Inside was a large hall. A meeting space, or possibly a recreation hall. Either way, the decoration spoke volumes about them. Birdlike designs dominated, but the figures depicted were lizard-like as often as not. Idealized murals of their ships and their pilots ran the length of the space.

At the opposite end of the room was a being draped in a winged and feathered cloak, his scaled, shortened head seeming drab and small above it. My request to see their leader had come through. I thought back, and was pretty sure that line had never worked before. Probably wouldn't again, either. But you take opportunity when it lands on your porch, and this was that.

They walked me close to the throne the leader sat in, pushing me down to my knees a good ten feet away from him. The claws on my shoulder stayed there. Even knelt, they wouldn't take any chances at this stage. I didn't blame them.

"Who," he began in thick halting English, his voice croaking out each word, "are—"

"Where. Is. My. Wife?" I spat out each word as its own curse. My chin up, eyes locked with his. I didn't care one whit about their plans. What they wanted with me didn't matter. But they'd give up Shae, if nothing else.

"What is this wife you inquire about?" he asked me, brow furrowing in what seemed to be confusion. No reason to trust him, though.

"Nice. Where is she? Tell me now, let her go, and I won't have to send this entire ship down in flames." I admit, this was as far as my plan took me. Get on board. Find out about Shae. Get out.

Certain people might argue with my tactics, thinking that starting right off into threats wouldn't help my cause. But they're only threats if you can't carry though. When it came to Shae, I'd burn the galaxy down. Details of how didn't factor in. I would. Simple as that.

"I do not know what you're talking about," he insisted.

I sighed in frustration, "Yes, we all look the same. While you were scouting Earth. Earth? Remember it?"

"No. We do not know of this planet."

"Do you know Trasker Four?" I asked, forcing myself to stay on my knees and not fight the guard holding me down. I could think of six ways to get up and free, and only one of them would maim the guard for life. Regardless, I waited.

"Yes, the planet we are currently being forced to harvest." The note of sadness in his voice was either a great bit of acting or I had no idea what was actually going on here. I didn't think he could act quite that well in a language he wasn't that familiar with.

"Wait," I said, "who's forcing you to level a planet? Another planet, mind you. This isn't the first, and eventually your path will take you to Earth. And it needs to stop."

"And yet it cannot," he said, "must not, in fact, for our own survival. Regrettable but necessary."

"You would kill whole planets of people for your own survival? Not even try to find a different way?"

"There has never been another way. Would you not do what is needed to survive? So that your people could? Didn't you come in here, threatening me, despite knowing I could simply have you killed, to save this one you call wife?"

"Stop talking in questions. Just explain to me why you're doing what you're doing."

"First," he said, raising a finger to make the point, "you must explain to me who you are and why you tried to sneak aboard our vessel in such a manner."

I tried to stand and the hand on my shoulder pushed back against me. So I grabbed his thumb and wrenched it back, feeling it dislocate. His shock left him unprepared for my kick to his ankle. He went down, I came up.

I stood, unmoving, while the guards in the room circled me. No attack from me, I just needed to prove a point. I brought my hands up in front of me, palms toward the leader, to show I was unarmed and uninterested in fighting. He gave me a look, one of understanding, it seemed, exactly the point I'd made.

"My name is Jonah, and you are attacking my people," I said, not even looking at the guards around me, focusing my attention solely on their leader. "And I am a member of the forces trying to stop the slaughter. I wanted information and I had a feeling someone on this ship - you, I think now - could provide it. Also, you have my wife." I bared my teeth in a cruel grin. "And this is the last time I intend to ask nicely for her back, unharmed."

"Stand down," he commanded the guards, I could guess from their reaction, in his own language. "Not many of us know your language at all," he told me, "apologies. My name is Tslakog. Once again, we do not have this wife you request. We have no prisoners, nor have we been to this Earth you speak of. I do, however, understand your actions. We would do no less. However, I also feel that if you knew of our problem, you would not judge us as harshly as you currently do."

I laughed. Right in his face. His guards bristled but didn't make a move toward me. "So you want me to believe you don't have Shae, and you want me to listen to your supposed tale of genocidal woe?"

"I will be happy to allow you, escorted of course, to explore every inch of this ship looking for the one you seek," he said.

"Which wouldn't prove anything."

"Then what would?" he asked me. It was a good question. What would prove it? I could search the ship but they could move her. Hell, they could have her in a different ship anyway. Or have just spaced her.

"Let me explain our predicament, then," Tslakog continued, "and afterward we can continue the discussion of these whereabouts."

"Giving you time to—"

"Yes, yes," he said, his voice growing an edge, "we can go in circles on this all day. I know of no way to convince you, and by your silence, you cannot think of one either. So these, then, are your choices. You can try to take this ship by force, alone and weaponless. I gather you would get fairly far, but we both know you would die here without ever finding this person you seek—"

"My wife."

"Just so. Or you can choose to trust me, just enough to listen and resume this core concern after understanding has been achieved."

"Go on, then."

"Let us walk," he said, standing.

205

"You trust me to not make a break for it and cripple the ship along the way?"

"No, I trust my guards to kill you should you try."

I was starting to like this guy.

Chapter 29 – Jonah

MY PEOPLE ARE CALLED TYFARSIANS," Tslakog said as we began our walk. "We are, truthfully, quite peaceful."

I raised an eyebrow at that, but let it pass for now. Three guards walked alongside us, and I'd spotted at least five behind us. They moved quietly, too, damn it.

"We have existed far longer than your own species," he continued, "keeping to ourselves. Our planet is far beyond your own settlements, which is why you have yet to discover us, I assume. There are many planets, races teeming across galaxies that your own people have never reached."

"Well sure," I said, "who has time to see the entire universe? But give it time and I suppose we'll get there, assuming we stop you from wiping us off the face of creation, right?"

"The Tyfarsian have no desire to rid the universe of you. It is a regrettable fact of our own existence that we have crossed paths in this way at all. We could have been allies."

"So those other races, the ones you know about and we don't. Did you slaughter any that you called ally, in your regrettable fashion?"

"Yes," he said, bowing his head in shame or honor or both. "We warned them of our need to progress and they shrugged and assumed they would be spared because of friendship. We did warn them. Tragedy, in truth."

"I'll say. More so for them, though, huh?" We turned a corner and took a flight of wide, softly sloping stairs. Made for their bigger feet, the rise and run were spaced so that walking up them was almost no different than a shallow hill.

"No." Tslakog said firmly, turning to face me there on the stairs. "We have to live with what we have done to those we considered our friends. That is not the sort of stain that eases from one's soul. Ever."

"Then why do it?" I demanded.

"This," he waved a hand and started to walk again, "this is what I am trying to explain. Our race did not start at the planet we recently left."

"Wait, you left? All of you?" I wondered how many this ship could possibly hold. Either their race was tiny or there were far more ships out there than we had a clue about. Not good.

"All of us, yes. But we shall get to that in time. I was telling you about where we came from. And in all honesty, I may be mistaken. There are, you see, two planets. The one we left and the one we head to. We have lived on both for so long that we, as a race, are no longer sure which planet gave us life originally. That does not matter.

"What matters is that long ago we were discovering space travel. Starting to go further than our own atmosphere and explore the stars. Evolution had allowed us to rise as the dominant life form of our planet, and we used that time well. Too well, in fact, for while we excelled at technology, we fared far worse at ecology. Our planet was dying. We had no choice but to speed up our exploration and leave in search of a replacement."

I looked at him as we walked. Comfortable in his role as leader, tall and proud. I kept my own counsel, thinking about what he was telling me. We turned again and entered a large space filled with what seemed to be a tiny city. The ceilings ran stories high and buildings lined the sides, breaking into streets. From the windows came lights and sounds and along the ground his people walked and lived. He wanted to show me his society.

"We searched from out beyond your knowing, through your own spaces and back out again until we found the second planet. The first journey proved almost impossibly hard. Many lives were lost. History tells us that the Tsyfarsians almost did not make it. However, of course, we did arrive in numbers enough to support future generations. We found our second world. Settling there, we tried to be more diligent in our treatment of the land, but even then, after many generations, thousands of years, we found ourselves in need of moving. Our scientists conferred and we set out once more. Unerringly we found ourselves drawn to retrace our steps, directly back to the world we had left.

"And so we returned. The land, in our absence, had restored itself and we were able to live there once more. But, in the fullness of time—"

"You had to leave again, didn't you?"

"Yes, you understand."

"How many times have your people completed this journey?" How long had they been around? They were already, based on the time needed for his stories to be true, one of the oldest races we'd heard about in the universe. If they hadn't encountered us the last time, that meant that the periods between their moves was thousands of years, never mind the actual travel time.

"We are unsure. That is why I cannot tell you which planet is the original home of the Tyfarsians."

We walked among his people, and they greeted their leader warmly, keeping their distance from me. The alien. The invader to their home. Wasn't the first time I'd been treated like that. Understandable, really.

"And so now we are on our journey. It is necessary for our survival," he said, turning to leave.

"And necessary to wipe out countless billions along the way?"

"We do not have the capacity to build enough ships to transport all of our people awake while on a journey this long. Nor could we possibly feed them. Much of our race lay in our ships in a torpor, fed minimal amounts needed for persistence, but even then we must cultivate that sustenance for them. For that we must raze what is in our path to collect enough to ensure our own survival. It is deeply regrettable, but what must be done."

"And you've tried different paths?" I asked.

"No, our path must remain true. We are drawn to it, it is the only way."

Something clicked hard in my head.

"You're migrating."

"Excuse me?" Tslakog asked, sounding slightly offended. Maybe he didn't know that word.

"Birds. Do you have birds on your planets?"

"Yes, I know the word, and the concept you mean by it, and we have such creatures on our worlds."

"You're like them."

"Birds? They are lower species, brainless! Are you saying—"

"I'm not saying you're brainless, no. But - do your birds travel with the seasons, follow the good weather? Ours do." I felt like an idiot for not seeing it sooner. Their ships, their suits – no matter what they looked like, they thought like birds.

Tslakog was watching me process the idea that I might be able to trust him.

"So you do scouting runs to each planet, to see what has changed and to see if its life can sustain your needs?" I asked carefully.

"Yes, of course," he answered. "I see what you are saying, we replaced evolution with technology, replacing what we may have been. Our dress, our ships, our very culture speaks of it. Though I admit, the idea you seem to have that we need you to come and tell us about ourselves is not one I am comfortable with. Still, I suppose, go on."

"I mean no offense. I am an outsider, of course. That just permits me an ability to see you through different eyes, not better ones," I said.

"And yet," Tslakog, said, "keep in mind we are not a backward race needing to be saved by you. You will approach this with respect, or not at all. Do not think yourself a savior, human."

"Of course," I told him, choosing my steps carefully. "You only range out toward the next planet you'll be approaching, not the entire path at once. It'd cost you too much fuel, wouldn't it?"

"Yes, precisely. Much as this battle being waged now is costing us dearly. Much longer and I fear for the future of our people."

I had to replay what he'd said two or three times to grasp it. I'd been lost in my own thoughts at first. I believed him, everything I'd seen supported it. Which meant that they didn't have Shae. Earth would have been far too far for them to bother with yet.

I didn't know who did have her, but I'd work it out soon enough. Back burnering that for a minute, I looked at the problem at hand. I didn't want planets wiped out, but I also didn't want this race to die. Neither would be acceptable to me. Which meant I needed to find a third option and convince everyone involved that my plan would be the only one worth trying. All I'd need was a plan worth pushing.

"Do you trust me?" I asked Tslakog.

"I have no reason to, I suppose," he said, truthfully, "and yet I find that I do. You listened, when you had no cause to."

"Look, I want to help you guys."

"And your wife? The one you call Shae, who you are convinced we have?"

I waved off his words with a hand, "You don't have her. Never did. It doesn't add up. Fool that I am, it doesn't add up, but something does. And I'll find out the truth soon enough. In the meantime, Tslakog, why don't we work on the problem of making sure everyone survives?"

"How would that be possible? We must hold to our route and must strip bare the planets along the way in order to live. Be wary of demanding our culture is somehow wrong because it does not fit your view and therefore needs…fixing."

"No," I said, "in general, of course not, I would not presume. But this trip - for the first time, I'm guessing - the planets you come across are inhabited."

"Not for the first time, but certainly far more of them, and better equipped."

"Well then let's solve the problem. Together."

"I bristle at the idea our culture is a problem."

"Not the culture," I said, stumbling for a second, "but only the effects. Now, I'll have to contact my people and get more of us working on this, it won't be the simplest thing in the world. But in the meantime, we'll have to stop the fighting out there. That is non-negotiable."

"We can agree to that, for now. So long as there is no buildup of forces. But the time we take for this may doom us by stalling. You know that."

"I do," I assured him, "and I also trust my people to find a solution."

"Where we have not?"

"Let's be honest, Tslakog, you guys haven't looked for one. Not really," I said, locking eyes with the reptile leader. "You apologized and felt terrible but never actually looked for a solution."

"Because it is not a problem,"

"It is now. Look, trusting me, risking it all on saving lives from here on out, is the price you pay for that. For risking the lives of my people. I mean no offense, or to imply a problem with your ways, outside of this event."

"That is agreeable," he said. We had arrived back at his throne room. He'd showed me his people, the size of his ship, and done his job. Now it was back to work for him and for me.

"Good man. I'll need my equipment back, and yes that includes my gun, though you can keep the charge for it. I just feel naked without it on. While you gather that stuff up, I'll work out how to phrase all of this to get us working as fast as possible. Faster."

CHAPTER 30 – SHAE

I INCHED PAST NEWT and took a look at the door controls. Popping out the plate and shorting it got easier each time. The door hissed open and we both ducked inside. The *Dozier* stood on full alert. We moved against a clock that would run down on us no matter what we did.

The thing of it was that they'd captured me for no reason, held me captive, chased me through these halls more than once, and were supposed to be on my side. I'd run out of my capacity to care around the time I had to set off explosives that I was standing next to for a second time.

I no longer gave a damn who they were or why they'd done it, I just intended to deal with them. Mud breathed thickly right behind me in the dark of the room we hid in. He'd come to rescue me. My son. I felt so proud of him, breaking into a Government command-class ship like this. Wasn't easy, I knew.

I also knew he was looking to me for direction, now that we were together. I'd been letting him lead to try and shake that out of him. Once you break onto a ship this scale, you better have a much more complete plan than Follow The Person You're Rescuing. But he'd learn.

Because we would both make it out of this intact. That much wasn't even in question. No, if needed, we could bring the whole ship down. For now, however, we didn't need that much.

"Mud," I whispered, "did you bring a wide-band frequency matcher?"

"I have one," he said, and I knew the answer before he finished, "but it's on my ship."

"Supplies don't do you any good if you don't have them in arm's reach."

"I know, Mom." Great, now he was talking to me like he was a kid again.

"I want to try and find your father, is all. Which means a communications room."

"Which will all be heavily guarded," he felt the need to point out.

"Exactly," I said, "and you've done a great job getting us this far, but I think this will be more up my—"

"I can still sneak, Mom, and from my glance at the layout, we're a hallway away."

"All right, lead on." I smiled so he couldn't see it. Good, he wanted to take charge and didn't sound like he was doing it to prove himself, but because it would be the smart tactical move. That's my boy.

We crept back out into the hallway and Mud stood, listening, just as I did. Stealth would rule the day for a little while longer. Once we accessed the communications array we'd become disgustingly easy targets again. But that wasn't just yet.

Mud sprinted down the hallway to the turn and took the risk of a quick glance. Turning back to me as I caught up with him, he held up his hands in a series of quick signals. Four guards outside the room - they'd learned from my first escape. He indicated he wanted to go first and that I should follow after a ten count. Then he vanished around the corner.

216

I counted to ten, keeping my breathing calm, making sure I wasn't rushing the count. Surprisingly hard to do - right before a fight or explosion, your brain just wants to get the whole business over with.

On ten I sprang around the corner, cursing inwardly at the pain in my shoulders and foot. The guards saw me, acting very surprised at seeing anyone in the hallway they were watching. I didn't see Mud. Maybe they'd gotten him and shoved him into the control room already. Their guns raised and I made a quick choice: I'd leap directly at them and hopefully the sonics at close range wouldn't take me down, but either way my mass would at least entangle me with one of them.

As I coiled my legs under me, one of the guards vanished into the door well next to the communications room door. He'd fallen backward. It surprised me and the other three guards, who all turned in wonder of what the flash of motion had been. Of course, stupid me.

Mud had camouflaged himself to the hallway colors and waited for me to spring his trap. I sprang too, at the nearest guard, while Mud took another one in the rear of the small pack down.

I landed badly, on my injured foot, and caught a sonic blast to the left shoulder. Biting my lip hard enough to draw blood so I wouldn't scream, I fell on the guard who'd shot me and wrenched his helmet off. Then I beat him with it. That felt good, better than it should've, probably. My left arm hung uselessly, though, thanks to his blast.

Another blast hit the ground near me and I rolled away from it, taking some of the bounce along my right side. I looked up, getting my feet under me, to see Mud dislocate the shooter's arm and drop him. Mud'd been hit, too, though. I could tell from the way he walked. He did worse with sonic blasts than humans.

"Mud—"

"I'll be fine. You?"

"Of course," I said. I had to be, same as him. We had no choice but to be fine and keep moving. I started to grab the door lock and Mud shook his head.

"Once we do this, they know who and where we are. Getting out of the room will be an interesting fight, no?" he asked.

"Pretty much the way it'll go, yes," I said.

He raised his sonic weapon at the door lock and fired, point blank. The lock shattered and the door shook loose. It didn't open but it didn't lock, either. "The hell with it, then," he said, and grabbed the edge of the door, pulling it open.

The techs inside the room fell too quickly to matter, Mud's aim true and fast. I limped over to the console, my left side still a fading ball of pins and needles from the half blast I'd caught. I called up location codes and shot them to Jonah's secure frequency, along with a coded message to let him know where I was. Time mattered, so I didn't go into detail. Just a location pickup, really.

"We have about two minutes before all hell breaks loose here," I told Mud. "I could disable the entire communications array from here."

"I know this is a Gov ship, Mom, and they...I don't even know what's going on, neither do you. Do we really want to leave them drifting like that?"

He had a point. I didn't like it, I wanted to set fire to the entire ship, but he might have been right. I considered the issue as quickly as possible. If I cut communications and Jonah did come in screaming, he'd have no way to let them know. Could work for him or against him, depending on his plan.

That assumed he'd come this time, granted. Even if he didn't, though, we'd been knocking out guards and doing no lasting harm to them mostly because they might not know what the actual score was. And as Mud'd said, we didn't know yet ourselves.

"All right," I conceded, "what if I just locked it down and encrypted it so they couldn't use it?"

"Can we?"

"I can," I said with a grin. "The array would be usable, and get incoming messages, but no one could reply without knowing our codes. It'll still cripple them, but—"

"It'll also give us a good out. Nice. I'll guard the door, you set it up."

Mud moved to the door, sliding it shut. We couldn't lock it, but they couldn't lock us in, either. One point of entry meant we had a better shot of keeping people out. That didn't account for gas, of course.

I got to work, pushing that all out of my mind. I'd need to reroute all communications to this station, which was an ugly hack but doable. Then I started to encrypt all outgoing messages using an old code my father used when I was small. I locked access to the console using one of the older family codes we had, so if something happened to me, Jonah or Mud could unlock it and restore the ship. Without that code they would have to flush and reinstall the entire software array, which would take days. Messy. Better to ensure the key sat with more than one person.

The rumble of sonic blasts went off and I glanced around at the doorway. Mud was firing shots at angles against the walls of the hallway. He had four sonic guns slung over his shoulders. Must have taken them from the downed guards.

"We've got incoming," he said, voice perfectly level and normal. Like telling me the weather. Not fazed or worried. I felt another surge of pride for the man I'd helped raise.

"I heard," I shot back, and I turned to finish my own work. "Almost done here. Do we have an extraction plan, or is it too late for that?"

"Too late, I think," he said.

"If we got into the floor below?" I asked, stomping my foot to see if it would even be possible.

"Not sure we have enough firepower to do it, and an explosion," he paused to fire another volley of shots, "would be too painfully obvious."

"I do not intend to get recaptured in this tiny room, Mud. Now let's think."

I paced the room, my left side feeling much better, though my right arm was still limp. We had some explosive paste left. We could get to the floor below, sure. But then what? Given the last blast, they were probably even expecting us to try it again but actually go through this time. I'd be expecting it, if it were me in charge.

The consoles were too heavy to move, but...I yanked a panel free and traced out the electrical wires. You shouldn't be able to short out the whole section from here, but with a tiny bit of help from a sonic gun to disrupt a conduit or two, I might be able to do it. Wouldn't last long, but in darkness, if we ran as fast as we could while shooting in front of us, we might be able to clear a path.

To go where? That was the bit I got hung up on. I decided to ask the family sneak. I was good, but he could blend - he'd grown up thinking of ways to sneak that, honestly, me and Jonah couldn't always keep up with.

"Mud, if you had a full minute of darkness—"

"In the whole corridor?"

"The whole thing, for at least this section."

"Emergency shaft to outer hull crawlspace to the command center," he rattled off, before firing yet another burst. He'd moved on to the second gun already.

"The outer hull crawlspace? There's no air there."

"We wouldn't be in it for more than two minutes, and it'd be a straight drop down."

"All right, I can see it. But it's thin," I said.

"Thin is what we have. We can use it. I see in the dark better than you, so hold my hand and if we move for all we're worth, and I keep firing to clear a path...Mom, I think it'll work."

"Then let me get you your darkness."

Chapter 31 – Jonah

WE WERE AT PEACE. Surprisingly easy to arrange, as a matter of fact. Once Tslakog's people stopped shooting, Bushfield stopped firing and held her people back. Mostly they were confused. If you pressed her on it, I know she'd admit she didn't want to kill anyone in the process of surrender, either. Which wasn't what was going on, either, but hey.

The important part remained that the shooting stopped long enough for me to tell Bushfield the score, and to ensure that no one outside of the battle group knew. That felt important to me. Hodges was up to something. I could tell.

Ships like the *Washburne* don't pop into battlefield situations with no ready support. There were no support ships anywhere. I'd sent my own guys, untrained and scared, to rescue damaged *Washburne* escape pods. They'd performed fantastically, according to Bushfield, but there should have been medical out there. There still wasn't. I kept chewing on the problem, but until I figured it out, I wanted to keep Hodges in the dark.

Then there was the problem of Shae. If the Tsyfarians didn't have her - and I really found myself convinced of that - where could she be? Of course, I also had to work out how to get the Tsyfarian migration back on track without leveling more civilizations. Looked to be a full day.

My problem was figuring out what to solve first. The Tsyfarian invasion wave threatened the most lives. The Hodges issue came a close second. None of it mattered in the face of Shae. Could I put her first, though, and risk everyone else? If she could talk to me she'd tell me no, of course. But listening to her about this sort of thing didn't tend to be my strong point.

Which left me nowhere, still. So, Shae. Where was she? The Tsyfarians didn't have her, but someone did. Why would they take her and why did Hodges—

Everything fell into place. Or close enough. Hodges called me to get involved. I said no. Not long after, Shae vanishes and it looks like a Tsyfarian abduction. Except when it happened, we didn't know the Tsyfarians. Hodges told me what it was and I went along, not knowing any better. There wasn't a good reason to mistrust him, then.

But all I'd had to go on was his word. And this was a guy who had refused to send proper support to his own field operation. He hadn't wanted me to come out here, either. Almost as if he was setting it up to fail.

But then why involve me at all? I'd have to ask him. I intended to ask hard. But if he'd kidnapped Shae, it would make sense. Mistake number one. He knew it'd get me into action. He'd also counted, I guessed, on being able to control me. Mistake number two.

For whatever reason, he seemed to want to make a show of stopping the invasion but also to fail. What he'd managed to do, though, was give me everything I needed. All of the pieces fell into place and I saw a plan.

I clicked my comm unit and saw a queue of family-encoded bursts waiting. I keyed them. Sure enough, Shae. Just a location and ship designation and extraction request. She was on the *Dozier*. Chances were, when I last stood on the ship Shae'd been nearby. I didn't bother to listen to the rest of the messages, fuming. Hodges had faked concern while he held my wife prisoner on the very ship we discussed her rescue on.

And now she had escaped, at least enough to send a message. Knowing Shae, it meant there was a lot of smoke on the *Dozier*. She asked for extraction: a pickup, not a save. I gave it a bit more thought. What were the chances our little Newt had joined her? Pretty good: he was a smart kid, and she would've pinged us both with that burst. He'd be on the way, too, if not already there.

I sent a location ping but got nothing off of him, which meant he'd gone dark. Which, to me, meant he was already on the *Dozier*. So one of my missed signals was from him, that much felt clear to me. Regardless, I was certainly on my way now.

I saw a way that might solve all of my problems, or at least delay one of them a bit longer to my advantage. I asked the Tsyfarian guard nearest me to tell Tslakog I needed to speak to him. They'd let me roam mostly free around the ship while I considered their problem, but with a guard always shadowing me. Luckily, this was one of the few who spoke English.

While waiting for Tslakog, I keyed Bushfield.

"Deep Water this is Jonah, copy."

"Jonah, any more peace treaties for me to agree to? I have the afternoon free, it seems."

"Cute. Listen, I need a favor."

"Name it, Captain," she said. I could hear her smirk over the hiss of the radio.

"Don't call me—"

"You're an easy mark."

"And you're in a good mood, with all this chatting," I said.

"No more of my people are dying. We're not actively having to shoot anyone. That sort of thing calls for celebration today. Do you know how long I've been in this ship? I think my ass is fused with the—"

"I'll make sure a med tech takes a good look at your ass later, Bushfield. I still need that favor," I reminded her.

"Make sure the med is cute. What's the favor?"

"In a little while you'll see activity. The sort that might make you open fire. Do me a favor and don't."

I waited, listing to silence for longer than I liked before she came back on. "What are you up to, Jonah?"

"I can't tell you. You'll know it when you see it."

"That hardly sounds good."

"It isn't," I admitted, "but trust me."

"Jonah—"

"Gotta go, thanks, Bushfield. Jonah out." I turned to a different frequency before she broke in to tell me off. She wouldn't want to help, not when this went down, but she would stay out of my way. I was certain of that. Pretty certain.

Flipping the frequency over landed me on something else I'd planned as an emergency measure. The ship with Bee and the others had a backup communications unit. Before I'd left, I'd switched it to a frequency. The same one I stopped on now.

"Bee, this is Jonah. Copy."

Silence. I tried again and waited. Nothing. Either they'd been shot down - no, Bushfield would have told me - or they'd blown out the main comm unit and resorted to the backup, changing the frequency. I started to run down a list of alternate ways to get their attention when my comm unit crackled.

"Jonah?" Bee's voice said. There was a garble and pop to it - the backup unit on that ship wasn't great, but it would do.

"Hey, you guys all accounted for?"

"We are," she said, and I could hear banging, "this backup communications unit, did you set it before—"

"I left? Yes. That's not important—"

"It's crap," I think she said. "Do you need a pickup? Where are you?"

"I'll be near where the main fighting took place soon enough. I want you to follow. Just that. Follow," I said, hoping she could understand me through the interference of that backup useless unit. "At the rear, got me? Keep your main communications array on the normal frequency until you start to follow, then switch it over to this one so we can hear each other. Copy that, Bee?"

"Enough to work it out. But what will we be following?"

"You'll know when you see it. Jonah out."

Near the end of that exchange, Tslakog came in. He waited while I finished, without interrupting or drawing attention to himself. A leader who respected the people working for him. I really liked this guy.

"Now, Tslakog," I said, turning to him, "it's time to move this whole fleet."

"Yes?" he sounded surprised. "You have found a solution to our problems so quickly?"

"Not quite," I admitted, "but I need to prove a point."

"You need our entire fleet to prove a point? Jonah, this does not sound prudent."

"It isn't, but it will get you a solution to your problem and get me one to mine."

He sighed a reptilian sort of sigh and nodded. "Is there risk to my people?"

"Of course. But minimal. Our forces will not attack, I promise," an empty promise, to be fair. I knew that Bushfield wouldn't attack, but further down the line it could get messy. I'd do my best not to let that happen, but I also knew Tslakog wouldn't agree if he knew the whole truth. A small lie and reasonable risk in exchange for Shae was all right by me.

"I shall recall the fighter group," he said.

"No," I said, stopping him before he could turn to start the recall. "We'll catch up with them soon enough. We need to go right through the battlefield, at full speed."

"Full speed?" he asked. His eyes got wide. I'd seen that look on countless people in my career. Often when I started to tell them my plans. I considered it a good sign.

If my allies were shocked by what I had in store, chances were my enemy wouldn't see it (and, by extension, me) coming either. That sort of advantage was priceless.

"Full damned speed."

CHAPTER 32 – JONAH

THE TSYFARIAN FLEET tore through the sky. Looming, the fleet looked to perch above the battle that we had all finally stopped. The simple presence of the body of ships, moving at such a speed, threatened to ignite hostilities again.

Bushfield would see this and hopefully realize at least enough of my plan to not open fire. I couldn't key her again, though. Everyone would be listening in. Bad enough I'd given her any warning at all. That ran a dumb amount of risk. Doing it twice was going out of my way to ask for trouble.

Of course, it could be argued that leading an invasion fleet against my own people was asking for trouble. But anyone who'd argue that would never understand the fine art of negotiation.

We reached the battleground and kept going. I saw telemetry of the battle groups reacting. Bushfield pulled the human forces out of the way, rabbiting to a clear distance quickly. The Tsyfarian forces fell in line with us the way I'd asked.

Bee and her tiny crew unfolded from Bushfield's scatter pattern and fell in line with the fleet as it ripped by. They fit into the pattern we built, as far back as they could, and I grinned. They were getting the idea.

Bushfield keyed me twice, but I ignored her. I waited for a much bigger fish to ask me to the dance. Meanwhile, Bushfield, realizing that this had to be me and torn between all of her options, had her group follow us. They didn't join our formation, or even get too close, but they followed us. Just in case.

I couldn't fault her idea. If everything I did was on the up and up, she would be close enough to help. If not, her group was close enough to start firing again. Either way, she both had us covered and had ensured she wouldn't get left out of next phase of this madness. She might be sick of being in that cockpit and having to get refueled and restocked along the way, but she didn't intend to stop now.

Neither did I. At top speed, we wouldn't reach Hodges and the *Dozier* for quite a while. But we were pointed right at him. The *Dozier* wasn't equipped to make a speedy escape, either. As Hodges's command center, it should have been slowly making its way right toward us. Surrounding it would be a full support fleet of smaller ships that could run. But with command-class ships like the *Dozier*, you had a general on board who demanded a certain style and air of respectability for diplomatic missions, such a ship's main function. So when it found itself preparing for a fight, everything tumbled around. They had to retrofit whole sections, fuel up, and coordinate everyone else trying to do the same thing. It left them vulnerable - something people had taken advantage of in the past, to varied success. Normally a fighter squad around the command ship would suffice. Not this time.

We passed through the battlefield and kept going. I asked the Tsyfarian near me to open a wide communications channel to the *Dozier*. We requested confirmation from the ship and got no reply. Strange. I could see, patched in to my own display, that the connection sat open. They just couldn't respond.

I laughed. Their signal had been encrypted and locked from the inside. They could receive messages but not send, not without the proper override. That meant Shae. I thought about what code she might use and tried a few family ones to no success.

Then I thought of an old one we'd used years and years ago. I sent it and the channel opened. But only that channel. I kept them locked down otherwise. Shae must've had her reasons.

"*Dozier*," I said, keying the channel, "this is Jonah Madison. Get Hodges on the line. Priority one."

"Captain Madison?" the voice on the other end asked. "Where are you broadcasting from? General Hodges is—"

"Hodges is going to jump on this line and he'll do it fast. I tell you what," I said, "I'll put this call on hold for a full minute. When I come back on the line, if Hodges isn't here...well, he'll want to be."

I nodded at the tech and left the room. My communications remained slaved to the Tsyfarians. I set my thinsuit for space and strapped my GravPack on tight. They cycled an airlock for me and I floated free, a speck in the vastness of space.

Wrapping a gravity shield around myself as tight as I could, I lashed the pack to the nearest planet in a straight line to the *Dozier* and went full-out. I knew it would do my bad knee in - the stress of a gravity shield that tight did bad things to wrecked joints. Not a big deal.

Flying at this speed and using the comms never ended up being smart, but I had no choice. Making sure my signal went to the Tsyfarian ship before bouncing to the *Dozier*, I opened the channel again.

"*Dozier*, this is Jonah Madison again. Where's Hodges?"

"He's on his way, sir," he said. I could hear the nervousness in his voice.

"Good. Actually no, not good. He's in his command center, lower decks, isn't he? Patch me through there."

"I can't—"

"Look up my auth codes, son. You can."

"Yes, sir. Hold on, sir." Hodges might be trying to avoid me and work out what I was up to, but I could short circuit that with his own hierarchy.

"Madison?" Hodges voice rang in my ear. "What's the meaning of this?"

"You know what it is, Hodges," I said sweetly.

"That's General Hodges, Captain, and I'll see you stripped of that rank the second you—"

"Shut up, Hodges," I told him, letting my voice go cold, "we both know you won't. Now. You listen to me. I want you to imagine something."

"Excuse me?" His confusion amused me, really.

"You. Right now in your command center. I've been in the room. It's rather sterile and cold. So let's warm it up with some mental images."

"What are you talking about? You're insane! Where are you, Captain Madison?"

"Imagine," I continued, paying him no mind, "a cone. An entire fleet of ships, flying in formation. Now imagine that cone is about the diameter of the orbit of Earth. Small fighters, command-class ships, personal transport, supply, the entire fleet. Spread out and in perfect formation. A simple cone. Can you picture it, Hodges?"

"Captain Madison, what are you—"

"*Can you picture it?*" I yelled.

"Yes, yes, a big cone."

"Good enough. Now imagine it bearing down on the *Dozier*. The whole thing. All those ships. Oh, some of the support ships could avoid it, sure. Your personal fighter squad could rally and get out of the way. But the *Dozier* itself? No way, Hodges. No way at all."

"Are you threatening me, Madison?" His voice remained confident, but I thought I could hear the faintest crack.

"Yes. And I'm not done yet. And really, call me Jonah. It'll make you feel better. Because that cone, even if your fighter group could blow it all to hell and back, is moving at a good enough clip that the flaming debris would still smash into you with the fury of the fist of God. Do you understand what I'm telling you, Hodges?"

"That you're mutinous and insane?"

"That I'm coming for you. The tip of the cone, the thing that will personally hit you so hard you won't have existed, is me. That whole fleet - all of those ships bearing down on you - I want you to picture them, the damage they can do, the raw destruction headed your way, and then I want you to realize something."

"And what is that?" The crack in his voice started becoming more and more apparent.

"The fleet bearing down isn't your problem. You shouldn't even worry about them. They're nothing. I'm the problem. I, personally, will be the one do deal with you. That entire fleet is nothing compared to what I plan to do to you with my own hands."

"Madison—"

"Jonah."

"Jonah! Fine, Jonah! Think about what you're doing! This is insane! And for what? What is your problem?"

"You took my wife."

"I don't know what you're—"

"You took my wife. You had her on the same ship I stood on, and you looked me in the eye and told me to go fight your war for you in order to save her. Did you think I wouldn't work it out? Better yet, did you think when I worked it out that this would end any other way?"

"You're deranged! You can't turn on your own species like this! Think of all the innocents you'll kill!"

"You. Took. Shae." I slowed down and pulled up alongside the *Dozier*. In a GravPack, most sensors found you too small to deal with. That wasn't as much of a problem as it was back when people used them regularly - there are ways of checking, but no one thought of it anymore. Hodges would - or someone on his team would - soon enough, but it was too late. I was on their doorstep.

"It wasn't like that, Jonah!" he insisted. I didn't reply for a few seconds, to let him sweat.

While he did that, I cycled the airlock and strolled in. Sure, Hodges would burn me, but that would take an hour, at least, and he'd have to hang up first. He thought I was in a ship on the way to him. While he thought that, I could still enter the *Dozier* just fine. I had rank, I had codes, and no one outside the command room even knew there was a problem with my being here.

"You're going to have to do better than that, dead man," I said, and switched my mic to mute. I greeted a few servicemen as I walked through the ship. I hit the access shaft and went down to Hodges' command center.

"Hodges? Anything to say?" I asked, turning my mic back on.

"Damn it, Jonah, think about...what the hell?" His communications were lost in a screech and shatter, sonic blasts going off in his control center. I broke out into the best run I could manage with my knee threatening to give.

I shouldered the door open, still moving, and dove into a painful roll as a sonic blast *spanged!* above my head. Luckily I'd been moving the other direction, so the reverb didn't hit me. I finished my roll and popped to my feet. Then I laughed.

Shae looked me in the eye and smirked.

Chapter 33 – Shae

MUD AND I HAD MANAGED the strange and dangerous path to Hodges' command room with minimal additional scrapes and bruises. We burst in, avoiding a small number of guards going the other way, and raised our weapons.

The room went into a panic. Mud shot the nearest chair at a structural joint to make it shatter. The noise caused Hodges to drop the headset he had pressed to his ear. That said a lot about Hodges, to me. He wouldn't bother putting a headset on during a command session, instead choosing to just hold it there, as if he had more important things to do. Well, he did now.

I walked right up to Hodges, one of Mud's spare sonic pistols in my hand, and jammed the barrel right against his side. "Wanna bet I can liquefy your kidney?" I asked. I couldn't, of course, but I could do a lot of damage regardless. Hodges looked appropriately worried.

Mud shut the door and kept his gun out, scanning the room with eyes and barrel to keep everyone else in place. I turned back to Hodges. "Did you really think it wouldn't come down to this?"

I heard the door burst open and Mud fire a shot at about the same second. A blurred shape shot into the room, rolling, and sprang up, recovering easily. I smirked as Jonah got his feet and laughed.

"If this is a rescue attempt, you're late," I told him.

"Baby, I think I'm rescuing him from you, not the other way around." Jonah walked over to me and Hodges, and I could see him hiding a bit of a limp.

"Why would you want to do that?" I asked, jamming the sonic gun hard against Hodges' side.

"You won't bother asking questions first," he said. He wasn't wrong.

"Hey, guys," Mud asked, "should we clear the room first?"

"Good call," Jonah said. He started to wave everyone out, and when the room stood empty except for the three of us and Hodges, he secured it tight. "Now. Hodges. You want to tell us why you thought it was a smart idea to kidnap my wife?"

"It-it isn't what you think," Hodges insisted. Sweat beaded on his forehead. I tried to tell myself I didn't enjoy the sight of it. I did.

"Then what was it?" I asked.

"The invasion was coming. Planets had gone dark. We knew they were out there—"

"And so you called me up," Jonah said.

"But you said no!" Hodges tried to draw in on himself out of fear. "If you had just said yes—"

Jonah laughed again and slapped Hodges in the face, hard. "So you kidnapping Shae is *my* fault?"

"You should've said yes!" Hodges yelled. His fear turned to anger, "But you were stubborn and left me no choice! Don't you see that? The Council is weak, they didn't want to believe there was any real threat! I had to get you involved, but you said no. So I thought, and realized that you would chase your wife."

"And then what, huh?" Jonah raged, grabbing Hodges by the shoulders. "What then?"

"We were going to let her go, eventually—"

"Dead," I cut in, "I assume. Made to look like the Tsyfarians had me the whole time?"

"What choice did I have? We needed to fight back!"

"Wait," Jonah said, letting go of Hodges, "when I did show up, you still didn't commit enough forces to possibly ever win."

"If we lost, with you involved, the Council would have no choice but to commit to the fight."

"You tried to make sure we'd lose?"

"We would have! Admit it, you all know it! If you hadn't worked it out, if your...your son hadn't...it would've worked!"

"So," Jonah said slowly, "your plan was to toss a small battle fleet down the drain, just cast them into the fire, and me and Shae with them, because you wanted to score points with the Council and make sure I was out of the way. This was seriously your plan?"

"After I took your wife—"

"My name is Shae. I'm right here, your little Plan B," I said, drawing closer.

"Yes, yes, after that, what choice did I have?"

"So all the men and women who died out there, you're trying to say this is my fault?" Jonah swallowed hard.

"If you'd just have said yes in the first place," Hodges said, growing a bit of bravery, "this all could've been avoided."

"Did you try *talking to them*?!" Jonah suddenly raged.

"We tried the normal channels and there wasn't time for anything else!"

"And I was able to get on their ship and talk to them and find out what's really going on. Where in your plan was that attempt even discussed? What made you think hinging your plan on throwing your own men to the wolves was ever going to be a good idea? What in the known universe made you think you'd get away with this?"

I hadn't seen anger like this bubble to the surface in Jonah in decades. Not since the Artesian Battles. I still wanted Hodges' head on a pike, but I needed Jonah to be calm as well. "The important thing is," I said slowly, "Hodges thought he meant well."

"We should let him live for that? Thousands have died, baby. On both sides. Both. And it could have been prevented if they'd just talked. Or if, I don't know, someone other than a complete psychotic imbecile was in charge."

"They're incredibly stupid and sure, Hodges meant to kill me and make it look like the Tsyfarians. And soldier, we'll dismember them soon enough. But right now we have to stop the war for good, no?"

Jonah turned to me, eyes full of incredulity. "Wait, now you want me to listen to this idiot and let him keep sucking air? It isn't even like I ever gave him a reason to want us dead!"

"It's just for a while," I admitted, "long enough to do our jobs. We'll need his access codes, I bet."

"Oh, I could get those," he said, and he flashed a grin. It wasn't a nice or pretty expression.

"If I could just—"

"Shut up, Hodges," we both said at once.

"Mom? Dad? Can we at least make sure this room isn't flooded by security first?" Good, smart Mud, thinking ahead.

"Right," I said, before Jonah could speak. "Hodges, call off security."

Hodges nodded and did so, picking up the headset he'd dropped earlier. "We're gonna need a few biologists, some med techs, and a whole lot of cooperation," Jonah said. Hodges nodded again and kept muttering into his headset.

Mud unbolted and stepped away from the door, reluctantly, and lowered his weapon. I pulled my own weapon away from Hodges and stuck it in my belt. Jonah stood, fists still clenched.

"There's still the matter of a bit of kidnap, and, from the look of it, torture," he said softly.

"Oh, no, soldier," I told him, "the wounds are self-inflicted. There are times you need to do a little damage to get out of a tight spot."

"Why is it," he said, softening, "those times always seem to center on you?"

"Luck. Planning. Style."

"Mom! Dad! Flirt later. Save the world now?" Mud said, shaking his head at us. Poor thing, we embarrassed him. But he was right, we needed to focus.

"Regardless, the kidnapping," Jonah said.

"We'll deal with him later," I promised him, "but Mud is right."

"Fine. Hodges, you hear that? You have a bit longer to live. Now get those people here."

The room filled quickly, fear being a great motivator. Jonah cleared the wreckage of the broken chair and everyone sat around the planning

240

space. Jonah proceeded to tell us what we were up against. The bird people who weren't birds. The migration and the problem inherent in it.

Everyone looked interested. This was a problem that, under normal conditions, would result in years of research. Careers would be made on the studies done and papers written. Under normal conditions. This was the calm of the storm, though. We sat right in the eye, and chances were it would pass quickly.

I grit my teeth as everyone discussed what could be done, tossing time frames around that were so unfeasible I wanted to laugh. A med tech came by with fresh bandages and painkillers for me. I took half the dosage suggested; I thought keeping sharp sat further up the scale of necessity than feeling no pain. It still helped.

Out of all of us, Mud looked the most pensive. He had something brewing in his mind, but I didn't know what. Hopefully he'd come up on the right side of a solution. Someone had to, and this room of brains didn't seem like it could in anything like the allotted time.

"All right!" Jonah barked out, stopping the discussion. "We're getting nowhere and we don't have time for that, do we?" No one spoke. Jonah looked at me and I nodded. I knew where he was about to go.

"So here's what we're gonna do. Hodges, get on the line with the Council. Explain to them exactly why they need to respond to this, and not with guns. Don't mention our little personal problems, we'll get to those as we go. For now, focus. This is your chance to do this right." Hodges nodded and actually put his headset on, instead of just holding it to his head. He might be worth keeping alive after all.

"Someone find me Mills. I'm going to need a liaison, ongoing. He'll do the job well."

"Soldier—"

"I won't keep him, baby," Jonah said, "but you know he's right for this."

"Fine."

"And, baby, do me a favor and unlock their comms, huh?"

I laughed.

"Also, you med tech guys and science division folk, open a channel to the Tsyfarians and compare notes. We might not have anything ourselves, but they know their biology better than we do, Lord knows. Let's see if something they know already sparks something worthwhile."

People started to move, taking his orders without any more questions. I'm never sure how much Jonah knows that he does that to people. How much was intentional and how much he just assumed as part of the natural order. I guess it doesn't matter, in the long run. It's still something to watch, every time.

"Shae, I need you to work with Bushfield. Call sign Deep Water. She's out in the thick of it, and the shooting's stopped but she'll want tactical reassurance and ideas. You're our best bet." I nodded. Truthfully, Jonah outstripped me on battlefield tactics, but he'd be busy.

I checked myself and thought about it. No, on normal tactics: yes, he outclassed me. Desperation and pulling a rabbit out of an empty hat, though - he was right. The answers I came up with alongside this Bushfield might not be pretty, but I could promise they'd work.

"What about me?" Mud asked his father. He was the only person there with no specific job.

"You and me are going to go for a walk, and you're going to tell me whatever it is that you've been chewing on this whole time. I don't know what it is, but I know you, Newt—"

"Dad!"

"Mud. I know you. You have something close to an answer. We're gonna need it. Let's go. Everyone. Let's go."

Chapter 34 – Mud

DAD'S HAND CLOSED over my shoulder as we left the room together. There were guards posted outside the door and I started to reach for my gun. I stopped when they saluted my father and moved aside. Not even thirty minutes ago they were trying to take me and Mom down, and now we were back to saluting and supposed to be all right with that?

Times like this I didn't envy my parents. This was their world, not mine. I liked to operate small and solo. The military, with all of their rules and quick turns, just wasn't for me. Holding a grudge wasn't always a bad thing, and operating by myself was just all-around simpler.

We wandered, Dad and I, for a few minutes in silence. He steered me clear of crowded spaces and waited until we seemed alone before he spoke. "So what do you have for us, Newt?"

"Dad," I said, holding in a sigh, "I'm not a kid anymore. You can use my name."

"You sound like me. And you're right. Mud. What've you got?"

"Nothing. I don't know."

"Nothing, or you don't know?" he asked. "Because you spent that whole time obviously chewing over a thought or two. This is the time to speak up."

I rolled over my thoughts slowly. He was right, if there was an idea I should be open about it, but I knew where it would lead and really didn't want to have to go there. No other choice I could see, though. "The Hurkz," I said.

"What about them?" He raised an eyebrow at me, not seeing where I was pointing yet.

I stopped and leaned against a wall. "They're… we're reptiles, too. Sort of. Almost."

"You think the Hurkz have something that could help?"

"I've been trying to think. But, you know, it isn't as if I spend a lot of time with them, or ever have. They sort of don't enjoy my company, don't forget."

"No, of course. But still, that might be a good way to point a search. The Hurkz are the best-known amphibian species. Is that close enough to what the Tsyfarian are? I don't know."

He tilted his head back and stared at the ceiling. He did that a lot. In his head, I know he saw stars, not tiles. It was how he thought when he had a strange problem to sort out. Or when he had to count to ten to calm down after you've set fire to the couch.

Dad keyed his comm unit and asked to be routed to the biologist meeting with the Tsyfarians. I guess he wanted to sit in on it. He nodded to no one and smiled at me. "Come on, Mud. Let's get you involved in this."

We wandered back the way we came, hit an access shaft along the way, and went up a level. I could already see the guards standing in front of a door and, correctly, assumed that was our destination.

Inside the room, eight scientists of various specialties sat around a table facing a large screen. On the screen, a life-sized vid feed of what had to be the Tsyfarians looked back. They'd assembled their own collection to join in. The whole room went quiet as we entered.

"Hey, Tslakog! How're you holding up?" Dad said, loudly, pulling out two chairs and dropping into one of them. I sat in the other, slowly, unsure of myself.

"Jonah, it is good to see you," Tslakog said, "you were correct, our two races may yet find a solution that will spare many lives."

"Good. Stopped the fleet easily enough, huh?" Dad smirked as he said it, knowing that the human fleet still stood on alert due to the increased proximity of the Tsyfarian fleet, which had been his fault in the first place.

"Of course. We can stop as easily as we can speed in flight," Tslakog said proudly, "but this is not our purpose here."

"Sorry," Dad said, looking around the table. He caught the eye of a tech and nodded. "Catch me up quick as you can, will you? My kid here, Mud, needs to be in on this. He's Hurkz and thinks that may help us. I'm inclined to agree."

They got us caught up fairly quickly. Nothing much had happened, really. The basic problem of how to allow the Tsyfarians to deviate from their known route didn't feel like it could be worked. Too many planets in every direction with life, and those that weren't wouldn't sustain the Tsyfarians anyway.

How to get them enough food to not need to raid planets was the current focus. The major issue there was whether anyone could provide that amount of food fast enough. Tslakog remained honest, and you could see some of his friends didn't enjoy it. The gist of it was simple - if a source of food wasn't found within a few days, the fleet would have no choice but to raid again, or perish.

Nothing could grow enough food at the speeds needed, much less harvest it and transport it. This was a purely useless train of discussion. I looked at Dad, but he had that far-away gaze he got when listening to something in his headset instead of in the room. He muttered something and refocused on the goings-on.

We continued to discuss our options, getting into Tsyfarian biology. Their consumption rates were slightly higher than the human species'. That only made everything harder. I kept thinking over Hurkz biology - what I knew of it, past my own - to see if something stuck out, but so far nothing did.

While we were hashing out a possible plan to land the Tsyfarians on a growth planet and ferry them along their route in smaller batches, a guy I'd never seen before came in and walked over to Dad. They talked quickly and then the guy went out again. Dad looked at me and nodded. "Mills," he said, as if that meant anything. Oh, right, his assistant.

"Well, people," my father said, looking around, "that was a report from every other angle of this mess."

The room drew silent as everyone wound down to listen to the state of things.

"The Council is fighting back, but Hodges is doing his best to bring them around," he said. "Carefully," he added, "so that they don't know the extent of the problems we've had. We don't want them deciding a war is the right answer. Shae and Deep Water are working out a plan to keep both fleets moving, as slowly as possible. We can't do a full shut down.

They've worked out a sluggish route that will allow the fleets to travel and keep the engines hot but not come near any planets." He looked at the screen with Tslakog. "They're also making sure the fleets don't stray far enough from your route to cause any panic or problems."

Tslakog nodded his thanks. Everyone around the table just listened and made notes. Many of them looked relived. As if what Dad said he had invented himself. He controlled the room without trying.

I shook my head, admiring the effect but not getting drawn into it. When you've seen the man sing songs from your cartoons as a kid it stops working as well, I guess. I thought, instead, about the problem at hand.

There was something gnawing at the back of my brain. A fact, a memory, that felt connected to this. Something I'd learned the last time I was on the Hurkz home world. I'd overheard a mention of some plan of theirs. A long-range plan. What was it?

I kept my brain working on it while I refocused on the conversation around me. One of the Tsyfarian scientists was going on about a plant he had heard stories of. "When I was but a child," he said, "there were tales of a root that would suspend all functions for days at a time."

Another Tsyfarian we couldn't see scoffed audibly at the idea. One of our scientists offered up the concept of true hibernation, not the process the Tsyfarians used that still required full feeding tubes. Humans hadn't worked out long-term suspended animation yet, but they'd come close.

Closer than the Tsyfarians, at least, and maybe that would be enough.

The heart sizes and glandular differences were too varied, though. Everyone seemed to realize it, but kept working it out just in case. Which is when it hit me.

"Hey, wait a second!" I blurted out. Everyone stopped to look at me, confused. I just carried on, heedless of the looks. "The Hurkz have hibernation tech, I think."

"You think?" asked one of our techs. "How much of a guess is this?"

"When I was on the Hurkz home world last, I heard two people mention it. They were being sent to explore a distant world and they were nervous about using the new hibernation technology. They, I remember now, they mentioned that the technology worked fine but it scared them because they hadn't tried it, personally. It felt unnatural to them, 'returning to a hibernation state,' one of them said."

"So this is new tech," a Tsyfarian said, "and not widely tested, on top of being for a different species?"

"It was then," I told him, "but that was at least ten years ago. So if they were starting to use it a full decade ago, by now there's a good chance it works just fine."

The room burst full of conversation after that. Everyone talked over everyone else, trying to work out the implications. No one knew for sure if Hurkz biology would be compatible enough with Tsyfarian to allow the science to hold. Then there was the problem of how to get our hands on it.

The Hurkz are an isolationist people, for the most part. They didn't expand much, or interfere with other races. They hadn't in centuries. The Hurkz Empire did its thing across their worlds and left everyone else alone. Outside of the occasional foray to human-controlled spaces to kill or retrieve those who'd left without permission, or who were aberrations.

There was a ton to work out. Dad was pleased, though. He practically beamed at me. I'd proven him right, was why. He'd brought me in as someone who could solve a problem and I'd given them the biggest idea they'd had yet. That reflected well on him.

Which sounds like bitterness. No, just acceptance. This was who he was. He was the hero. The guy who found answers, or found people who could find answers. Every time it worked out well, it just added to the belief people had that he could be counted on.

I stood up to stretch my legs, pacing around a corner of the room while everyone else debated how best to go about getting the Hurkz to play along. That wasn't a discussion I wanted any part of. It'd be hard to distance my own feelings toward them, even with the fate of two species hanging over it. Not something you admit to a room full of strangers.

The more they tossed around opening diplomatic channels to the Hurkz again, the more I felt my skin crawl. The pinch of the needles going into my skin, the pain of the tattooing, all of it just kept flooding my senses.

I had to get out. The room grew smaller and smaller. I left quickly, without another word.

CHAPTER 35 – JONAH

MUD BOLTED from the room. I think he meant to be subtle when he started pacing, but he moved like a lion in a cage and I knew it was a matter of time till he gave in and left. My question was why. I stood to follow.

"Jonah," Mills said over my headset, "latest on the fleet issue is—"

"Hold that, son, dealing with something else." Outside of the room, the guards started to salute again. Did they intend to do that every time I walked by? It made me want to get up to hit the bathroom every five minutes. Pushing past them, I spotted Mud turning a corner up ahead. I sped up to catch him.

He managed to not flinch when I put my hand on his shoulder, but I could see a twitch in his neck.

"Hey, kid," I said gently, "what's eating you?"

"Nothing, Dad, it's...nothing. I just needed to stretch my legs."

"You're not a bad liar," I told him, "but that was pretty sad. If this is going to affect us here, we need to know. At the very least, I do."

He sighed, his hands clenching and unclenching. "You know how I've been off and about recently?"

"Sure. You like your space, it's good for you."

"I've been on the run." He looked at me with shame.

I fought down my first reaction, which was to ask who and why and then go and smack them around for trying it. This hurt his pride, though, and that would just set him back. He needed to deal with this like an adult, so that he could make his own peace with it. I couldn't just jump in and save him, even though I wanted to.

"Oh?" I asked. I couldn't ask him if he'd deserved it, or what he'd done or anything like that. I wouldn't mean the questions to be accusations, but I knew they'd play that way. He was a teammate, sure, but he was also my son. My son who was starting to laugh.

"That's your reaction? All you can do is go 'Oh' and leave it as a question for me to jump into? You don't want to ask what I did, or if it's connected to you?"

"Is it?"

"Not at all. This is all me." He held up a hand, asking me to let him finish. "Not something I did. Stupidly enough, it's all just about who I am."

"You're my kid," I said.

"Yeah," he laughed, "but the Hurkz don't care about that."

"We could fix that, you know."

He laughed again. Good, he was calming down at least. "Not what I meant. They've been sending Reclaimer squads after me."

"For what? For how long?" I asked in quick succession.

"For being tribleless. For still being alive after all this time, without my original markings."

"Wait, that?" I sighed at him. "You said that whole thing was dealt with almost a year ago. Right after you turned legal age for Hurkz. They contacted you and you told us you'd straightened it all out. That it wouldn't be an issue."

"And then I took off to wander—"

"To get your own space and find your way, you'd said."

"To hide and work out how best to deal with the problem, without dragging you or Mom into it."

"And how'd that work out for you?" I asked. Maybe I should've been nicer, but finding out my kid has been on the run for a year without telling me put me in a mood.

"Hey, I'm here, right? They haven't been able to catch me." He puffed out his chest a bit. He wasn't wrong, a year on the run like he'd spent wasn't a small feat. It was still, though, a stupid one when not necessary.

"That's not the point, Mud. I could've helped. Your mom could've helped."

"By blowing them up?"

"Diplomatic means. I have favors owed."

"Uhm. Dad? Do those favors include Mom getting kidnapped to try and force you to do things? I think maybe you're further off the reservation then you like to think these days."

"I may be, all right, I admit that. But we still could've helped and you know *that*. But even with that problem, why is it going to factor into this? We just don't have you ask and we're fine."

"I don't think so," he said. He'd been thinking this over. There was still information I was missing. Great. "They probably know I'm here."

"How?"

"I dodged a Reclaimer crew right before I headed here. They wouldn't dare try to get on board one of our ships or even ask the Government to hand me over, but if they tracked my ship, then they know."

I saw red for a second. "Wait, your escape plan with your mother had to include going back to your ship. How was that going to work for you and not against you?"

"I had no choice or time!" he yelled. "I was working with what I had! What would you have done?"

"Not put the people I was trying to rescue into more danger by rescuing them!" Shouting wouldn't help either of us, I knew. I couldn't stop myself, though.

"Oh, really? Like that ship of people you had out on the front lines? They're well trained, are they? You do what you have to when the situation needs doing, Dad! You and Mom both! How can you act surprised if I do it?"

I ran a hand over my hair slowly, thinking. "No, you're right. I'm sorry, kid. But we still need to hash this out in full later. But, fine, damn it, here and now. How does them knowing you're maybe here hurt us?"

"They know who raised me," he said, relaxing some himself, "who my parents are. By now the information that you're here and in charge has spread. You think they won't monitor the channels to make sure of that sort of thing? So they know I'm here and you're here. A request comes through asking for their help. What's their first move?"

"To demand you in return."

"To demand me in return, exactly," he agreed. "And that's fine, I'm even all right with that, but I don't think they'll bother with the 'in return' part at all. They'll just demand me and still refuse you, on principle."

"They're that bad? I knew when we adopted you they were harsh, but that seems cold even for the Hurkz. To be willing burn two species over one person?"

"Trust me."

"I do. So what's our next move? If you're right and the tech exists, then we have to ask. So how can we swing it to get them to agree?"

"I don't know that you *can*," he said, sounding defeated.

"Everyone wants something. But we need a clue."

"Permission to hunt outcasts in the human territories, even across Government ships?"

"There aren't that many."

He thought, thumping the wall with a hand rhythmically. "You're right. I don't know. They don't expand their spaces."

"And maybe that's it. What if we offer them a nearby world. We leave it and they move in."

"Can we even do that?"

"If we had to? Yes. If it comes down to two races versus one planet, when we can relocate the population? I don't see why not." I didn't want to have to try and sell that to the Council. I couldn't even remember the name of the planet I'd be selling out. Still, if that was the only card I had to play, I'd play it.

I decided that we'd have to go through with this and the negotiation would have to be lead by me. That way any fallout would also hit me. Technically I still carried rank - the worst they could do would be to throw me out and cancel my pension. Well, no, the worst would be jail time, but I doubted that. I also didn't care about the pension.

So I'd have to make the call. Which meant it was time to think sideways. I'd dealt with the Hurkz once before, which had ended up with us adopting Mud. If their memories were as long as it seemed now, they'd go into this with a grudge. Hunt my kid down for a year or more, and I walk in with a grudge, too, though.

"So that's the move, then?" Mud asked me, the uncertainty in his voice making him sound much younger than he was.

"That's the move, unless you can think of another."

"Stay creative, Dad. That's my only other move."

I grinned at him and clapped him on the shoulder. "Always."

We walked back to the conference room together. As we got close, my earpiece went off again. "Jonah. Mills. We need to discuss the fleet situation."

"What's up, Mills?"

"Shae says she thinks she's got everything worked out now."

"All right," I'd assumed she would handle it. "So what is there to discuss?"

"Deep Water requests docking for her fighter group to get a break and send out some fresh pilots, at least a shift's worth."

"Except she's at the back of the fleet, and if we swap them all out we could spook everyone."

"Exactly, also they would be new pilots, not used to the situation. I wonder how much problem it could cause."

"Good point. All right. Tell Deep Water she can send in half her squad for this shift and then rotate out the other half next shift. But either her or Frogger remain with the squad for now. Her choice."

"Got it. I'll pass it along."

"Thanks, Mills. And send my wife up to my location, and come up with her."

"Roger."

We sat back down and I explained to the room that we would shortly open communications with the Hurkz. I ordered them all out and told the Tsyfarians the same thing - this needed to be done small and simple. A minimal amount of people, so as not to spook the Hurkz or make them feel attacked in any way.

No one liked it, on any side, but I wouldn't budge. Hodges came down with Mills and Shae as the scientists left. The Tsyfarian screen shut off and Hodges looked mad. That made me want to laugh, but I decided against bothering.

"You can't negotiate on behalf of humanity with the Hurkz," he said, anger simmering. "You aren't authorized! I will handle the—"

"Hodges," I said calmly, "I'm in charge, remember? That will change when this is all over and done with. Which will happen after I deal with you." I glanced at Shae slowly, so Hodges could note it. "Remember?" He paled and left the room. I'm sure he would tell the Council about this and they would balk. But by the time they did, it would be too late and all of this would be a done deal.

I pulled Shae aside and told her about Mud's troubles quickly. She grew angry as fast as I had but relaxed before Mud could catch it. We'd have to deal with that along with everything else, and she was sure to enjoy that part.

We all sat and arranged ourselves for decent viewing of the screen, except Mud. He sat off to one side where he wouldn't be seen. If they spotted him, everything could go to pieces. Assuming seeing Shae and I didn't do that off the bat. Either way, I wouldn't refuse him the right to be here and listen in. Even advise, if he felt the need, so long as he did it silently.

Mills set up the call and we sat back while he handled the preliminaries. Basic diplomatic stuff, the sort of thing Mills could handle easily - I was sure of it, given his usual job.

I sat back and fought the urge to put my feet up on the table. Despite what I'd been saying and heading toward, these guys had hunted my son for over a year. I was going to enjoy this little chat.

CHAPTER 36 – MUD

MY VIEWING ANGLE wasn't the best, but when the first Hurkz diplomat came on-screen I still had to suppress a small twitch. Mills took care of him, flashing credentials and requesting to go higher up the chain.

The first flunky was replaced by a second and Mills discarded him too, his language precise and professional. I started to see why Dad wanted him as an assistant. While obviously a bit unsure of himself, he focused when it counted.

We went up the chain like that for about an hour until someone worth talking to finally came on. I recognized him and signaled Mom. I jotted down a note and got it to her without him noticing. This was the guy who'd signed my death warrant and forced me to flee in the first place. Not a friend.

Dad read the note as Mom flashed it to him under the table, and he actually grinned. He ran his hand across his short hair, rubbing his scalp, and settled back into his chair. Spreading his hands on the top of the table, he ran them over the surface, looking for all the world like he was smoothing it down.

"We need Hurkz help," he said as a starting point. Brave tactic, just asking right off the bat. It wouldn't work, and I think he knew that. Dad was playing a game, and had made some sort of choice that the rest of us weren't aware of.

"You are the criminal Jonah Madison," Slon said, his sneer crystal clear even from my angle of sight. "Why would we ever consider helping you?"

"Because you don't want to be responsible for the loss of life that will occur if you turn me down," Dad said smoothly.

"What do we care for your lives?"

"Diplomatic ties, for a start. But no, really, what you care about is the material you buy from human-governed worlds. If that took a substantial hit, you would feel it, too."

"We would adjust. Criminal, we will not deal with you."

"That's twice you've called me a criminal—"

"Because you are," Slon said, cutting Dad off. "You refused to return the one named Mud, the tribeless, to us. Instead you raised him as your own and denied basic Hurkz law."

"I saved his life, you mean?"

"Criminal—"

"That's three. And twice you've interrupted me. I don't think you get how diplomatic talks are supposed to go," Dad said.

"Do not lecture me on—"

Dad leaned forward, slapping the table with both palms as he did. He got that look in his eye, too. The one that none of us liked being on the receiving end of. "I will lecture you on anything I damn well please!" he shouted. "You wanted to kill a child for the bad luck of his being tortured. I refused to let you. You branded me, my wife, and my child as criminals. And make no mistake, I don't consider him anything other than my kid. We agree on that one thing - he isn't a member of your people anymore. But you will not continue to try and reclaim him, or make a move against me and my family."

"This is how you ask for help?" Slon looked faintly amused. "Throwing threats around and posturing? Am I supposed to cower and give you what you want now?"

"Naw, I'm just saying hello." Dad leaned back again and folded his hands behind his head. "Now, to business."

"There shall be no business with you unless you return the tribeless one to us."

"We need hibernation tech. I've heard rumors you have some."

"Did you not understand me?" Slon shook his head in disbelief.

"Yeah, I did. Let's assume for now it's on the table." Dad smiled at Slon and sat there.

I blinked, hard. He couldn't mean it, could he? Mom looked at me subtly and we locked eyes for a second. No, of course it wasn't what it seemed. Still scared me to hear.

"Excuse me?" Slon asked, seemingly as taken aback as I felt.

"You heard me fine. Assume it's on the table."

"This is a trick."

"No, it's diplomacy. I've made my feelings on my son clear, so you'll understand how important he is to me. So when I offer him up to you in exchange for this consideration, you'll realize how much I am giving up and, hopefully, part with the same in return."

"This must be a trick," Slon repeated.

"Nope," Dad told him, and my blood turned to ice. I knew it had to be a trick, but Dad was selling this. "It's one life for countless lives. Even an old fool like me can do that math. So let's move this along before I lose my nerve and can't go through with it."

"Yes...you were asking about...," Poor Slon didn't know which way was up anymore.

"Hibernation tech. We need some. Not for us, but for a reptilian species. We're hoping they're close enough to you that this might work."

"It would not. The adjustments would be large and unpredictable."

"Willing to go with that. Do you have the technology?"

"Confirming or denying state secrets is not something I am prepared to do right now."

Dad sighed heavily. "We don't have *time*. If we did, fine, go upstairs and make some calls. But there, quite seriously, is not time for this. Do you want to be known as the man who bested the criminal Jonah Madison? Not many have. On top of which, bringing in the longest-escaped tribleless Hurkz? It would be an incredible coup for you. But it's on the table now, not later."

"I..." Slon looked down. He ran the numbers in his head, I'd guess, and muttered something we couldn't hear. "Yes, we have this technology," he said at last.

"Not in testing, but working technology?" Dad pressed him.

"Yes, it is in normal usage when required. But I do not think even for the price offered I could give such a bounty to you." Slon actually sounded sad.

"So what could you give it to me for?" Dad asked, face serious. "What else could I provide?"

That made Slon think again. "Your gravity tech," he said slowly, running the idea around in his mouth while he spoke.

"Huh. Well I'm not sure if I can authorize that," Dad said, raising an eyebrow.

"There is not, as you told me, time for you to go and find authorization. But a deal brokered here will be binding. Your gravity tech, and your son, for the hibernation technology you seek."

Slon was going to play hard now that he felt he had the upper hand. Mom tensed. Dad put a hand on her knee and gave it a squeeze and she relaxed. He was still playing some game. Mills blanched as well. Dad gave him no reassurance. To his credit, though, Mills didn't speak out or run off to tattle.

"The gravity tech is worth far more."

"Is it?" Slon asked. "When you say species hang in the balance. Can you truly say that giving us your gravity technology would result in more loss of life than your current situation - or, truthfully, any at all?"

Dad spread his hands across the table again and nodded at the screen. "Fair point. Fine, the gravity tech and my son. In exchange you give us the hibernation technology we require."

"This is agreeable."

"It isn't to my soul, but what choice do I have?"

"None."

"So we're agreed?"

"Make no mistake, I am prepared for trickery from you, Captain Madison—"

"Call me Jonah."

264

"But if you deal fairly with me, so shall I with you. Cross me, however, and you will start a war."

"No tricks. We will approach in a standard transport, unarmed, and make the swap. Agreed?"

"Yes," Slon said, "I will send you coordinates."

"All right."

"And...Jonah?"

"Yeah?"

"Thank you." Slon switched off. Dad told Mills to unhook the data feed to make sure there was no way Slon could still be listening or reconnecting. Mills yanked a cable out and we all started talking at once.

"Dad! You can't mean to actually—"

"Jonah, if you think I'm letting you give our son or gravity technology to those—"

"Sir, you can't—"

"All of you, relax!" Dad bellowed. He put his feet up on the table and smiled. "Here's what we need. Mills, get Tslakog on the phone and see what he has in the way of incredible pilots and fast ships big enough for a party of six. Then rustle me up one of our crew carriers, small. Shae, Mud, you're with me. We leave," he looked at Mills, "inside thirty minutes. So you best get going on those ships and pilot."

"Jonah," Mom said, looking like she might slap him, "what's the plan here? How do you pull this off without starting a war, since I know you aren't about to give them what they want."

"Oh, that part is easy. We invade the Hurkz home world. Take what we want."

"That's easy?" Mills asked.

Dad laughed, loud and happy, "Have you met my family yet, Mills? I just rescued three planets in the last while, my wife escaped your own security twice from what I hear, and my son waltzed onto your ship and made sure she got away with it. You're gonna bet against the three of us together? Son, that's not a smart bet."

"And the war issue?" Mom asked again.

"They already want us all dead. What will this do? Make them want us *more* dead? I'll take that chance."

"No, you smiling idiot, they'll start a war with humanity."

"They're not that dumb, they can't afford to be. Newt pointed it out, earlier, they need more space. A full on war would decrease, not increase, their expansion." Dad insisted. "They'll lay it all on our heads. What's one more race that wants us dead? Seriously. At this point, what should we care?"

"How many," Mills asked tentatively, "races want you all dead *now*?"

"Four," Mom said with a sigh, "last I checked."

"Wait, what?"

"Mills," I said to him, putting a hand on his shoulder, the way Dad did with me, "you get used to it. Most species declare you an enemy of the people and swear to see you dead, but really, they're not going to go far out of their way to find you. Sometimes, sure. But mostly it's just something you get used to."

"Which is why," Dad said, "you should have told us the Hurkz were still after you this hard."

"I'm sorry, I wanted to deal with it myself."

"Honey," Mom said, "this is what family is for."

"I'm not sure," Mills broke in, "if you're all crazy or not."

"Neither are we, honestly," I told him, "but we're still alive, so that has to count for something, right?

"Hey, Mills," Dad asked, "when I came in I had three lockboxes with me. Are they still in storage somewhere?"

"Of course," Mills said quickly, "Hodges wanted to get into one to see what you were bringing on board, after you left, but we couldn't."

"That's why they're called lockboxes. If anyone could get into them, what good would they be? Regardless, we're going to need them. Get someone to bring them to the flight deck where the Tsyfarian ship will dock."

"What if the Tsyfarians don't supply the ship, sir?" Mills asked, making a note.

"They will. Tslakog is an agreeable sort," Dad said, turning to look at Mom. "I like him. He's a smart guy. Gets involved. Gets his hands dirty."

"You can take him to brunch after we save his species. And ours," Mom said with a headshake. "For now, don't we have a planet to invade?"

"Right," Dad said, "let's get on that."

CHAPTER 37 – JONAH

I KICKED THE STORAGE BOXES and looked at my family. "And you always think I over prepare for these things." I reached down to unlock the first box.

"In general, you do. Days like today, that's all right," Shae said.

I tossed her a thinsuit that looked like mine. Same black with blue along the outer leg. The line vanished at about the waist and reappeared on the back, where it scooped up and over the shoulders. Down again across her chest, the blue faded out. Over her left breast was the standard five arrows in an upside down V, with SHAE in standard block letters under the crest.

She laughed, snatching the suit out of the air, and went to change. That left Mud. I reached out to hand him a suit of his own, crest and name in place.

"Dad, I have a suit," he told me, not grabbing it. I sighed at him. This discussion again.

"Mud, you're family."

"I've never been part of your team. I have my own suit. It's fine, Dad, really. I don't need," he waved at the suit I still held out for him, "the symbolic gesture."

"Yeah, you do," I said. "You are part of my team. We've never gone into full combat before as a family. We're gonna do this right. As a team. Take the suit."

"I can't fade in that suit. I can in mine. I mean, look at that blue, it'll mess everything up. Even if it was flat black I'd have some kind of chance, and..."

"Mud, you think I'm stupid?"

"What, no—"

"Of course the suit has your tech in it. The needles and all, though you know I hate them."

"No other way for me to access the color shifts."

"Doesn't mean I like the idea. Either way, of course the suit has them. The blue is a default static charge, not a true color. It'll default to this mode, think of it as a standby. But when you need to shift, it will, just like yours. Even the insignia will fade."

"Put on the suit, Mud," Shae said, coming back wearing hers. It felt good to see her in the colors. Real good. Made me feel twenty years younger in an instant. "We go as a family." Mud nodded and went to go change. "As for you, soldier," she turned to me, her face serious, "what was going on in your head that you thought we'd, all three of us, need this stuff?"

"Baby, this is just how I pack for trouble. Coming up here, all I knew was trouble sat just over the horizon. You were gone, I didn't know where Mud was, but these are the ready boxes."

"Your panic boxes are built for the whole family?"

"Yours aren't?"

"Too many grenades to worry about proper attire."

"Can I just hope we don't have to blow ourselves up again today?" Mud said, walking back. He looked great, though he walked as if he was unsure of himself.

"No promises," Shae said with a smirk.

I opened the second lock box and pulled out a bunch of chargers for my Acadian blaster and stuck them in pockets. One I slotted home in the gun. A full charge to start just made me feel better.

I pulled out some fresh sonic pistols for Mud and underhanded them to him. He caught each easily, affixing them to his suit with quick release hooks. I lobbed some packs after them and he nodded, sticking the battery packs in the pockets of his suit.

Shae snatched her own Acadian blaster out of the air when I tossed it to her. She didn't like to use it, but they were handy weapons. Mud had never gotten used to it and hadn't used one in too many years, which is why he didn't get one. They weren't a weapon to wield unless you knew them backwards and forwards. I added some extra detonation caps and grenades and the like to Shae's load and closed and locked the second box.

I opened the third and Shae laughed, reaching in the box for herself. Mud groaned.

"I hate GravPacks, guys," he said.

"We're not gonna get close enough in anything else," I said, handing him his pack.

"This is why we have ships. You can ride inside the transport instead of strapping it to your back, now."

"Not as fast or hard to spot," Shae said, grabbing extra air canisters from the box and checking their charge. "We'll use both, I assume?"

"Of course," I said, handing Mud extra air for his suit. "We're gonna need every advantage we can find, Mud. You know how to use the GravPacks, you know why we prefer them."

"I hate them," he said, "they just feel...odd."

"You get used to it," Shae said.

"I never did," Mud insisted.

Mills came up as I locked the third box and he told us the Tsyfarian ship would be docking soon. Hodges heard our plan and lined up completely against it officially, while not even trying to stop us. Good. That was the right move. The smart one. The Government needed to be able to deny their backing.

It would enrage the Hurkz to have agreed to something they thought was sanctioned only to be told it wasn't. They'd cast blame and puff their chests and threaten all sorts of things. But they would not go to war. Not against humanity. The cause was obvious but deniable. The only thing they would have remaining to go after would be us. And we really didn't care.

Maybe we should have. We were, Shae and I at least, getting old. When I thought Shae had been taken, it could have easily been someone like the Hurkz instead of Hodges' stupid idea. Could we ever really retire and stop fighting and running if we also kept adding names to the list of people who wanted us dead?

Which brought me to Mud. What kind of life were we giving him? He was just starting out on his own, but he'd inherited the enemies of the family. I tried to think back to how long I would have survived if, back when I'd started, I'd been hunted by multiple species and marked for death. Probably not half as long as I had. Were we ruining his life?

No, these were an old man's recriminations. I had a job to do. No time to let myself wallow in answerless questions. It was, instead, time to throw myself into the breach yet again and find a way through the darkness of the sky.

Shae caught my eye and nodded. As always, she knew exactly the pit I'd almost fallen into there. And as always, she stood there ready to pull me out of it. I loved her, more every day I knew her. That was true back when we first met and it was still true, graying and cresting decades together.

She was my constant. The thing I could always come back to. No matter how lost I felt out there, Shae would be exactly where I needed her, when I needed her. And to think I'd wasted all that time, fighting a war, trapped on planets and working my way back, when she'd been sitting right here.

"I'm sorry," I said softly to her.

She understood exactly what I meant. Of course she did. I could see it in her eyes. She nodded at me slowly. "I know. You had a job to do. Don't regret doing it well."

"We're too old to be doing this," I whispered, moving to hold her to me.

"Aren't you sick of saying that and proving it wrong?" she asked against my ear.

I laughed and let go as the Tsyfarian ship settled into the dock. It was a beautiful ship. Painted bright colors, like their fighters, it also had the same quad engine placement, except they were twice the size.

The ship just *looked* fast. Curved like a stretched egg, it sat in the dock and seemed almost wrong for sitting still. I walked up to it and ran a gloved hand along the side. The hatch opened and a Tsyfarian stepped out, bird helmet in place. He took it off with a slight hiss of escaping air and nodded at us each in turn.

"I am Chellox," he said, holding a hand out to Shae.

We introduced ourselves and climbed on board the ship. The colors continued inside, the interior of the ship laid out brightly. Seats and storage compartments all sat about where I would expect them, with slight differences accountable to the species' thought patterns. A personnel ship is still what it is, though, and we buckled in after a short look around and went over the plan again, in great detail.

Chellox grinned as he plotted our course. He loved to fly, and felt confident he could get us even closer than we'd originally planned without any problem. I discussed it with him and described the vectors needed - and speed changes required - for the sort of flight plan he suggested.

He just nodded and assured me it wouldn't be a problem. Turning away from us and grabbing the controls again, Chellox eased us out of the dock.

"Mills," I said into my headset, "got the other carrier ready to go?"

"Yes," he said after a second's delay, "someone will fly it remotely from here. It'll catch up with you at target."

"I really don't think it will," I shot back. "Either way, see you back here when we've achieved mission."

"Good hunting, Jonah," he said, and I clicked off.

Chellox took us out and hit the engines, hard. The internal gravity field reduced the effect, but even with it we were still slammed about like ball bearings in a washing machine. Chellox shot through space with the grace of a dancer and the angles of a pool shark.

Sitting in that ship, looking out the viewport as we dodged and needled our way through the fleets, I wondered how we'd had a chance at all against the Tsyfarians in open dogfighting. This ship was amazing and so was its pilot. Chellox did rolls and hairpin turns that would've taken me twice as long just to work out, and he did them with the smallest twitches of his hands.

"I've always wanted to fly free like this," he said over his shoulder. "With the fleet, it's always just formation and the occasional small skirmish. You, Jonah, you caused me some trouble, though."

"When was that?" I asked, shrugging at Shae and Mud.

"Whose ship do you think you hung onto to invade our command?"

"That was you?"

"Flying under orders to search and go slow. Otherwise you would not have clung to me like a branch."

"No," I admitted, "I would not have. So you got this duty as punishment?"

"There was no punishment for being fooled by you. It was a masterful strategy. So simple that we never would have seen it. So we learn from it, instead of punishing for it."

"Your people aren't stupid," Shae said.

"No," Chellox laughed, "we are not. Still, it is good to be able to meet you, and your family. And to help both of our races."

"And to fly until our stomachs leave our bodies?" Mud asked.

"And, always, that!" Chellox agreed with a laugh, and he spun the ship. We turned again and aligned with something unseen. Chellox hit the engines harder than ever and we shot forward fast enough that the only thing I could think of that would possibly outpace us would be a GravPack on full.

Scary speed. The ship didn't feel it. No creaking, rumbling sounds from the hull or strange strain from the engines. This ship was simply built to go flat out like this when it needed to.

"Relax," Chellox said, "we're mostly a straight line from here to Hurkz space."

Next stop, then: invasion.

Chapter 38 – Shae

I WOKE UP AND BLINKED several times to make my eyes come back into focus. We still rocketed toward Hurkz space. Hitting my restraint release, I stood and stretched slowly, doing basic small-room calisthenics. Even at full speed, which broke a few minor laws of physics, it would take about two days to reach Hurkz space.

The thinsuits could provide water and nutrients as well as dispose of waste for us, that wasn't an issue. But you felt like you were living in a suit. So while we were on a ship, might as well take advantage of it. The Tsyfarian ship was well equipped. So we slept in shifts, just in case, and managed to not say much at all to each other.

That silence ended up being fairly normal for Jonah and I. In the middle of a battle we could be chatty as a way of diffusing tension. Before we left we would be all about discussions. But those dark hours, the ones spent speeding across a vast star field between deployment and action, we spent in silence.

Rest when you can rest, Jonah used to tell me, back when we first met. Back before we started fighting side by side and he would go off on missions and I would stay home and hope he would find his way back to me. So we did. Those precious hours or days between deployment and the mission became a time of quiet for us.

We slept. We worked out when we could. Double- and triple-checked equipment, went over maps, all of it. Whatever needed doing to ensure that you survived when everything went sideways. Because no matter how hard and careful you were, every plan went sideways eventually. When it did, you could die or you could be so prepared for life that you could manage regardless.

And so the time passed. Mud looked tenser the closer we got, but that only made sense. I wanted to talk to him about it, but it wouldn't help. We both knew why, his father and I, and nothing we said would change the fact of it. He was headed right to the last place he wanted to be. But he had us, and he knew that too. We both had to trust that would see him through. That and his own natural ability to get a job done.

About halfway through the second day, Chellox flicked a warning light and told us to make sure we were awake and strapped in. Jonah looked at me and flashed me a grin. I returned it and then gave Mud a wink. He just nodded at me and checked his straps.

The turns and insane maneuvers started up again, not long after that. Chellox threw us around space hard and fast. As we entered Hurkz-controlled space he had to. A large part of this mission depended on us getting close before they knew we were here. Which meant Chellox had to stay at the extreme edge of sensor rage at all times.

That wasn't easy when there were multiple ships to consider. His display flashed and he hissed at it, correcting course over and over. There was no way possible to avoid total detection, but Chellox flew us fast enough and moved in confusing enough ways that nothing picking up our presence would know quite what to do with it.

Soon enough we would have to abandon the ship and go to GravPack travel. Three of us, small as could be and moving quickly through their system, would be close to invisible. We just needed a ship to get us close enough. Technically we could've made the whole trip on pack alone, but Jonah's knee wouldn't take that sort of travel well, Mud hated it, and I was a bit out of practice. So instead, we cut down the time for that and left ourselves an escape ship just in case.

It also bought us time for the rest of the plan to kick in. The other ship, the human one, entered Hurkz space about the same time we did. It went a far more direct route, trying to be noticed. Along with it came recordings and normal activity to make the Hurkz think we were in it.

We needed it to fool them, but also to make them show us where we were headed. They gave it docking instructions toward a certain spaceport on a specific planet. That became our new goal. Chellox dipped and spun us far away from that location. We swung around again and made a few maneuvers that even I couldn't quite follow. The Tsyfarians had certainly sent us one of their best.

We finally reached a good drop point and unbuckled.

"We'll comm you when we need extraction," Jonah said, reaching for the airlock. "Stay out of sight."

"I intend to get far enough out that they won't be able to find me," Chellox said.

"But still close enough to meet up, I hope," Mud said.

I laughed. "This is a bad place to hitchhike out of."

"I'll be there when you need me," Chellox promised.

We entered the airlock together and readied ourselves as it hissed shut. A count of five and the outer lock cycled. Jonah jumped first, followed by Mud and then me, taking up the rear.

Open space greeted us with cold arms. My GravPack came online and the HUD flashed into life. I opened a short-range communications channel between just the three of us. It would only work within about six hundred feet, and wouldn't bleed much signal at all.

"Free flight or formation?" I asked Jonah.

"Free flight while we get bearings. Formation for the ride in, and back to free a bit out. Sound good?"

"Sure thing." I selected a few gravity wells and started off in the general direction of the eventual landing point. Mud wobbled a bit, selecting odd points, I'd guess, while he found his footing with the packs again. I figured he hadn't used one since we last made him train.

We flew easy, a good distance apart but all in the same general direction for about ten minutes. Not going anything like as fast as we could, giving the decoy ship a chance to get closer. We needed to arrive at about the same time it did, or the plan could fall apart.

"That's us," Jonah said, and a request for formation flight came up on my HUD. I keyed acceptance and he took over my selections and controls. Mud, too. I could tell by the way his flight pattern synced up quickly. "We're gonna burn hot for a while. Hold on," he said. As if there was anything to hold on to.

We accelerated hard. My HUD showed me what we were doing, what points Jonah was choosing, and I could concentrate on my own body instead of flying. The gravfield around me constricted down when we went into hard flight and pressed all of my joints hard. It wasn't a comfortable feeling, like being tightly wrapped up in blankets made of steel.

Jonah's knee must be killing him, and his shoulder couldn't be far behind. Mud's eyes must have felt the pressure worse than ours, too. The packs were still the best way in.

Jonah dipped us around the dark side of the planet, scouting out satellites and other near-orbit debris. We caught sight of the decoy ship going in for a landing and Jonah cut into the atmosphere. We came in hard, flames licking around the shields that kept us alive. Jonah cut an angle that wouldn't put us on the same screens as the decoy ship.

My selection screen switched down field resolutions to show my choices on a planetary level. Jonah flew us in hard, just under the speed of sound. This would be the point where we would start to show up on sensor arrays. Nothing to do for it but hope they didn't put two and two together.

Chances were, we'd decided, that Slon would have us dock near the actual tech, just in case we were being upfront about making the trade, but far enough from it to protect himself in the event we were about to double-cross him.

The problem was we wouldn't know where he actually intended to place the tech. Until we'd arrived, we didn't know where he would have us land, even. We all looked around as Jonah did a fly-by. Mud keyed the comms with an idea.

"See that bunker?" he asked. "Fortified, near the spaceport, and guarded like the King lives there."

"It's a good option," I said, "so is something underground. Harder to get in and out of."

"Check your selection screens, both of you," Jonah said. "I think you're both right. The bunker has something massive under it. Too much space. So you build a fortress and then build a second under it. What do you think?"

I looked at the masses on my HUD and saw Jonah had a point. "Seems like a good bet."

"So how do we get in?" Mud asked.

"Front door," Jonah and I said simultaneously.

Jonah took us up and over hard and then cut us free of formation flight.

"Mud, you go in from the right. Shae, surprise from above. I'll go in level," he said, and he split off.

Mud looped around, his flight pattern much more stable now - he must have spent a bunch of the flight in going over controls in his head. I went straight up and stopped dead, holding there carefully.

Jonah leveled off, dangerously close to the ground, and started in, zipping between buildings and vehicles for maximum confusion. Mud circled and came in higher, from the right. As they moved, I targeted the ground and dove.

The planet came up to meet me fast, air rushing to get out of my way. I extended my shield a good ten feet, just in case, and soft-selected a ninety-degree turn, not keying it in but letting the selection hang there, waiting.

As the last second, maybe eleven feet from the ground, right above a set of guards, I broke hard right to cross Mud's path. The guards dove for cover and Mud screamed by them. The combined effect gave them no time to work out what was going on.

From their point of view, something had almost fallen on them, turned impossibly, and then came back the other way within half a second. They didn't even have time to reach for a radio before Jonah hit them full on. He came to a stop and Mud and I circled around, landing by his side. The guards lay on the ground, unconscious. Jonah had hit them with his shield as he barreled through them, hard enough to put them down for a while but not kill them.

The door in front of us was huge. Huge and solid. I could crack the lock, but it would take a while. Probably more time than we had.

Jonah took a look at it too, and he sighed. "Door knocker, I think."

I agreed but didn't want to. I could blow the hinges, but no, Jonah was right, it would use up too many supplies. We should get in as fast as possible. I dragged a guard clear of the door and Mud followed suit.

"What's a door knocker?" he asked as he set down the last guard.

Jonah and I stood in front of the door, about thirty feet back. I motioned for Mud to join us. "Target your pack on the ground," Jonah told him. "Anchor there." I did the same.

"A door knocker," Jonah went on, "is simple. With one hitch."

"A hitch that will kill us, I assume," Mud said.

"If you want to get technical about it, yes."

"Dad…"

"Best way to do this," Jonah insisted. "Now, target a pull on the door. Keep the ground anchor in place and then reverse the pull so you pull the door to you, instead of you to the door. The only problem is—"

"The door is going to come at us at roughly the speed of sound," I finished. "When it pops, key a push on the door. If we time it right, the door will land clear of us. If we don't, be prepared to jump."

"Jump," Mud said, "faster than the speed of sound."

"Well," Jonah said softly, "that's why we want to do it right."

I set up the selections and keyed them. The door and ground fought with my body as a focal point. I wanted to look and see how Jonah and Mud were doing, but couldn't risk taking my eyes off the door. A second would make the difference here.

The door started to creak, buckling. The locks were ripping free and the hinges were coming out of the wall. It broke free and I keyed the push, trying to make the door stop. It kept coming.

Chapter 39 – Jonah

THE DOOR KEPT COMING. I could feel it before I saw it. My eyes caught up and I realized there was no way we'd get clear. So I reversed my ground tether. Instantly I started to move toward the door.

I jacked my shield up to a good ten feet and braced myself to meet the door anyway. I slammed into it and Shae hit it not long after. The door slowed, our combined gravpush making sure we weren't pancaked by it.

The door hit the ground hard, toppling away from us, and we turned off our packs. We dropped the two or three feet to the ground. My knee gave and I hit, sitting. Shae grabbed my hand and yanked me back up. I increased the pressure on my brace and tested my leg. It'd hold.

Mud came over, shaking his head. "You guys could've told me about the alternate plan."

"We made that up," Shae admitted. "Never tried that before."

"Worked though," I said with a nod. "Good idea to remember it. Now let's go find this hibernation tech."

I selected a five-foot distance from the ground. Shae and Mud started running on foot and I kept up with them in the air. My knee would hold me but I couldn't run, not now. I felt every one of my years just then. Watching my son run was fine - watching Shae, still fully able-bodied, hurt a bit, I admit.

My body wouldn't keep up with my needs anymore. Not always. I didn't want to adjust to that, but again and again, I had no choice. Not the problem that second, though: we were in the base but had no idea where we were going.

"Has to be down," Mud said, pointing to a stairwell. "Why build an underground bunker and keep something precious in the lobby?"

We hit the stairwell and I took point, partly out of stubbornness. My blaster found its way to my hand - I didn't remember drawing it, but that was fine. Guards started to floor the area; we could hear their boots above and blow us. I set my blaster for range, not power. It'd take a man down but not blow a hole clean through him.

We kept going down, watching the level doors get thicker. Boots above got closer and I glanced back to see Mud draw both sonic pistols. He sent a volley of shots bouncing up the stairwell. Screams replied.

Ahead of me, a batch of guards turned the corner and spotted us. They opened fire and I flattened against the wall. My blaster answered them and I heard two go down. There were still five down there, though, already calling for reinforcements. We were on a clock. Once we took out that door, any idea that we were playing fair had vanished.

Slon probably already knew, regardless. That decoy ship had landed and purposefully botched the landing, turning into a skidding ball of fire on the landing pad. Between those two events, Slon must have been making sure the tech we needed was being moved and put under extreme guard.

Something small and dark flew forward over my head and I turned away just before the grenade went off. Shae, helping clear a path. We kept going. I fired a few shots randomly through the smoke, just to add to the confusion below.

We left the stairway and hit the larger passageways. No way to know if we were on the right level, but I figured a change of scenery might be nice, and might confuse them some. A shot came out of nowhere and hit me in the arm. I cursed and fired back, lucky it hadn't gotten my gun arm. We were being swarmed. Shae dove in front of me and threw herself at the guards. Mud wasn't far behind her, the two of them going hand-to-hand out of sheer anger.

It was like watching a dance. A violent, brutal dance. I was never much of a technical fighter. I could take a person down easy enough, but I didn't bother with grace. A fist was good enough for me. Shae and Mud though, they both loved to get their hands dirty. Limbs went everywhere and guards fell. Mud punctuated a few kicks with a sonic blast, just to make a point.

A guard got a shot in and hit Shae in the shoulder, right over her injury. She made a noise, a half-bitten scream, and said something to Mud. He came running back to where I was.

"Mom says duck and cover," he told me, and he looked at me for an explanation. I shook my head.

"Anchor yourself to the floor and wall and ceiling. Just solidify yourself in place with the pack," I told him, "and hang on." Shae went down, curling into a ball on the floor. Guards piled on her.

The first few did it by choice. The rest found themselves flying at her uncontrollably, slamming into their comrades. We stayed silent as bits of loose debris from the hall added itself to the pile Shae was making. Seconds passed, feeling like they were creeping by. Then, suddenly, everything and everyone exploded outward, hitting walls and ceiling and floor with enough force that I was sure bones broke. I know I heard a few, through the din.

Shae stood and glared at her shoulder. She took a pill from an arm pouch and swallowed it. The pain pill would kick in fast, but wouldn't be enough to dull her senses at that dosage. I popped one myself and bandaged my arm.

As we went over to her, I noticed one of the guards was in far more armor than the others. I reached down and grabbed him up. It took a few shakes to wake him up and his left arm dangled brokenly, but I didn't care.

"Where were you coming from?" I demanded. More armor meant bigger thing to watch. Where he came from, we wanted to be.

The guard opened his big eyes and stared at me, uncomprehending. He said something in Hurkz and started to pass out again.

"Mud?" I asked.

"I don't speak it much or well, but I'll try." He came over and I shook the guard awake again, adding a slap. Mud asked him something in Hurkz and made him repeat the answer, slower. "One level up, other side of the compound," Mud said.

"Think it's where they took the tech?" Shae asked.

"I don't have a better idea," I said, "either of you?"

They didn't, so we set off. I took point again, by virtue of not being on my feet. We hit the stairwell door hard, Mud coming up and letting a few volleys of sonic shots go ricocheting up and down the stairs before we entered. We went up a level and left the stairway as fast as we had entered it. Guards were everywhere, all of them wearing thicker armor, same as the one we'd questioned.

Shae and I opened fire before ducking into the doorway to avoid the return volley. She held up a hand and nudged me aside. The hand she'd used had grenades in it. I watched them fly: one, two, three, and four, sent off in different directions. The hallway shook as they all went off at once.

"Baby," I said gently.

"They're down, aren't they?" she replied before I could even finish my thought.

"Yeah, but we need the hallway still standing."

She rolled her eyes in response and ducked out of the stairwell, crouched low. I followed, on foot now since we weren't running, and Mud came out with me, facing the other direction, sonic pistols at the ready.

He fired two shots in quick succession and said "This way." Shae and I came over and followed him. A thick security door stood there, glaring at us. "Door knocker?" he asked.

Shae shook her head and stood in front of the panel. "I'll get it." She pried the panel off and started to look around for her tools, patting her pockets down.

"I packed them. Left thigh, pockets three and four." The thinsuit pockets were blended into the light armor in each, so they didn't stand out unless you knew where they were. She dug into them and came out with a handful of tools.

The panel popped off the wall and Shae went to work. The door beeped once and she stuffed the tools away. "They really think people are stupid," she said, sounding annoyed that it wasn't harder. I reached for the door to help open it, forgetting for a second I'd been shot in that arm. I winced and dropped my arm to my side.

The room past the door contained nothing but another door. The lock looked far more complicated. Shae started working on it while Mud and I took up positions at the first door to watch her back.

A few shots came zinging out of nowhere and Mud and I returned fire toward the point of origin. The guards had taken up the same stairwell we'd used as protection. Mud slid a grenade down the hall toward them and started to shoot after it, confusing everything with noise and smoke and fire.

The guards fled the stairwell and made a straight, head-on run for us. Mud took a shot to the leg and I almost lost a hand. They were playing for keeps and we were still playing nice. Killing people isn't good for you. I didn't like to do it if I could manage to avoid it, but they were making it hard to keep that idea in my head.

Shae poked her head out between Mud and I. "They had the plans just sitting in there. All but under a spotlight. Either they think we're really bad at this or they're convinced they're really, really good."

"The Hurkz are convinced that they're superior to everyone else," Mud said, "and don't seem to learn fast enough."

"Their loss." Shae shoved the plans in tight against her GravPack, sealing them into a large pouch there. "Now, do we have time to find Slon?" she asked.

I considered it. I would love to get my hands on him personally. I know Shae did, too. But no, it would be a bad idea to stop and try to find him. We still had two days' travel to get back, and fleets that didn't want to wait. A full week of waiting might do bad things as it was.

"I wish," I said, "but we need to get out of here and get back as fast as possible."

"Are you going to tell Chellox that?" Mud asked, "Because I don't know if I'll survive his fastest."

Chapter 40 – Meanwhile

KNOWN AS JONAH'S TEAM, the small ship had found itself primed to take messages from one fleet to the other. They flew between the rear of the Tsyfarian fleet and the start of the human fleet that had flown here after them from Trasker Four. For a while everything had been peaceful.

Where once their main job had been search and rescue, the small group found themselves acting, unofficially, as diplomats. It was a role that none of them, save the Seer, enjoyed. And yet they carried on because it was their job.

The space between fleets grew tenser the longer time dragged on. The human fleet changed shifts, which required it to send half of its ships through the Tsyfarian fleet. The first few times the maneuver was done, no one minded. Each passing attempt brought more resentment, however.

The human shifts flew closer and closer to the Tsyfarian, almost daring them to react. It was the sort of tactic one uses when trying to provoke shots being fired. On the other hand, each fleet - knowing the other would be listening - had recently started to openly gripe about the other.

A Tsyfarian flight commander tried to put a stop to the verbal volleys as best he could. He knew, of course, that humans did not speak Tsyfarian, but also felt that the tone could be understood. He was not wrong. The human pack leaders, on their side, were doing the same, for the same reasons. The human flight leader also threatened to dock shore leave for any pilot who flew too close to a Tsyfarian ship.

They tried to hold the peace together. They failed.

The third day after the mission to Hurkz had left, fighting broke out on the border of Tsyfarian and human fleet space. It started by accident, as these things often do. A Tsyfarian pilot made a course correction, through sheer exhaustion, that took him into what was considered human space at that moment. He did this at the same time as the human shift change.

His drift across the paths of the human ships, full of pilots tired and overworked, was seen by one of those pilots as an act of aggression. A shot was fired. The shot was returned. War blossomed.

And the little ship flew straight to the start of the aggression, hoping that sight of them would return a level of calmness to the fleets. It had worked before, barely. It might have worked again, except this time open fire was being exchanged. The ship took several hits. The cabin filled with smoke and screams. From the outside, the ship poured smoke and fluid. The volleys of shots ceased as both sides wondered who had shot down Jonah's hand-picked team. No one wanted to be responsible for it. That was, they all felt, a ship of nonaggressors. The neutral party, tied to the man who would help.

Destroying it would serve no purpose, and that fact, as the ship spun out of control and drifted out of the field of danger, stopped a full-scale war from erupting. Instead, both fleets sent in help.

Inside the ship, no one knew that their work had been successful yet again. They were trying to stop the loss of air, and of fuel. They tried to clean the cabin air and regain a breathable atmosphere. They fought for their lives, those four people, inside a small metal box that spun silently in the vastness of space.

Steelbox put out the fires as fast as he could spot them. He moved to the engine compartment to make sure that it was not on fire as well. His left leg had sprouted a shaft of metal, thrown there by the ship when it had first been hit. He slipped on his own blood once, but he knew better than to take the shaft out. He carried on with his job, knowing that if the ship could be saved, he, too, had a chance - but if not, bleeding out would be the least of his problems.

Olivet tried to work both communication consoles, finding the backup one shorted out but the main one functioning. He called for help and was answered. Thankful, he listened to directions and went to prepare the airlock for docking.

Bee tried to regain control of the ship. She called out to Kem, asking for diagnostic readings so that she would know how badly they had been hit. Kem didn't reply, and Bee called out to him again, growing frustrated. Without that information she would be flying the ship blind. Bad enough that they were damaged. Trying to get the ship under control while not even knowing what systems fully worked would be impossible. Bee decided right then that she never wanted to fly again, if it meant piloting. She loved tech work, not this.

She called to Kem a third time and when he didn't answer, Bee shut down her controls and unstrapped to pull his chair around so she could get his attention. What she saw caused her to scream loud enough that everyone else on the ship came running.

When they saw what was left of Kem's body, and the half a navigation console that sat where his chest cavity had been, they grew silent. No one could help him. All they could do was mourn. Steelbox demanded that they put even that off until they had assured their continued existence. That way, they would have time to mourn. Olivet took Kem out of the chair, carefully, and laid his body aside, under an emergency blanket.

He then sat in the chair, ignoring the condition of it, and asked Bee if they could still fly the ship without the navigation console. Bee just stared ahead. Olivet asked again, in a calm whisper. Bee blinked, nodding. Together they worked to bring a secondary, emergency navigation console online. Olivet didn't understand the wiring, or what he was actually doing, but Bee's cold calmness directed him well.

By the time the Tsyfarian and human ships sat outside, helping right the ship with brute force slams against its sides, they had stopped the fires and brought the ship under control. They took boarders, then. They also accepted assistance gratefully, though they refused to abandon their ship.

Steelbox explained: they had been given a job, and that job wasn't done yet.

Both fleets went back to waiting – a little more patient for another day.

Chapter 41 – Jonah

WE CLEARED THE BUNKER by inches, Shae bringing another wall down behind us. Rubble and dust were everywhere, and we used the confusion to take off with the GravPacks. We went straight up like greasy rats squeezed in a fist. Shooting clear of the gravity well of the planet, we each hit a different direction and signaled Chellox.

He tossed back an encoded burst with his location. We each zeroed in on and boarded the ship, even as the Hurkz started to fire.

"Chellox, I think we might want to get out of here," I said, reaching for the first aid kit.

"That was the general idea," he said. "You three might want to strap yourselves down."

We did what we could, passing the kit back and forth. We were running out of bandages. That was never something you wanted to realize. I ached, and I hated it. Shae looked tired, too. Mud, though also battered and shot once that I'd seen, looked like he was ready to go at least one more round in the breach.

Good for him. For my part, though I didn't want to admit it out loud, I was ready for the fighting part of this mission to be done. I sat back and let the ache take me over for a while, feeling the twists and turns of Chellox's flight plan.

At this point, anything in the sky that wasn't Hurkz was being fired on. That really ended up meaning only us. Chellox had his hands full trying to keep from being shot down while still working a way out of the area.

He pulled a few turns that felt, even within the ship's compensating gravity, like a broken rollercoaster about to go off the tracks. I tightened my straps and glanced at Shae. She shook her head, not enjoying Chellox's flying either.

We leveled off and hit a clear patch. "I think they're all behind us now," Chellox said. "Which means they can't hope to catch us if I do...this."

The acceleration wasn't something you could brace for. Not this hard a jump. It felt like we went from zero to infinity in one jolt. I'd assumed we'd come in as fast as the ship could go, but now I saw Chellox's plan. Just in case the Hurkz had spotted us, he'd kept something back so our getaway would work.

The speed kept up, but we all got used to it by the middle of the first day. The three of us rested as much as we could, using the last of the first aid supplies to do the best we could. Our wounds would close and not get infected. Everything else got tossed into the ignorable clutter of details.

Around the middle of the second day, I reached out to Mills.

"Mills, we have the stuff. The Hurkz won't be happy, but we've got it. Get everyone who might be able to help and keep them together. We're gonna come in hot."

"Jonah, there's been—"

"Mills, has war broken out?"

"No, but—"

"Then right now we need to focus on making sure it won't. Best way is to get this tech working."

"All right, but Jonah—"

"Mills, I need you rounding people up. We'll talk when I get back." I cut off. I didn't know what he wanted to tell me, but I knew it would be bad news. The problem was, from where I literally sat, I couldn't do anything. If it had been something I could cleanly advise on, he wouldn't have given me a bad-news lead-in.

Not being able to do anything would just make me focus on the problem and chew on it. No, I needed to focus on these plans and getting this hibernation tech running.

Assuming that the Hurkz had allowed the real plans to be stolen. The fact that Slon had actually agreed to this bothered me a bit. Mud knew them better than I did, and he was right - they were incredibly confident - but this was plain stupid. It might've been as simple as a hunger for power that made him think he could taunt me with the plans, take Mud, and then double-cross me by leaving fake, deadly, plans out for us.

Some belief like that sure could've led him to miss seeing my own double-cross, or at least to assume he could deal with it handily. But I could also explain it easily enough if he'd made the plans fake. Something that looked real enough to fool us but that would kill anyone it was used on.

We landed after too many more hours and were met by a whole crew. They took us straight to a briefing room while a team of medical personnel followed, treating us as best they could on the move.

Techs took the plans from Shae and the medical crew started to discuss them. We all did. Thankfully, everyone else landed at the problem of it potentially being fake as well. Tslakog sent over a few of his scientists to help us with their biology. Even if these plans were real, they would need adapting.

It became a race against time that I could do nothing to further along. This sort of thing isn't in my skillset. I hung around to make sure everyone else stayed on track and because I felt possessive of the problem. If it blew up in our faces, I wanted to be there to pick up the blame myself.

Everyone was on edge. The scientists, human and Tsyfarian, worked around the clock, but time kept slipping right by. Tests were run and rerun. Models were made and discarded. The plans seemed close to real but there was a problem with them. Damn.

Still, no one gave up. New models were made. It came down a question of time. The Tsyfarians didn't have much left. As it was, another incredibly large shipment of food was on its way to them from our stores; even if the hibernation tech worked, we'd cost them too much time to make it without an influx of sustenance, and the size of it would be the last we could possibly do. Without the tech, they were finished.

Mills cornered me somewhere around hour twenty.

"Jonah. We need to talk."

"Now, Mills?" I asked. "We're right in the middle of this."

"Jonah, you're pacing. That's all you're doing. Let these people work and talk to me. You need to hear this." He sounded insistent enough that I followed him out of the lab and into the hall.

"All right, Mills, what is it? I know it's bad, just come out with it."

"Fighting broke out while you were gone. It was stopped, but not cleanly. Shots were fired from both sides."

"But it was stopped."

"Yes. But one of your crew, that ship you had doing rescue duty? With the refugees?"

"Bee and them?"

"Yes. One of them didn't make it. Kem, I think his name was."

That hurt. They'd agreed to help out because they didn't know what they were getting into. By the time they realized, they'd kept helping anyway. I wanted to race out, to do something, anything, be the leader they'd needed me to be while I wasn't around, but I knew nothing would do. They were all good people - some of the best, given what they'd tossed themselves into to help others. And now one of them had died because my plans ran into a snag. "The others?" I asked, looking for a small bit of light.

"They're all fine. The ship is limping along, and they've been insisting on staying where they are, patrolling the empty space between fleets as a showing of the cost of a breakdown in peace."

"Call them in," I said thickly.

"Jonah, they refuse."

"They refuse you. Tell them I'm back and they need to come in now." I turned away from Mills and walked down the hallway by myself for a while. This was part of why I'd retired in the first place. Losing team members cost my soul, every time it happened. I was sick of it, physically sick.

I met them down on the hanger deck about an hour later, and greeted them each warmly, even Olivet. I told them, in quiet words, how amazing they each were and how much two entire species owed them. They swelled at my pride in them, and that hurt like a dagger to the chest. That desire to please me that they now wore as a badge had cost Kem his life, and far too soon.

But I didn't say anything. I smiled at them and made sure they got the medical attention they needed and told them again how proud I was of them. My pain at their pride would only serve to hurt them when they needed only to know that the cost had been worth it. And it had been - if not to me, but to them. They needed that reassurance, and though it hurt me to do so, I wouldn't deny them that. Ever.

Leaving them and finding my way back to the labs, I ran into Mud. He entered with me, and I asked where we were in this whole problem. He shook his head. It didn't look great. They'd been using blood samples from Mud, trying to get his cells to go into hibernation and come back out. They'd managed it once, and then twice, but there was something still not quite right.

Until they fixed that, there wasn't a good way to go forward. Mud stepped to the lab bench and rested a hand on it heavily. "What we need to do," he said slowly, "is test it on me. Not some blood, but me."

"Mud, that's crazy. They've gotten this to work, but only mostly. It could kill you," Shae said, coming around to our end of the room.

"Sure, Mom, but we've all made incredible progress. And this is the final test we need. We all know it, including you and me and Dad."

"He's right, baby," I said. I didn't want to put our kid at risk, but like before, I had no choice.

Shae shot a look of hatred at me but then turned away with a brief nod. She knew it, too.

Mud hopped up onto a test bed and rolled up one sleeve slowly. He relaxed back, staring at the ceiling.

"So let's do this thing so we can adapt it for the Tsyfarians," he said to the techs in the room. "We don't have all day."

CHAPTER 42 – MUD

THE TABLE WAS COLD, and the lights too bright. A needle pierced my skin and I wanted to laugh when they said it might sting. If they knew how many needles and how much stinging I dealt with…but of course they didn't. So I nodded at the med tech and closed my eyes.

The medical guys felt sure the formula would work. It had managed to work on my cells fine, in multiple trials. The problem was, no one was sure how it would work on organs, much less my brain. So they would drop me into hibernation for twelve hours and see what happened when they tried to wake me up.

The serum started to take hold and my eyelids grew too heavy to open. They fit a mask over my nose and mouth and flooded it with the gas they'd prepared. I breathed deeply and started to drift away. I had a moment of panic as I grew convinced I could feel my heart stopping and my life draining away. I fought back the urge to struggle, to strike back against the darkness. I gave in to it and hoped I would live to see the other end of the experiment.

My eyes opened slowly and I cursed under my breath. The serum hadn't taken. This was going to be a problem. Or so I thought until I caught sight of a clock. Twelve hours had passed. They'd done it.

Mom and Dad helped me off the table and both gave me hugs. I returned them, once my brain processed what I'd just done. The science techs smiled at me and drew some more blood to see how the hibernation had affected my system. A short test, but still one that would be telling.

I felt fine, but knew that wasn't enough to go on. The Tsyfarians looked pleased, though. This might be the answer they'd needed. The tests started and Dad took Mom and I to meet some people. Three folks who had flown a rescue ship and then held the peace, in a tiny rickety ship. Untrained, even. Dad was proud of them, but I could see it hurt him to be around them. They'd lost one of their own, and Dad felt it worse than they did. He hadn't been there, and I knew that was what ate him up.

The five of us talked while tests ran. We didn't discuss anything important, tell any deep personal stories. We just talked as if we were five people who hadn't been to war that week. It was a nice illusion.

Eventually Mom, Dad, and I were called back to the lab. The tests had come back and everything was a go. The Hurkz had given us bad data, but hidden it inside too much good data. Now it just needed to be adapted for the Tsyfarians. They gave us some blood samples and all the work started over again. This time, though, it wasn't about "if" anymore. It'd become a conversation about "when." We left them so Dad could call Tslakog.

"If you haven't heard, we're almost there," Dad opened with, instead of any sort of greeting.

"The food you sent has also arrived. There is a chance, my friend, this will all work."

"Or at least enough of it to scrape by, huh?" Dad leaned back.

"I am truly sorry to hear about the loss of your comrade. That was a regrettable mistake," Tslakog said.

303

"No one is placing blame," Dad reassured him, telling him a pretty lie since both Mom and I knew he placed lots of blame squarely on his own shoulders. "It was a mad, tense time. Still is. A mistake was made and, thankfully, stopped."

"You speak with wisdom."

"Not wisdom," Dad insisted, "old age. I've seen too many wars started over something stupid to not recognize it."

"I, too, am sick of war. Jonah, truly, your whole family is a friend to the Tsyfarian people, now and forever, for all that you have done. Possibly sparing us from the slaughter we partook in before, no one can calculate how many lives you may have saved."

"Thank us when the job is done. We're not there just yet."

"But we will be soon," Tslakog said, full of confidence.

"We hope. But we won't know until we are."

"You play your joy close."

"I've run afoul of being too confident before," Dad said.

"Well then, I shall let you go back to your work, and hope to hear soon that we have found success." The screen went dark and Dad sighed.

"He's right," he said after a minute, "we should get back."

"I was sort of enjoying just sitting here, as a family, without gunfire for a change," Mom told him.

"It is nice," I agreed.

Dad laughed. He also stayed where he was. We sat there like that, in silence together, for at least an hour. No one came to find us, no one bothered us - we just relished sitting there and not having to be at war. Too often, growing up, I'd missed this. Both my parents had been off saving a world somewhere, and when they weren't I was demanding we go find an adventure I could be a part of.

I didn't regret it my choices. Deep down I don't think any of us thought we'd been wrong in how our lives had been led. It still that didn't mean it wasn't nice to try the other side for a while. I felt, for the first time, really, like an equal. They would always be my parents, always ready to rush in to help, but the three of us had never done this before. Gone into one of their situations - together. It felt nice. Really nice. I felt sure they knew it, too.

Mills came into the room. "Jonah," he said, after a quick apology, "they're ready for you, all of you." He nodded at us and stood by the door. We got up and followed him back to the lab.

"We're ready for the final test," one the techs said as we entered. "If this works, we've done it."

"And if it doesn't?" Mom asked, looking at the Tsyfarian lying on the exam table. They were injecting the serum into his arm and readying the mask.

"Then," the Tsyfarian said, raising his head before the mask came down, "they will try again, without me." He lowered his head and we all grew silent. They were a brave species, the Tsyfarians. Loyal and true, at least the ones we'd met.

Shame about the genocide. I suppose if something happens so infrequently that whole generations pass between each occurrence it becomes almost religion, and you don't question those openly too often. But when you did, the whole world could change around you.

We stood watch while he dropped off, sinking into the same oblivion I'd found. He'd be back. The Tsyfarians were different from the Hurkz, but closer to each other than either were to humanity.

We stood watch over him, not wanting to move even though it would be twelve hours yet. Eventually everyone in the room had to leave: to eat, to nap, to deal with other problems big and small. We went in shifts, though, making sure we all knew where everyone was. When it came time to wake him, we all wanted to be there. There was a notch in the clock, it felt like, a single notch that could tell the tale of two species. All we could do was wait for the clock to strike.

Eventually, of course, it did. They pumped the reviving gas through the mask and nothing happened. We quieted, watching as his vital signs didn't peak. They laid flat, almost imperceptible. One of the med techs reached for a defibrillator, thinking that might kick-start the cycle, but suddenly the levels all jumped. The gas was working - it just took longer than it had on a Hurkz, namely me.

He woke up, sitting up and glancing at the clock. Then he smiled. "Let us begin the after-effect tests," he said, holding out one arm. We cheered, every last person in the room.

While they ran their tests, Dad went to call Tslakog again, just to give him the latest update personally. No one wanted to deny him that pleasure.

"So, what about Hodges?" I asked Mom while he was gone making his call.

"What about him?" she gave me a look.

"Is he going to just get away with kidnapping you?"

"You're asking something I don't have an answer to. If you're really asking if I'd like to deal with him, you know that answer. But that doesn't mean I will, or that it would be the right move."

I nodded, and Dad came back in the room. I let the Hodges question drop for a few as the tests came back good. The hibernation technology would work on the Tsyfarians. And I thought we had all cheered before.

I went along this time, as Dad gave Tslakog the final update.

"It works," Dad said. Simple and direct. A war had been one, by avoiding it, and that made this a great day.

"Then we can go and decide our own fate," Tslakog said.

"Always," Dad replied. Behind him and allowed myself a smile.

"In return," the lizard-faced leader said, "we shall divert our fleet and aim it directly at the Hurkz."

"Uhm, what?"

"They are now your enemies and so we name them ours as well. Harvesting their planet will allow us to range even further afield from human lands."

"You can't," I cut in, stepping forward.

"We can, and we shall, stranger," Tslakog, said.

"Mud, mayb—"

"My name is Mud, son of Jonah," I said, cutting Dad off and trying to adopt a more diplomatic tone. "And committing genocide in our name is wrong."

"But Mud," Dad said, "I mean, it's wrong but I can't say it wouldn't solve problems."

"And you don't think they should, either. But you'd probably give in, wrongly, just for a second, right now." I shifted my focus back to Tslakog, "Which is why I have to step in. No."

"You can not order our fleet," he replied.

"This race you consider is my original race. They hunt me," I told him, "and wish me dead. That does not make it acceptable for me to kill them on a whim. Nor does it allow me to wish their destruction, even from someone I would like to consider a new friend and ally."

Dad looked at me and nodded. The joy of the moment, the rush of it, brought him close to an edge. Add in his exhaustion and hurt over the loss of that guy on the ship, would he have done it? Allowed it? No. But for a second he may have faltered and that could have dug just enough of a hole. It didn't matter. He didn't have to carry every load alone.

Tslakog kept a level gaze through the screen. "Son of Jonah you may be," he said, "but I have had my fill of being told how to direct my race recently."

"You can stand with us, with humanity, against needless slaughter like the actions you threaten, or you can stand against us. Against us isn't smart. Not," I added quickly, "because of war. But because it rejects newfound alliances. Ones we all need. It rejects the spirit of life we would all wish to live under. Including the Tsyfarian, I think."

"I shall take," Tslakog said, "your...wisdom... under consideration."

the word go, Hodges. And now, what, you'll walk out of this with a promotion, smelling of roses?"

"I understand you hate me, Jonah, but I did what I thought I had to, and everything worked out in the end."

He was right. I did hate him. As soon as I got home I would ensure he lost his commission. No point in giving him warning, though. Let him think he would get out of this clean, then destroy him through the channels he so dearly seemed to enjoy falling back on when convenient. And then, maybe, hunt him down and beat him into the ground, just to prove a point. It wasn't my normal way of dealing, not given what he'd done, but killing him outright seemed pointless.

"Furthermore," he continued, "I've been asked to offer you your old job back."

"I retired, remember?"

"And we're asking you to reconsider. Jonah, this wouldn't have happened with you and your family if you'd stayed. We all know it. Even I know it, all right? It would be a shame to lose you again."

"You have to get used to it. Even if I said yes, some day I won't be here. Then what? Get used to flying solo, Hodges. You need to move the best people up, like Mills. Not keep them down, tied up with protocol."

"So help us ensure that happens."

"I'm retired."

"So that's it? You'll go back home and pace like a lion in captivity?"

"Actually, Shae and I thought," I said with a grin, "we'd travel. Not for the Government, but for ourselves. See the universe without having to blow it up for a change."

"Don't do this, Jonah. You'll have full pick of your own crew and support staff. You can even have a liaison with the military of your choice. We need you."

"No, you don't," I told him, drawing close. To his credit, he didn't flinch. "But I do know what you need. I'm even willing to help with it."

Hodges raised an eyebrow, not sure if I was setting him up. "So you'll help?"

"Sort of," I reared back and head-butted him, spreading his nose across his face like paste. "I'll help you find a med tech to fix that up." I kneed him in the gut and dropped him on the floor.

But his words rang in my head. Would Shae and I ever be happy retired, sitting at home? Probably not. Even touring the galaxy might not work. We could visit the Tsyfarian planet, be the first humans to do so. Tslakog had offered. I didn't know if it would ever be enough to quench the occasional fire that lay in both our guts. Maybe Hodges was right. Maybe we should sign back up.

I looked to Shae, as the three of us stood there over Hodges' whimpering, bleeding form. "Maybe we should discuss this," I offered. She nodded and we started to walk off, looking for a quiet room to talk.

Mud stood there, not sure if he should follow or get Hodges help or just leave for his own ship again. "C'mon, kid," I called out to him, "you're a part of this discussion, too."

He grinned and caught up with us.

CHAPTER 44 – EPILOGUE

A RADIO CALL WENT OUT. Five communicators flashed a signal. Unsurprisingly to anyone else on the command carrier, they were together, seated at a table, talking and eating. They weren't elitist or exclusive, but left to their own devices each of them sought the others out.

At the call, they put down their drinks and cleared the table, rising to leave. Each one went to their own quarters to change. Within fifteen minutes, the five people were walking across the hanger deck. They picked up their conversation from where they'd left it around the table, never missing a beat.

They walked to a unique ship. Painted black with only a single symbol gracing its lines: five arrows forming an upside-down V. The same symbol each one of the five carried on their thinsuits. Each suit was the same as well: black, with blue coming up along the outer side of the legs, rising until it turned at the waist to slide up their backs and curve over their shoulders, coming back down their chests and ending at the bottom of the ribcage.

The ship itself was a mix of human and Tsyfarian technology. Engines from the Tsyfarians, giving it more speed than anything else in the sky, trailed down a teardrop body, elongated to hold up to ten crew rooms. Slim, hidden armor plating along the crew sections and engine compartments allowed them to sleep safely, knowing they could fight off anything they might run across with minimal damage. Weapons gleamed along the clean lines of the hull, looking like they'd grown there. A hybrid of speed and power, the ship was known throughout the fleet as the *Arrow*.

The hatchway opened and the pilot climbed on board. Though he wore a thinsuit identical to the others, his Tsyfarian bird helmet still sat proudly over his head. He went directly to his chair and fired up the consoles, putting the engines through pre-flight.

Behind him came the navigator, a Trasker Four native who'd found he had a gift for keeping up with the data sets needed by the Tsyfarian while in flight. He kept the name he'd earned in the gangs back home, refusing any other call sign.

Next through the hatchway was the science officer, from Bercuser. He mixed science with his own predictions, carrying with him two jars of fog from his home world so that he could predict both the past and future for the crew of the *Arrow* as needed.

The engineer, also from Trasker Four, entered, running her hand along the side of the ship as she did. She loved the *Arrow*, considered it the most beautiful thing she'd ever seen. There was a part of her that wanted to fly the ship some day, but she still couldn't force herself to sit behind the controls. When she tried, all she saw was her friend, dead, in the seat next to her. She checked the hull integrity and readings from around the ship, sending a green light to the pilot. The *Arrow* would, as always, fly true.

Lastly came the leader. He walked slowly, still not sure this was the best choice he could have made, while at the same time knowing his choice was not only right but wonderful. He sat down in his seat and adjusted straps to buckle in. A call came in not long after.

"It's Mills," the voice on the other end of the communications unit said through their earpieces. "You're cleared for takeoff. Deep Water will escort to the edge of the fleet."

"Sounds good to me," their leader said, reaching down to run his fingers across the butt of the Acadian blaster that hung heavily along his right thigh.

"It's just a small revolution on the largest moon around George Six. If you need backup—"

"Deep Water will be there on call for us as always. Thanks, Mills," he said, giving Chellox the signal. The ship rumbled to life, a caged beast in a tiny hanger, waiting for its chance to roam free once more.

"Good hunting, Mud."

With that, the *Arrow* took off, plunging far and fast into the dark space between stars once more.

COMING IN 2017...

Oh God, oh God, oh God, Mud's leading the team this time. Aw shit. Duck.

Stepping into his parent's boots, Mud Madison (Please stop calling him Newt) is still breaking in his new Insertion Team. Everything is going smooth enough, until the answer to a long standing mystery forces them to deal with a multiversal incursion that no one was prepared to even accept as possible.

It's five against the impossible. Luckily they have each other. And gravity packs. And blasters. And grenades.

THE ENDLESS SKY

ALSO BY ADAM P. KNAVE

PROSE

Crazy Little Things

Stays Crunchy In Milk

Strange Angel

NYCWTF

I Slept With Your Imaginary Friend

COMICS

Amelia Cole

Never Ending

Artful Daggers

Laser Joan and The Rayguns

Sensation Comics Featuring Wonder Woman

ABOUT THE AUTHOR

Adam P. Knave has been telling stories since he was a small child. He never stopped, and hopes he never will. A New York native, he self-exiled to Portland, Oregon, not long before his fortieth birthday and now spends many evenings on his patio, whiskey in hand.

www.ingramcontent.com/pod-product-compliance
Lightning Source LLC
Chambersburg PA
CBHW050551260626
47157CB00002B/523

* 9 7 8 1 9 2 6 9 4 6 0 3 0 *